Secrets of the Chimes

John Vance

Black Rose Writing | Texas

First printing

ISBN: 978-1-68433-602-9
PUBLISHED BY BLACK ROSE WRITING
www.blackrosewriting.com

Printed in the United States of America
Suggested Retail Price (SRP) $19.95

Secrets of the Chimes is printed in Palatino Linotype

*As a planet-friendly publisher, Black Rose Writing does its best to eliminate unnecessary waste to reduce paper usage and energy costs, while never compromising the reading experience. As a result, the final word count vs. page count may not meet common expectations.

Special thanks to Reagan Rothe and Dave King at Black Rose Writing; to my children Hope and Jimmy for their love and support; and to my wife Susan for her enthusiasm and keen editorial advice.

Secrets of the Chimes

"We dance round in a ring and suppose,
But the Secret sits in the middle and knows."
—ROBERT FROST, *The Secret Sits*

CHAPTER 1

The anemic lighting barely illuminated the west-side stairwell that led up to each stack level of the venerable Hendley Library. In recent years, little care had been given to the stairwells on either side. Each was swept every other month, and the walls of both were last painted sixty years earlier, on the eve of President Eisenhower's visit to New England and to the university in 1959. No one had even bothered to scribble graffiti on the pasty and yellowed walls, for students hardly ever used the stairs. Indeed, they rarely needed to examine the older books housed on the upper stack levels, which rose as a tower from the main three floors of the library. Although little used now, the steps still bore evidence of the labored treks of scholars from decades past. The stairwells were currently relics with little utilitarian function, because an elevator serviced all the floors in the Hendley Tower. Yet any alteration of the stairwells was vigorously opposed by a powerful minority who wished to preserve as much of the august Hendley as would have been familiar to later nineteenth-century and earlier twentieth-century students and faculty.

Jackson Lawrence walked up the west-side stairwell more cautiously than normal. Was it because tonight he had chosen the seventh stack level for a clandestine meeting? He smiled at the thought. But he understood that tonight the elevator was out of the question. He didn't wish to be seen or be forced into small talk with a fellow passenger, explaining why he was doing research this late at night. When he reached level four, Lawrence glanced at his pocket watch and noted both the time but also the date—February 7, 2019. He was certain it was the 7th, but he couldn't help checking. It was part of his scholarly character to confirm such things. Check, then double check. Leave little to doubt.

By the time he reached level five, he no longer felt the chill in his body. It was 25° when he left his car and headed to the Hendley. The grand old library was always well heated, if nothing else. Besides, Lawrence was warmed by the reason he had come to the Hendley on this splendid Northeastern winter's night. As he reached level six, he began to breathe more forcefully, which reminded him that as soon as spring arrived, he needed to get more serious about his exercise regimen, including a return to the jogging he had given up six years earlier, right after he turned forty. Yet he believed the acceleration of his heart rate was as much the result of heightened anticipation as it was a reflection of his poor conditioning.

The idea to meet on the seventh stack level was his. Owing to the wholesale shifting of the library's older volumes still labeled according to the Dewey Decimal system, these vintage texts covering English Literature to the arbitrary date of 1920 had been moved up to the lonely seventh stack level, visited only occasionally by faculty seeking an antiquated straw man for their critical arguments. Otherwise, these moribund volumes gathered much dust but provided little service as they rested on the cracked wooden shelves that marked all the upper stack levels of the Hendley. The area above stack level five was also the repository for the hidden and unspeakable history of the structure—a history, it was said, one could attempt to uncover at one's own risk. Within a week of each other in December 1929, for example, two members of the faculty took their own lives on stack levels five and six, and all attempts to attribute the deaths to the infamous stock-market crash were met with ridicule. Misfortunes ranging from facial cuts and broken noses from falling books from upper shelves, mysterious voices causing long-lasting psychological distress, and severe lung damage from inhaling the residue from the flaking covers of the moldering tomes were all part of the library's history. It was more exhilarating, after all, to believe that something evil lived in the upper reaches of the Hendley Tower.

Always delighted by such spirited tales, a few of which he embellished before a classroom of fascinated students, Jackson

Lawrence found further justification for arranging the meeting on the seventh level. As he entered the stacks, he went to the row housing the older books devoted to his academic specialty—the writings of Victorian England, including many older volumes devoted to the major subject of his research, Charles Dickens.

The noise startled him. Startled him more than the sensation of having just caught his foot against one of the rolling steps wedged partially into the bottom of one of the shelves. It was a single step twelve inches high. Just enough to assist shorter patrons in their attempt to reach a volume at the top of the stacks. But the rollers hadn't been oiled or replaced for at least a generation. The movement of the step emitted a crying metallic sound, the kind to unnerve even the heartiest of patrons. One of the custodial staff told Lawrence that none of them wanted to go to the upper stack levels late at night, and when they did, they briskly pushed their brooms down each aisle while their coworkers, keeping up the same rapid pace, only lightly snapped a cloth at the spines of the aging books as they hurried through the narrow corridors. They wouldn't have stopped to reposition a rolling step unit, even if it had disarranged the books on bottom shelf.

A moment later, Lawrence thought he heard another sound and turned to see if the noise announced the arrival of the expected visitor "to the land of forgotten lore," as he dubbed the meeting place. He would greet the visitor by gesturing with his hand that the two of them must keep their conversation to a whisper. The last thing Lawrence wanted was to have additional company amid these aged volumes. But when he saw no one coming down the aisle as he had just done, some of the chill returned to his body.

Lawrence again checked his pocket watch and altered his position so that he faced the books on the shelves immediately in front of him. He reached to the shelf several inches above his head and touched a little-disturbed 1931 edition of Dickens's Christmas book, the lesser-known work *The Chimes*, which rested among other early editions of the great English novelist's works, some going back to 1910. Only students of Dickens were aware that the Victorian author wrote four additional Christmas books in addition to the beloved *A Christmas Carol*.

Lawrence turned to the section devoted to *The Chimes* and began thumbing through the volume, searching for a specific passage he knew well. Wondering who had last opened this edition and in what year, he had a thought. He smiled and ran his left hand lightly across his full head of hair while still holding the volume in his right. But this thought was soon eclipsed by another. His face sagged into a frown as he contemplated his next move. Finally satisfied, he replaced the volume on the shelf, but didn't push it all the way back.

Shortly afterward, Lawrence walked to the end of the aisle and took a quick glance at the elevator door and checked the time yet again. 11:53 p.m. Eight minutes had passed since the agreed-upon meeting time. He stepped back down the aisle and positioned himself directly under the specific volume of Dickens he had previously opened. He bent his head so he could hear the elevator doors open. What he heard were only the last two footsteps. He hadn't been aware of the many others that came right before it. Lawrence had only begun turning his head to the left to see who had come from around the stacks and into his aisle from the west side. He delivered his words in a panicked whisper, "What are you...?" He felt a burning sensation under his jaw, followed by the spurting of blood from the jagged wound. Hearing footsteps moving quickly away from him as he staggered to his right, Lawrence reached up behind him and grabbed the green-clad volume resting an inch or so forward of its companions. It might appear to anyone coming upon the scene that Lawrence was unsuccessfully trying to keep himself upright by grasping at the shelves.

When he fell, he had the 1931 edition of *The Chimes* in his hand. He looked at the blood running down his sleeve when he opened the book. He managed to pull a pen from his pocket, but it slipped from his grip. With his last conscious effort, he touched his neck wound and brought his finger down and ran it across the two open pages, leaving daubs of blood in two places on the page. As he began to lose consciousness, he closed the volume around his finger. He thought he heard someone speak, but he couldn't be sure if the voice was his own or someone else's. In a moment, he lay dead on the floor.

CHAPTER 2

"The following morning, two students found his body in this very spot. Right down there—lying on his side. His head and left arm were thrust partially into the bottom row of books. From what the police told me, he had his right index finger wedged into an old edition of Dickens. It looked to the investigators first on the scene that he was deliberately attempting to keep the volume away from the blood seeping from his neck. A scholar's reflex, one of them noted at the time. Yet, there seemed to be some blood on his finger, which stained the pages."

The recently retired African-American professor sighed and then continued his narrative. "The medical examiner said it was a three to three-and-a-half inch blade thrust perfectly through the common carotid artery. It was as if the murderer knew his human anatomy very well. Obviously, every surgeon and pathologist in the city and surrounding counties was questioned. A few leads pointed to a local thoracic surgeon and even a dermatologist, for heaven's sake, but nothing came of it. No one was ever charged. So now, young man, you know just about all there is to know about the most famous unsolved murder in recent academic history. Oh—and by the way—welcome to the Hendley."

Jeremy Nichols smiled at the dramatic flourish that concluded the colorful tale told by Professor Emeritus Fred Beauchamp, who was giving him a guided tour of the impressive and undeniably intimidating Hendley Library. Nichols imagined that Beauchamp, whose name was pronounced BEE-chum as opposed to BO-champ, had no trouble turning thespian in the classroom before he retired as an active teacher. Even though he was over seventy, Beauchamp was still tall and lithe, his bronze features almost devoid of wrinkles, his hair only spotted with gray. But Nichols was most taken by Beauchamp's resonate and commanding baritone.

"I hope you enjoyed the account, Jeremy. It's been a while since I had a captive audience."

Nichols was certain the man's former students enjoyed their captivity, even if most of them never fully appreciated the splendid reputation this scholar of nineteenth-century American Literature had achieved.

"I admit I thoroughly enjoyed offering dramatic and appropriately frightening readings of Poe, and the students often howled at my attempts to sound like every one of Mark Twain's characters in *Huckleberry Finn*—even though they dropped their smiles and sat up straight when I read, in dialect mind you, the words of the runaway slave Jim. They seemed shocked that a highly educated black man would read Jim's dialect without any reluctance—not to mention my inclusion of the 'N' word. Anyway, in my twenties I was sorely tempted to try my hand at acting professionally. As a matter of fact, there were several in the department who thought I could have made it on the stage. My friend Jack Lawrence being one of them."

Nichols appreciated his good fortune in being shown the ropes by such a notable scholar, who even in retirement seemed to have a firm grip on the pulse of the department and the university.

"Jeremy, you'll find yourself here at the Hendley quite a bit in the next three years, and I dare say you'll look upon the coming period as perhaps the most fruitful of your career." Nichols smiled, but Beauchamp detected some doubt in his eyes. "I know, I know. You're wondering whether you made the right decision in taking a position with no hope of tenure. As you're aware, that's just the way it is in the upper echelons of the academic world. Institutions like this one simply don't tenure members of the junior faculty. But you have to remember that with your publication record so far and your accepted book on Dickens coming out while you're teaching here—plus the very fact that you'll have taught at this august institution—all of that will land you most comfortably on your feet when you move on in three years. Of course, you were but a year from a tenure decision where you were, so maybe you're of "the bird in the hand" school. Beauchamp paused to gauge Nichols's reaction.

It was immediate. "No, no. I made the right choice."

"I know you have. You're still in your early thirties, right?"

"I'm thirty-two, Professor Beauchamp."

"Still a baby, then. And please, humor me. Call me Fred."

Nichols realized that wouldn't be easy, given the sterling reputation of the man talking to him on the seventh stack level. Nichols was curious why Beauchamp remained in the aisle where the body of Jackson Lawrence was found six months earlier. Nichols wished to return to the main floor. It appeared as though Beauchamp wanted him fully to absorb his surroundings.

"You'll have to excuse me for not recalling all the facts in your *curriculum vitae,* Jeremy, but how did you get to where you are now?

"I did my PhD work at Penn."

"Right, right. You worked with Betty Grummond, didn't you?"

"Yes, I did."

"A first-rate scholar and lady—brilliant though modest."

"She was that. She never spoke about herself. The only professor I had in graduate school who didn't assign one of his or her own books as part of the required readings." Nichols bit his tongue. He hoped Beauchamp wasn't one of the self-aggrandizing types.

Beauchamp laughed. "I once had a senior colleague who included his vanity press novel on the reading list of his Modern American Novel course. A complete egomaniacal idiot. But to continue, you ended up teaching at one of my favorite unsung institutions in the great state of New York." Beauchamp examined Nichols's features. "Forgive me. I suppose you haven't been happy there."

Nichols hesitated before replying. "Let's just say, it was time for me to move on. And when I saw the opening here, I had to apply."

"Yeah, your department head Jim Yarborough is a first-class son of a bitch, I agree."

Nichols couldn't contain his smile. "Did you get to know Doug Finneran, who did a three-year appointment here in your department? He left a year ago."

"So you knew Doug, eh?"

"We're best buddies."

"How about that? Heard from him lately? How does he like UMass?"

"It's one of the three places he's always wanted to teach at." Great, Nichols thought, he ended his sentence with a grammatical *faux pas*.

"Okay, there you are. Your friend Finneran has validated my point about landing comfortably on your feet once you leave here."

Nichols made a note to call Finneran later in the day. His friend had just returned from a very important week in Canada with his estranged wife.

Beauchamp dropped his smile and looked around the aisle. "Yes, the murder occurred right here. Exactly here. The medical examiner believed it happened between eleven thirty and a few minutes before midnight. If so, Jack would have died in the waning moments of February 7th—a little over six months ago.

Nichols shook his head. "Are you sure that's the exact date?" Beauchamp nodded his assurance. "Jesus. February 7th is Dickens' birthday."

"Really?" Nichols thought Beauchamp's inflection hardly suggested that he was unaware of that fact.

"That's incredible. Jackson Lawrence, one of America's leading scholars of Dickens, was murdered on the man's birthday."

"Would one call that irony or mere coincidence, Jeremy?" Nichols was struck by the ambiguous though intriguing expression on Beauchamp's face.

"I imagine that this aisle, indeed this entire stack level, has been left generally unchanged since the murder."

Beauchamp seemed pleased by Nichols's question. "Not a bit changed in many, many decades, Jeremy. Not a bit. All the books in the exact place they were when they were moved up here. Hardly any of them disturbed in all that time."

Nichols noticed the rolling step unit farther down the aisle and wondered if it was in the same place the night of Lawrence's death. Without telling Beauchamp, he found the murder site particularly depressing. The highly respected Dickens scholar was slain in what was perhaps his refuge, his sanctuary away from faculty meetings and grievances, away from classroom disappointments, and away from any frustrations and loneliness in his personal life.

Nichols made a motion to go, but Beauchamp didn't budge. "It was odd that Jack wasn't wearing his winter coat that night, since the temperature was in the twenties. They found him only in a crew neck sweater and his sports jacket, but no coat. He always wore that coat when the temperature dropped below forty."

Nichols thought for a second. "Maybe he was in a rush or underestimated the chill. Perhaps he spilled something on it and sent it out to be cleaned."

Beauchamp nodded. "Could be, Jeremy. You're probably right."

"I suppose Professor Lawrence had been up here searching for some obscure reference in his research on Dickens."

"Yes, we all assumed the same thing. I'd love to know what it was, but then I'm not a Dickensian." Beauchamp paused and took another look at the books on the shelves near where they stood. "I don't know if the fates were unjust or kind, since he breathed his last within sight and touch of the material he so loved."

"Yes."

"You knew about this murder, didn't you, Jeremy? I mean, being a Dickens man yourself."

"Oh, yes. I attended a Dickens conference in the spring expecting him to be there—I really wanted to meet him, but that's when I heard that he'd been murdered in this library and that the killer had yet to be identified."

"Perhaps not as grippingly poignant as Thomas Becket's being dispatched in the cathedral, but close enough, I'd say. Well, let's head down. It's getting late. You and I have a dinner reservation at one of my favorite spots."

• • •

An hour later, the men were dining in the claustrophobic but elegant restaurant Fred Beauchamp had made his second home since the death of his wife two years earlier. Each man nursed a drink and offered his assessment of the unusually cool Saturday evening in early August and then began to regale each other with brief vignettes of recent academic foolishness and annoyance. Before shifting to non-academic topics of interest, Jeremy couldn't resist asking one further question about the murder.

"I hope you don't mind my continuing this matter, but had anyone ever said what Professor Lawrence was working on at the time of his death?"

"As you might have guessed, I used to serve as Jack Lawrence's tavern chum. The last time we shared a pint at our favorite local haunt—the night before the murder—he seemed nervous, as if he were sitting on something big."

"What? A new book idea on Dickens?"

"Don't know. Jack was a skilled poker player—and, even though we were close, he kept most of his scholarly epiphanies to himself until he published them."

"Something in his personal life, then?"

Beauchamp smiled in the same sly way he had at the Hendley Library. "It might have been, since Jack's personal life was both highly interesting and controversial. But you know, I can't help thinking he was behaving as though he'd made a discovery of some kind that disturbed or frightened more than excited him."

Nichols nodded. "Perhaps I can trace back what he might have been working on then."

Beauchamp flashed a broad grin. "So, you're saying you have a bit of Detective Bucket in you, eh?"

Nichols matched his grin, a bit surprised that Beauchamp knew the name of Dickens' character from *Bleak House*. "Well, I'm a little younger than Bucket and not as husky."

Beauchamp laughed. "In any event, I'm glad you might be taking an active interest in finding something out. I'm very glad indeed."

CHAPTER 3

It is the first day of January 1858. I will in a little over a month's time arrive at my forty-sixth birthday. Before now I have had neither the time nor the inclination to make entries into a personal journal of any kind. Yet at present I feel I have no choice but to begin one. I must have some way to express my feelings for the young woman who has taken away my heart. Perhaps I shall write very little in the days to come. It is possible I may even burn these pages next year and wonder why I ever wrote a single word about my passion for Ellen Ternan. Still, I can only enter my thoughts as I am prompted by my heart and allow my changing sentiments and subsequent events to continue or end this journal at whatever time is most fitting.

Some four months ago I was in Manchester, and I observed that Free Trade Hall was immense by comparison with some of the other places where I and my amateur troupe had staged our dramatic productions. I initially imagined the place full of patrons, looking like rows of living books sitting politely out there—the bindings of various colors, many impressive, still others unusually plain. It was warm—it was late August—and I hoped the title of the play we would perform, ***The Frozen Deep****, might make things a little more bearable for all concerned.*

And theatre was my true delight, after all. Not what I have made my name on, certainly, but what I most loved doing. It was gratifying to know that London audiences appreciated our little play, just as they had warmed to my public readings of my Christmas books— ***A Christmas Carol*** *and* ***The Chimes.***

But facing a performance of the play in Manchester, I understood that the size of the venue demanded more experienced actresses, women who knew how to translate movement in a large auditorium and who had the vocal strength to be heard over the distance and the din. I knew that my daughters Katie and Mamey, as well as others, would have to be replaced for these performances.

Before long, I was encouraged to obtain the services of Mrs. Ternan and her daughters, Maria and Ellen. I had known Mrs. Ternan for some time, admired her work on stage, and felt confident I would most enjoy working with her and her daughters, although what I knew of the youngest, Ellen, was that she was no match on the stage for her mother or older sister. But then she was only eighteen.

Yes, dearest, dearest Ellen, you were only eighteen then. This diary I now begin to keep is not **for** *you, but is rather* **because** *of you. These are my private thoughts that I must share in the only manner I can. It shall never be seen by anyone other than by me and by you, if you so wish it, my dearest one.*

The reader chose to glance at only the first two pages tonight. It was late and the effects of two drinks encouraged sleep. The pages were returned to their place with the rest of the diary composed a century and a half earlier by the greatest novelist of his century. Perhaps only one other person in the world knew of the existence of this diary, the discovery of which would command considerable international attention and the offer of an exorbitant price. In fact, three persons had seen these pages, but one of them was dead—murdered at the Hendley Library in early February of the present year.

• • •

Having driven back to New York early Sunday morning, Nichols set about finishing a book review assigned by a literary journal. The final two paragraphs came easily enough, and as he completed the last sentence, he tapped his fingers on the bottom edge of his keyboard. What academic address should he include with his name? He'd been assigned the review and written it while still teaching in New York. Should he say the hell with it and send in the review noting his new home for the next three years? He would do just that with his Dickens book now being copy-edited by an academic press. He had typed just the first two letters of his new academic address before experiencing sudden and intense pressure pulling back his neck and head. The pain was immediate. He struggled to maintain his balance in the chair.

"Daddy! You're home! Did you bring me a present?"

Gently removing his daughter's rigid forearms from around his neck, Nichols answered her spirited inquiry. "You bet I did, Belinda." He managed to spin his chair around, while turning both his body and hers so that she ended up sitting on his lap, kissing him sweetly all over his face.

Belinda Nichols was to her father the very embodiment of joy—a reward he never felt worthy of but always completely grateful for. Exactly a month shy of four years old, with a face that munched a thousand chips, he liked to tease, parodying Faustus's memorable description of Helen of Troy in Marlowe's play. And consumed a thousand Lorna Doone shortbread cookies. And a thousand chunks of chocolate. And still he worried about her comparatively small size. He was convinced she would at age fourteen either explode outward—that is, spontaneously combust, as did another of Dickens' characters in *Bleak House*—or she would be one of the lucky ones able to gorge with impunity on any and all the sweet treats and never gain a pound. Of which of these possibilities he couldn't be sure, but he was certain she was the most delicious sweet treat in his life.

Named for Belinda Cratchit in *A Christmas Carol* primarily because Nichols thought Bob Cratchit the model for any father, regardless of century, his little girl was a bright, vivacious, and inquisitive child, with that special gift of wonder so many talk about but all too rarely find. And her father believed she was moreover blessed with a kind of stoicism, if not heroism, for one so young—given what she had to endure since birth.

"I brought you back a paint set."

"You did?" Belinda's face radiated unqualified love for her father and relief that the one gift she so badly wanted was indeed the one he brought back home. As was her habit of late, she stuck her nose against his and heavily whispered into his nostrils. "I love my Daddy." Nichols thought she sounded exactly like a miniature Marilyn Monroe when she did that.

"Good gift, Jeremy."

"Thank you, Janis." Nichols gave the prim though still attractive woman the usual ironic smile when he saw her standing in the doorway to the converted small bedroom serving as his den. They had often discussed Belinda's pencil drawings and crayon sketches and agreed that the child would enjoy working with paints. Nichols had become intrigued by his daughter's drawings of empty fields and meadows, with one object in the right foreground of each sketch she did. The sun or the moon would also appear in every drawing—and usually the facsimile of rolling hills—but with nary a tree, bush, river, or house in the scene, except for what she placed in the lower right-hand corner. Belinda would at times draw herself, at other times her father, but never together. Only a single figure was permitted to take residence in that corner of her drawings. On other occasions, she would sketch a dog, horse, tiger, or bird. Once there was a multi-colored snake. The non-living entities were represented by a book, a bottle, a chair, and something her father couldn't identify. An empty oval—not quite a circle, but an oval. He couldn't bring himself to ask his daughter what that oval represented. He was afraid he already knew.

"Are you going to eat supper with us, Aunt Janis?"

"No, honey lamb, I promised to take both your cousins out to eat Chinese food tonight."

"Are you sure you're going to move with us, Aunt Janis."

"Absolutely sure, my love."

Jeremy's face radiated deep appreciation. His older sister and nieces were coming with them when Jeremy and Belinda moved to their new university town. Janis had already secured a part-time job, which would supplement the substantial funds she had at her disposal since the death of her husband. After informing her younger brother—by eight years—what Belinda had been up to while he was away, Janis blew them both a kiss and left.

In so many respects, Jeremy Nichols had an ideal family situation, and he rarely passed on the opportunity to spend time with his sister and nieces, to whom he felt closer with each passing year. He knew the loss of her husband five years earlier made Janis a far more empathetic confidant to her younger brother when Belinda's biological mother decided, on the very day she gave birth, that a daughter was the last thing she could handle at that time in her life.

CHAPTER 4

Sandra Stark thoroughly enjoyed the Sunday luncheon in honor of Lorene Williamson's completion of her twentieth year as the Hendley's Head Librarian. Having finished her first calendar year employed at the library, Sandra found Williamson an inspiration and supportive mentor from the time she entered the Masters in Library and Informational Science program two years earlier, right after she took her B.A. from the English Department, situated a stone's throw away on campus. How truly lucky to have been hired out of graduate school by the Hendley, when she assumed she's be cutting her teeth at a small college library—likely in the Midwest or South. Whereas she was strongly encouraged to do a PhD in literature, Sandra held that the life as a teacher-scholar wasn't best for her, although she refused to divorce herself entirely from research and especially from the pleasure of handling books.

Lorene Williamson saw to it that Sandra spent time in several departments in the Hendley, and at each stop the young woman impressed her superiors. Today, as she mingled with library employees at the luncheon, one of her senior colleagues proposed a toast to a "splendid career yet to come," which delighted Sandra and made the lunch-time champagne all the more enjoyable. Yes, a splendid career, with the exception of one horrific event and the guilt that accompanied it, which remained an invisible yet open wound.

And she had been unable to tell anyone. She hadn't spoken untruthfully to the police who asked her only three questions the previous February, two of which related to what she knew of Professor Lawrence's classroom and library habits. The third question she answered truthfully, yet not fully. To her considerable relief, the fourth was never asked.

• • •

Professor Jackson Lawrence had always been a bit of a flirt, and when the object of his interest was at least mildly attractive, he enjoyed tossing out bits of flattery like so many colorful Mardi Gras beads. Pretty department and administrative secretaries all enjoyed or endured the praise, flowers, and *ad hoc* verses to their beauty. But as each year passed, Lawrence found the climate more and more unreceptive to what many thought were outdated notions of chivalry, but there were still a few young women who at least cautiously responded to his effusive charms and accepted his seemingly harmless gifts.

One of these young women was the beautiful Sandra Stark, then adding luster to the circulation and reference desks at the Hendley and drawing to them more than her fair share of male admirers—all disguised as library patrons with their many questions about the location of books and journals, the answers to which most of them knew already. Jackson Lawrence was one of those frequent visitors and seekers of information, even though only a handful of professors knew the Hendley as well as he did. And only the most masochistic spent as much time there.

Before long and after being gently showered with compliments, small and sweet trinkets of affection, and personalized odes, Sandra Stark was privy to Professor Lawrence's eerie and mildly prurient tales of the library's history. She had earlier been captivated by his charming classroom manner when she took his Nineteenth-Century Novels course. Therefore, it was quite easy for him to pay her special attention when she started working in the Hendley. It seemed he had at least one tantalizing nugget about every stack level and reading room in the expansive cathedral-like structure. She enjoyed them all, with the exception of the two instances he cited of sadism and incest—for which Lawrence immediately apologized for having offended her sensibilities. Before long, Sandra worried that he would invite her to visit the scene of some of these tales of long-ago apparitions and romantic trysts. She wasn't concerned she would have to hurt his feelings by turning down such an invitation; rather, she feared that her desire to accompany him would jeopardize her employment and the chance to stay in the one place where she most belonged.

Even just six months after his death, she couldn't help smiling at the memory of his handsome face. She was still warmed from the knowledge that beneath the playful and eccentric demeanor was a deeply passionate man—one who desired her physically. And how much she reveled in the memory of his voice.

"Please, Sandra. I've asked you to call me 'Jack'—you know, like Jack Kennedy," he said that spring day she received her Masters as he walked with her to find her family after the ceremony. He claimed that as a boy he cavorted with some of the younger Kennedy clan at Hyannis Port and that once, in 1995, he was handed a bottle of beer from the then Senator from Massachusetts, Edward Kennedy. Sandra refused to believe him, causing Lawrence playfully to express his frustration. Although she refused at first to call him anything but "Professor Lawrence," by the end of the summer, she came to defy her better judgment and began to meet with him in a half a dozen public places—and several private ones as well.

• • •

"Doug! Got you at last. I tried your place three times last night."

"Sorry, Jeremy, but I wasn't at my apartment. You should have called my cell."

"No way was I going to interrupt you if you guys were...well, you know." Nichols felt it wasn't his place to ask directly.

"Jeremy, everything is good. No, actually it's great. We've had an incredible week with each other. I wasn't at my apartment last night because I was at the house. In my bed. With my own wife. Can you believe it? Mark it down. My life begins anew!"

Nichols realized his closest friend was trying his best to keep a check on his emotions. He'd talked with Doug Finneran several times by phone when his friend was in anguish over the direction his private life was taking. Nichols was certain it had to be another woman, but Doug wouldn't confide in him except to say that what he was going through was temporary—that it *had* to be temporary. But now Finneran couldn't disguise the joy and relief his reconciliation with Heather, his aggrieved wife, had given him.

"Doug, I'm proud of you, buddy."

Finneran's voice lost its exuberance. "Damn it, Jeremy, don't say that. Man, don't say that. I am such a...such a son of a bitch."

"Doug, you *were*, but not any longer. Okay?"

"Thanks, my friend. That means a lot." Nichols thought Finneran sounded less than sincere—more as though he wished to change the subject.

"Okay, so what are you doing at your apartment now?"

"Moving out, *mon frère*. That's what I'm doing here. Getting my stuff and bringing it all home."

"That's great, Doug. Just great."

"Damn. I forgot to ask. How did it go yesterday? Did you drive up and check out your new academic digs?"

"Yes, I did, and it all went very, very well."

"You'll probably get my old office. Hope they painted the damn thing. Hey, who showed you around?"

"You won't believe this. Fred Beauchamp. He gave me the guided tour of the campus, the Hendley, the town, and set me up with a realtor."

"Beauchamp? You're not serious."

"Yes, I'm serious. By the way, I never asked—did he show you around when you first went up?"

"Hell no. Another of the lost untenured souls gave me the tour. Fred Beauchamp. Jesus."

"What? Why the shock?"

"You better know this now, Jeremy. All I heard when I taught there was that Beauchamp did a little more with his time than teach American Lit."

"Doug, what the hell are you trying to say?"

"I'm trying to say that Beauchamp was or still is an agency man. 'Agency' as in 'Central Intelligence.' Scuttlebutt had it that he also knew more about the secret comings and goings in those hallowed halls than anyone there. He might still be serving the agency by recruiting young talent, so be careful."

"Come on, Doug. I long ago stopped sticking my leg out for you to pull."

"I'm not kidding. I couldn't be any more serious. Don't you get it? If he personally took you around, it's got to mean he's checking you out to see if you have what it takes to join the team. You can bet your sweet ass he's done his homework on you. Damn, you may have gotten the teaching gig there because you possess whatever the hell Beauchamp and his crowd is looking for."

Nichols could barely contain a laugh. "Beauchamp and his *crowd*?"

"Hell, you do know, don't you, that half the members of the past five administrations in Washington were professors or deans at your new academic residence?"

"Exaggerating a bit, aren't we?"

"Okay, a bit. But ye old campus where you're going to teach for three years has provided in the past three decades Secretaries of Commerce, Interior, Agriculture, Housing and Urban Development—twice, I think—and Energy."

Nichols imagined his friend counting the cabinet secretaries on the fingers of both hands.

"And that's not to mention one Attorney General, three Deputy Secretaries of Defense, one Director of OMB, and two press secretaries."

Had Doug kicked off his shoes so he could use his toes as well?

"And if that isn't enough for you, Professor Nichols—the university has also given Washington one Director and three Deputy Directors of the CIA and the man who's just been re-elected governor of your home state and is the odds-on favorite of becoming his party's next presidential nominee, although I wouldn't vote for him if they held a gun to my head."

"Wow. Are you the *facts-wizard*? Sure you're not shooting for a job with Alumni Affairs?"

"Don't laugh. Just watch your back, my friend."

"I promise. Doug, give Heather my love. I'm so, so happy for the both of you, and before the summer is out Belinda and I will be driving over to see you guys in Amherst."

"Jeremy, answer me this. Did Beauchamp ask to see you again before you begin teaching the fall term?" Finneran waited, but Nichols held his answer. "Come on, tell me. Did he?"

"I'm going back up Tuesday, but just for a few hours."

"I knew it."

"To see the realtor, Doug. To see the realtor. I need to make a decision on a place for me and Belinda and one for Janis and the girls, you know that."

"Right. And...?"

"Yes, I'm having lunch with Beauchamp."

"Jesus. You know how I feel about those bastards. Didn't we agree, when I was there, that they had no business recruiting on campus?"

"You're really worked up about this, aren't you? Most of that recruiting stuff was done forty or fifty years ago." Nichols easily detected the frustration and anger in his friend's voice but couldn't believe that it all stemmed from his Libertarian political leanings and his contempt for the intelligence agencies—FBI, CIA, NSA, DNI—it didn't matter.

Finneran finally calmed. "Oh, hell, Jeremy, I'm sorry. I'm just looking out for you, that's all."

"Thanks, but I'll be all right. Belinda and I will see you next month. Bye." Nichols shook his head in bemusement and muttered, "Oh, I'd be perfect for the CIA all right." Yet he couldn't help being somewhat flattered by the possibility that Fred Beauchamp saw something special in him.

CHAPTER 5

Fred Beauchamp examined the photograph taken fourteen years earlier, in May 2005. The three men were standing on the front steps of the Hendley Library. One was a well-known and respected teacher and scholar, one a bright young academic star on the horizon, and the third a brand-new graduate, fresh from commencement exercises on the university's main quad. They picked the steps of the Hendley for the photograph because it was there that Jackson Lawrence convinced Coy Mallory not to leave school without the degree and at the Hendley where Beauchamp had many conversations with Mallory about another line of work that would "complement" a Bachelor of Arts in English, another field of endeavor about which Mallory was quite enamored, making up his mind that there was more he could do to prove his fitness for such work. As it turned out, at the end of the summer, Mallory was given a teaching position, with limited classroom duties, at a university in Qatar, remained there for two years, and returned to the States, enrolling in the Master's program at Georgetown, in which he stayed only one semester when his path suddenly shifted into the political realm, and after working both a Senate and a presidential campaign in 2008, he was recommended for a formal position with the CIA.

But as was his pattern, he didn't remain long at Langley—"Not a good fit," Mallory wrote Lawrence—and after leaving Washington, he worked abroad for three years, doing what Lawrence and Beauchamp didn't know. Mallory returned to California in 2014 and the first of a series of movie roles. No one was quite certain why he decided to make a transition to film work. "I wanted to give it a shot before I got too old," he claimed—but his virile good looks, respectable thespian skills, and important connections led to his finding a series of small to mid-sized character parts. In 2017, Mallory acted in his last film and began lending his distinctive baritone to several historical and military features on several cable channels. Mallory was at present enjoying a general reputation as a leading voice-over talent, with several scheduled projects coming his way.

After recalling Mallory's peculiar career arc, Beauchamp chuckled at the photo, taken when he was in his mid-fifties, Jackson Lawrence in his early thirties, and the "punk kid" Mallory in his early twenties—a former student of both English professors. Beauchamp whistled, and his dog Usher came lumbering into the living room. When he retired from the English Department, Beauchamp got the dog, fulfilling a personal promise that he'd mitigate some of the expected postpartum depression of academic retirement with a canine companion. That he took advantage of his emeritus status and kept an office in the department and attended almost all social functions, as well as occasionally playing godfather to the younger untenured members of the faculty, didn't make him at all regret getting Usher. Besides, he always found amusing that fellow faculty members and some graduate students believed he named his dog to honor the frightening and morbid protagonist in Poe's "The Fall of the House of Usher." But in truth, the name was inspired by something even darker than a Poe short story.

After vigorously petting and wrestling with the English setter, Beauchamp stared at the telephone resting on the table next to his favorite chair. The discussion about Lawrence's death with the newly hired Jeremy Nichols was only the first the two men would have in the days ahead. Beauchamp had read enough on what to expect when one became a septuagenarian—most notably the sudden need to resolve old issues and to answer old questions. Perhaps young Jeremy Nichols might be his ticket to satisfying that long-standing need, one now made all the more important given the way matters had shaken out in the past several years.

Beauchamp's hand began to reach for the phone, but when it did Usher barked twice. Beauchamp thought better of the call—at least for now.

• • •

Nichols finally got his chatty daughter to sleep. When she was telling him about her day, he was often distracted by thoughts of the Hendley Library. He wondered how many murders had been committed in the smaller single- and two-story public libraries that dotted the communities outside the larger cities. It seemed such a ludicrous subject to consider, but the murder in an august academic library defied his desire to think of other matters. By the time Belinda closed her beautiful and expressive eyes, her father was completely absorbed by the horrendous scene he imagined on stack level seven.

From what Fred Beauchamp told him at dinner, the medical examiner believed the murder was committed shortly before midnight on February 7th. During the winter, the Hendley closed at the odd time of 11:50 p.m. Perhaps Lawrence was merely doing some last-second checking on a late nineteenth- or early twentieth-century critical assessment of Dickens. Still, what fact could have been so important to draw Lawrence up the Hendley Tower at that time of night?

Halfway through his beer, Jeremy pondered the killer's motive. Nothing seemed to make sense. According to Beauchamp, several of Lawrence's colleagues quarreled with him on matters of department policy, but surely there was nothing that would have prompted such violence. The professor emeritus added that other colleagues objected to Lawrence's charming ways—especially with women—but again nothing to suggest any deep-seated resentment.

Nichols recalled Beauchamp's words as he dropped him off at the hotel after dinner. "Jeremy, one strong belief is that the murderer was a bitter and disturbed former student, yet not a single suspect could be identified who accurately fit that description. Jack Lawrence never failed any student who gave an honest effort, and he worked very hard shepherding his graduate students to their degrees. Some in our department thought it was a drifter or homeless indigent who made his way up the stairwell and bedded down on the seventh stack level and was confronted by Jack, which then led to a violent confrontation."

Nichols recalled that as he shook hands with Beauchamp the two men smiled at each other, each finding the "drifter" theory more unlikely than credible. Beauchamp parted with the view that "Whoever he was and whatever his motive, the murderer likely followed Lawrence into the library and then up to the seventh stack level. Perhaps this intruder even lured Jack to the area."

Nichols once again recalled that Lawrence was found under the older Dickens editions and critical studies, with his right index finger wedged inside one of the volumes, almost as if Lawrence wanted the person who found his body to look at something on those pages. But apparently, the book was simply replaced on the shelf after Lawrence was removed from the Hendley.

• • •

Another page from the unknown Dickens manuscript was pulled out indiscriminately for perusal. *"Why do I care whether young Ellen Ternan has read and appreciated what I have written over the past twenty or so years? Had she grown up reading one of my books? She hasn't yet said anything about what I have written, and I feel bruised because she has not. It shouldn't matter, but it does. I am wise enough to know that infatuations are a natural and inevitable result of the theatrical experience. And I wonder, since I cannot love my wife, if I am in desperate need to love someone? Even if that someone is twenty-seven years younger than I?"*

• • •

The hood of the heavy dark blue sweatshirt was perfect for hiding all facial features from anyone who might happen to be walking by at this late hour. It would also keep anyone looking out a window from identifying the solitary figure standing on the street within the cul-de-sac and peering at the upstairs bedroom window of the Finnerans' comfortable house in Amherst. There was only a dim light coming from the window. The figure on the street debated whether the illumination originated from a bedside lamp or from the bathroom inside the bedroom. Perhaps it stemmed from the upstairs hallway light. Was Finneran awake and reading? Or was his wife the one with a book? Or were they having sex with the added enhancement of romantic lighting?

The hooded figure took two steps toward the house but then stopped. No, not now. Not with that light on. The pistol lying zipped and secure inside the front pouch of the sweatshirt wouldn't be used—not tonight. But soon enough. The figure in blue sighed bitterly and headed out of the cul-de-sac, but after walking only twenty feet, turned and looked back up at the window. The light was still on. No one heard the muted sarcasm. "What the hell are they doing? Trying to make a baby?" The figure in the heavy sweatshirt checked the time. It was just past 2:00 a.m.

In the dark, Doug Finneran sat downstairs in his favorite chair finishing a Red Sox game he had recorded. How pleasurable it was once again to be in such warm and loving surroundings. His wife had turned on the small reading lamp on her side of the bed and was likely reading a paperback novel. Although their reconciliation included a resumption of their sex life, tonight Finneran postponed getting into bed with his wife because he couldn't get the phone call from Jeremy Nichols out of his head. Hell, there was still much to think about. Too damn much to think about.

CHAPTER 6

Upon awakening, Nichols discovered a single sheet of stiff paper resting on his chest. As she liked to do on Monday mornings, Belinda rose before her father and drew him one of her landscapes, the first one she had done with the paint he brought back from "Daddy's new school" as a gift. Nichols rubbed the sleep out of his eyes and saw that his daughter had placed a book in the lower-right-hand corner of the paper. There was moreover a second figure in the space. It was a stick figure—male, since Belinda always put a triangle on her female effigies to represent a dress—but it wasn't standing. Rather, the figure was prone, with his outstretched stick arm touching the book.

Nichols was startled. All he could see in Belinda's scene was Jackson Lawrence lying dead, with his finger wedged inside the volume on the seventh stack level of the Hendley Library. Nichols couldn't understand his daughter's depiction in any other way. And yet how could she possibly know what had happened six months earlier? He had said nothing to her or to his sister Janis about the murder.

"Do you like my painting, Daddy?"

Nichols wasn't quite ready to absorb Belinda's little body slamming onto his thighs from what was obviously a flying start.

"Love it. Your first one with real paint too."

"I know."

He wanted to laugh at the proud and smug expression on her face, but he couldn't shake the nagging question from his mind. He sat up with all intentions to ask what she was depicting in the corner of her sketch. Who the man was and why he was lying with his arm outstretched like that. Previously, he avoided probing her about the human figures she drew. Again, he feared hearing her identify the person she thought of when she drew her empty ovals.

Over four years earlier, the woman's otherwise alluring and intriguing face revealed a depressing meld of panic and disdain. Behind her was the large bouquet of flowers Jeremy searched three florists to find. He wanted the picture of the new mother holding their darling child framed by the floral arrangement, with its eighteen pink roses and what seemed like forty sprays of baby's breath. They both knew she would deliver a girl, but she held off choosing a name, waiting until she saw the newborn's face. She was certain the infant's features would help her decide on something most fitting. Now, however, the new mother looked as though she didn't even want the nameless child placed in her arms.

Meredith Jamison had informed Jeremy Nichols that marriage was a destructive institution to both the individual and the family. Jeremy initially resisted her assertion, telling Meredith he truly wished to marry her and that any child they conceived would grow up far more secure if its father and mother were legally bound. But he simply needed Meredith too much to take arms against her view, which he knew he could never successfully combat.

Conceding to her desires and caprice had become a willing habit—a visible characteristic of the new Jeremy Nichols—a feature of his personality that especially disturbed his sister Janis and good friends like Doug Finneran. It was not as though Meredith had rewarded him with considerable passion or even special moments of undivided attention. She took all of his gifts, from flowers to his ardent attempts to please her physically, with the same attitude, one ranging in its expression from only mild satisfaction to utter indifference. But he needed her and acceded to her wishes, whatever they were.

Nichols hoped that Meredith's having a child would alter her insecure and debilitating view of herself and her future. He had devoted an inordinate amount of time attempting to repaint her gloomy portrait with as many shimmering tones as he could manufacture. He flattered her lavishly; he brought her thoughtful gifts of considerable expense; he took care of the cooking; and he made sure they had a housecleaner every other week.

Jeremy and Meredith lived together for seven months before she became pregnant with Belinda. He assumed their living together would brighten her general outlook, for such increased intimacy would certainly convince her she was worthy of a man's loyalty and devotion. When they met at a cocktail party, Nichols was taken by her looks and aloof bearing. As a result, her non-responsiveness when they first made love didn't bother him as it might have. But even though he soon realized she had serious problems regarding self-esteem, he maintained his belief that he would eventually make her appreciate her own worth, especially with his passionate love-making in spite of her evincing little if any pleasure in the act, although she always accepted him without protest, reluctance, or impatience.

But nothing changed between them until Meredith discovered she was pregnant. In the days following, she offered Nichols a reprieve from her deflated spirits, although she still wouldn't consider marrying him. She smiled more, though not effusively. She hummed frequently, which she had never done before. In her fourth month, she told Jeremy she was uncomfortable making love and wished only to be cuddled. He took the disappointment in stride, because he sensed a change in her demeanor—a change modest and subtle, but a change nonetheless. For the first time, she accepted without contradiction his pleasant predictions about their future. She listened to his university classroom tales and asked him specific questions about his research and writing on Dickens. Even so, she turned from him when he wished to kiss her passionately, and she specifically asked him not to buy her flowers for Valentine's Day or for her birthday. "Just get me flowers when the baby comes" was her request.

But when the baby arrived, she reverted to her earlier demeanor—now amplified by visible panic and disdain. She held her daughter for less than a minute and handed the infant to Nichols. Within four days, during which she refused to touch the baby, she left her new family without any indication when she would return and without any promise to contact Jeremy again. It was then that his sister Janis took control of Belinda's care, juggling her own young children and the demands of her part-time employment. Meredith never again saw her child or contacted Jeremy.

• • •

"Sandra, which of your latest admirers gave you the flowers?"

She handed the man a glass of prosecco and smiled at his question. He of course knew the arrangement was an early birthday gift from her step-brother. Her dinner guest, Rob Porterfield—a thirty-two-year-old attorney whom she had known for close to a year—never pushed himself on her physically or otherwise, a quality that led to their dating more frequently the past two months. Since she came to work at the Hendley, she sifted through a broad selection of interested men who paid her considerable attention—two coworkers at the Hendley, as well as four faculty members and men with positions in the Bursar's Office, Human Resources, and Legal Affairs. And there were the awkward flirtations and the clumsy flattery by tactless undergraduates and graduate students.

Following the murder of Jackson Lawrence, however, Sandra Stark refused to date for four months. When she resumed accepting offers, she had cut her beautiful long hair to a mid-length style and altered her makeup and accessories she wore. She sought now only quiet men who deferred to her in earnest and polite ways—Rob Porterfield being the best of the lot. She refused all party invitations, preferring dinner and movies to more spirited nights on the town. It was as if she wished to stay away from anything exuberant—and that included physical passion.

She never slept with the few men she dated; a kiss or two on the lips was as much as she would permit. Her best friends in the Hendley assumed that the murder of Jackson Lawrence had something to do with her retreating socially, but no one was sure what the connection was. They knew the professor was rather sweet on the beautiful Sandra Stark, but then who wasn't? Perhaps she developed a kind of bond with him; perhaps he served some avuncular role in her life, advising her about career choices. In spite of her unashamed affection for Lawrence, after his death she wouldn't speak about him in any way.

When Sandra began dating Rob Porterfield more frequently, her friends thought he was absolutely the wrong man for her. He was pleasant and on the threshold of a partnership with a respectable

Manhattan law firm, but he failed to impress in social situations. At first, her friends tossed off the old chestnut "Be careful of the quiet ones" in an attempt to relieve their anxiety over their good friend's misguided choice of a mate. Porterfield wasn't completely devoid of wit and humor, but he had little if any sexual aura. Simply put, none of Sandra's friends believed he could satisfy their gorgeous colleague in bed. At weekly gatherings at their favorite haunts, these same friends, well-fortified with champagne cocktails, chatted up the hypothesis that Sandra already had a lover or two lined up to do the satisfying, with a well-off potential husband there to provide the entrée to all things socially desirable down in Manhattan.

Rob's quip about the flowers was the first thing he said to Sandra after having been away for several days. He had flown back from San Francisco two days earlier but went directly to interview with two law firms in Manhattan. Sandra assumed that if she continued her relationship with Porterfield, it wouldn't quite be a long-distance one, given the proximity of the university to his office in Manhattan—that is, if he accepted a position there—but every week, except for vacations, they would be apart for at least four and up to six days at a time, given the kind of position he was seeking. Her knowing friends asserted that Sandra wanted this kind of relationship or marriage and therefore wasn't going to hitch herself to a man she was sexually attracted to, a man she would need far more frequently than his career would allow.

After Porterfield kissed her goodbye—again failing to get an invitation to stay the night—Sandra stepped outside to her deck and heard the slight rustle of the wind chimes. Usually comforted by the near haunting Far-Eastern sound, on this occasion she stepped back into the house and looked toward the ornate bookcase in the living room on which rested a thick green volume—a complete edition of *The Christmas Stories of Charles Dickens*, with critical commentary by Jackson Lawrence, published a mere six weeks before his murder in the Hendley Library.

• • •

The seventh stack level was just as empty of patrons on this late Monday afternoon as it had been on that late February evening six months ago.

Added to the usual sparse illumination, the natural lighting gave the area less of an intimidating air, and the dust rag lying in the aisle was freshly moistened, evidence of the custodial staff's early Monday morning pass through the area. The traditional middle-of-the-night cleanings of the upper stack levels ceased after Jackson Lawrence's body was discovered. The changes in the custodial staff since that night didn't matter. The new employees learned immediately what had happened up there. The tales of books on the seventh level having the ability to whisper warnings were now part of the library's folklore, as were the whispered beliefs that another body or two remained undiscovered somewhere among the upper stacks. Still, even the more coldly rational couldn't be completely dismissive of the effects this part of the Hendley had on those with more vivid imaginations.

The Dickens volume slipped easily from its place on one of the upper shelves. The lone patron on the seventh level paused a moment before opening the pages. The section inside the volume was soon located; the covers laid as wide open as the book would allow. It was still there. Six months later, it was still there. As it should have been. The visible streak of Jackson Lawrence's blood. Blood from his fingers. Fingers that touched his neck as he was dying. Blood that Lawrence perhaps used as some kind of ink to leave a clue or message. Perhaps to identify his killer. But all Lawrence managed to get on the two pages was a jagged streak of blood most resembling a check mark. Or was it merely that? Might even this streak be some kind of sign or hint? The visitor was well aware that the past was alive—was always there. Always reminding. Always imploring.

Within a minute, the seventh stack level of the Hendley Tower was again devoid of all patrons. The Dickens volume once more rested comfortably in its sanctuary in the stacks.

CHAPTER 7

His classroom responsibilities having ended with the May graduation, Nichols's plan for this Tuesday was to run at the track, return home and eat breakfast, shower, dress, drive back up to his new academic home, and meet with the realtor who would be showing houses for him and his sister, where both would be living for the next three years. And he'd also have lunch with Fred Beauchamp. Doug Finneran's warning, whether justifiable or not, had disturbed Nichols off and on since their conversation Sunday night. A soft knock on the front door interrupted his musings.

"Good morning, Jeremy."

"It sure is now."

"Belinda still asleep?"

"Haven't heard a peep."

Nichols looked at the lovely woman standing inside his front door and found it hard to believe she was in his life at all. He wished he could proclaim how lucky he was. But he knew better—they both knew better. In one important and very painful way they saw themselves as the unluckiest man and woman in the world.

"You look fetching today, Elizabeth."

"In this old thing?" Elizabeth Ellertson giggled in that slightly raspy way he so adored. She had just turned thirty, but when she laughed like that, she sounded all of six. And on those occasions when she and Belinda started laughing together, Jeremy believed that a listener might think they were two lively young children expressing their unadulterated merriment. In every other way, though, she was a mature and highly desirable woman. A woman he deeply loved. A woman who was, in all ways, different from Meredith Jamison, except for the outline of their faces—not the specific parts but the outline—which in his mind was identical in structure. It was as if someone had replaced Meredith's eyes, nose, lips, and mouth with the corresponding features of Elizabeth Ellertson. Just kept the bone structure and oval shape and replaced the individual parts. As she had been doing for several weeks, she dropped by to watch Belinda while Nichols followed his periodic morning regimen of running at the university track.

Elizabeth Ellertson was rounder and softer than Meredith, and Nichols always felt a welcoming "give" of her flesh when he put his arms around her. Meredith's body was more naturally sinewy and resistant to the touch. And there was another significant difference between the two women. Meredith disdained the very idea of marriage, while Elizabeth entered the state eagerly. But as yet she had not exited out of it, which was the painful reality they both confronted.

Jeremy was very much in love with Elizabeth Ellertson and desirous of spending every night with her. And he was confident she was equally in love with him. Her insistence that he call her "Elizabeth" and not any of the seemingly endless diminutives of the name charmed him. She demanded all four syllables. She told him playfully she would answer to no less than four, so he could save his "Beth," his "Liz," and especially his "Betty" for some other Elizabeth. Her husband, who was at work early on Tuesdays and Thursdays, had the infuriating habit of calling his wife—the married Elizabeth Ellertson—"Double-E."

What mitigated Jeremy's guilt over their clandestine relationship was the fact that she wanted out of her marriage even before she met him the previous September at the university's fall convocation. Steve Ellertson was a newly tenured associate professor of Music, and he had struck up a lively conversation with untenured assistant professor of English Jeremy Nichols regarding movie versions of the novels of Charles Dickens. Ten minutes into their discussion, Elizabeth Ellertson wandered over and introduced herself to the man with whom she would soon fall in love.

Nichols felt an immediate attraction, but it was so unlike the one he experienced upon first meeting Meredith. Without question, Elizabeth was more than simply pretty, although her husband seemed neither proud nor protective of her. When she joined Steve Ellertson that day, holding a plastic cup of punch and small paper plate of *hors d'oeuvres*, Elizabeth appeared preoccupied, if not fatigued and unhappy. Yet the moment she put the plate down in order to shake Nichols's hands, her face came back to life.

As Nichols tried to broaden the conversation to include her, he found himself taking on the role of interviewer, asking if the Ellertsons had any children—they didn't—and what Elizabeth did with her days—she taught piano from her home and often accompanied in the evenings for miscellaneous community theater productions, as well as the occasional recital. Jeremy also inquired where the two of them had met. Ellertson answered, "Near Orton Hall's Chimes Tower, on the Oval at Ohio State. I happened to see her strolling across the grass, a vision of female pulchritude—both barefoot and bra-less."

Nichols winced at Ellertson's gratuitous and inelegant description of his wife and diverted his eyes from Elizabeth in order to save her further embarrassment.

"Double E here was just a sophomore. I was a few months shy of graduation. Okay. Long story short. I showed her the best of my charms, and within a year we were married."

Nichols found pathetic Ellertson's vulgar emphasis on "charms," and he didn't ask the man to explain the "Double E" reference. A month later Elizabeth would explain it, as well as a host of her husband's other objectionable idiosyncrasies that made her so often uncomfortable and depressed. At the convocation, her face wasn't flushed with embarrassment; rather it was almost pallid. Fortunately, Ellertson shifted the conversation to the prospects of Ohio State's current football season—that is, after he trained his eyes briefly in an intimidating fashion on Nichols, who apparently looked at his wife's sweet face one time too many.

Ellertson informed Nichols that he'd been a walk-on linebacker at Ohio State as a freshman, but that a "fucked-up shoulder" put an end to any hopes he had to play big-time college football. Jeremy wasn't surprised. Ellertson's body still reflected the linebacker/fullback physique of most men who played either position. The man's body type, personality, earthy vocabulary, and vulgar allusions made Ellertson's being an associate professor of music simply incongruous.

It was only after Jeremy began seeing Elizabeth alone that he learned of the four or five times Ellertson had agreed with his wife that they should divorce. She said he even remained calm and reasonable when they spoke with a counselor about the future of their marriage. But that night and for the first time he threatened her with physical harm for having complained to a stranger about his shortcomings. Elizabeth didn't mention any further threats to her person, but she did admit to Jeremy that she had stopped loving her husband in the second year of their six-year marriage. She also emphasized that she never had an affair—or had ever sought one.

Nichols tried to assure himself that the state of the Ellertson marriage had nothing at all to do with him and the love he professed to Elizabeth, for she often expressed dismay that the couple hadn't yet secured divorce lawyers. She told Nichols that Steve frequently promised, "As soon as this semester is over" or "Just as soon as I get tenure." But semesters came and went and tenure had been secured. Nichols listened to Elizabeth's refrain, "Why won't Steve accept that he would be happier moving on from what he surely must feel is a loveless marriage?" She assured Jeremy there was no longer any sexual intimacy between them, although though Nichols understood, even without her telling him, that the Ellertsons were still sleeping in the same bed. The thought left him angry and frustrated.

At one point, he asked why, since Steve wouldn't budge, she hadn't seen a lawyer and started the process.

"Jeremy, I just can't. Not now. It's just that I need for us to be in agreement from the very start of the divorce proceedings. I need to talk more about this to someone I really trust before I do anything on my own."

Jeremy assumed she wasn't telling him everything—for example, about this unnamed confidant she alluded to—but he couldn't bring himself to push the matter, although his patience was sorely tested.

But now he had another issue to contemplate. The murder of Jackson Lawrence had played with his imagination since the moment Fred Beauchamp pointed to the spot where the body was discovered at the top of the Hendley Tower. Nichols was amazed he never found the event worthy of his attention before now. Since graduate school, he'd read all of Lawrence's work on Dickens and accordingly found the man's death a serious blow to Dickens scholarship. After all, Lawrence was an exceptional scholar-critic in his early forties, with many years of productive scholarship and writing ahead of him. Even Doug Finneran's three-year stint at the university hadn't influenced his thinking about the crime. Nichols had twice in those years visited Finneran at the university, but both occasions occurred before the murder, and at neither time did the men go over to the Hendley.

But now that he'd been there, Nichols couldn't stop dwelling on the event. Perhaps those with a historical bent who visited Ford's Theatre or Dealey Plaza found themselves coming away inordinately interested in the assassination of a president, leading to further reading on the subject and a return visit to Washington or Dallas. Besides that, there was his daughter's haunting and inexplicable sketch of the man lying face down with his hand touching a book.

Even as he leaned forward to kiss Elizabeth, Nichols knew there might well be more to learn about the murder than what Beauchamp told him. He smiled at a fresh thought. Perhaps he could get a nice article out of his further probing published in *Dickens Quarterly*.

• • •

With much relief, Finneran pulled into the parking lot of the apartment complex in Amherst where he lived after he and Heather separated. He couldn't be happier that this was the last time he'd enter his "bachelor pad." Once he removed the rest of his books and miscellaneous possessions, he would lock the door, return the key, and begin to put the most disastrous period of his life behind him.

As he stepped into the living room, he noticed something was amiss. The bedroom door of the apartment was open. He was sure he'd shut it when he left, after loading his car the previous evening. Conceding to instinct, Finneran stood to the side of the bedroom door, turned the knob, and gently pushed it open. He looked inside and saw that everything was as he had left it. The bed was stripped of his personal linen and covered with the bedspread that came with the furnished apartment. The alarm clock he no longer wanted remained on the bed stand; the drapes were still pulled shut, letting him know that no one had entered through the window.

Finneran cautiously opened the closet door. Nothing different—the same four wire hangers remained where they were the previous evening. Coming out of the bedroom, Finneran headed for the kitchen. He recalled he hadn't emptied the drawers of the silverware, knives, and assorted long spoons and spatulas. As he placed these items in a cardboard box, Finneran discovered several printed pages of emails he brought from his office before he and Heather went on their trip to Ottawa and began mending their broken marriage. One of the emails was from his friend Jeremy Nichols.

"Doug, haven't heard from you in a while, so I thought I'd write and ask how you are. All's well with me, although nothing's been resolved regarding Elizabeth's marriage. Anyway, I'll be heading up to your old stomping grounds in a week to get the lay of the land. But if I have any questions about surviving as a member of the junior faculty, I'm sure you'll advise wisely.

"I'm also sure you're wondering what I'm going to do about Elizabeth and my relationship when I make the move next month or so. To be honest, I don't know. Fortunately the drive is not that long from where I am now—about two-and-a-half hours—so we'll see each other when we can until she ends her marriage.

"Anyway, I'm thinking about you and Heather and your forthcoming trip to Canada. You have all my prayers and good wishes. —Jeremy."

Finneran clenched his fists in anger at himself. "God damn it, Doug. Why the hell did you...?" His voice trailed off as he quickly regained his composure.

Emptying the last of the drawers into the cardboard box, Finneran realized something was missing.

Before he could turn his head to look for it, he felt the sudden rush of heat radiating up his back and neck. In another second, when he sensed the heat touching him below both ears, he felt the pain right before he dropped to the floor after being stabbed by the carving knife he didn't see in the box.

• • •

Heather Finneran picked up the phone. "Hello?" The line went dead. She checked the caller ID. It was her husband's cell. He's probably on the road, she thought. She wouldn't ring him back because, being inordinately safety-conscious, she never called if she knew he was at the wheel. She'd just wait until he called again or came home.

• • •

So Heather Finneran was home alone. Wrapping the carving knife in a dishrag, the caller noticed the printed email from Jeremy Nichols.

CHAPTER 8

After making arrangements to speak with the realtor at 2:00 p.m., Jeremy called Beauchamp, who suggested they meet for lunch at a little coffee and sandwich shop across the street from the Hendley. Nichols had only just been seated in the quaint 1950s-style booth, when Beauchamp arrived.

"Jeremy, so good to see you again." The men shook hands, and Nichols was again impressed by the firmness of the retired professor's grip. Everything but the deepening cracks around his eyes belied Beauchamp's seventy-three years.

Nichols insisted up front that he pay for lunch, but Beauchamp waved him off. It all seemed so bizarre, Nichols thought. Fred Beauchamp was as far removed from Nichols's academic league as he could possibly be. He was a distinguished scholar, an honor graduate of Howard University in 1969, and later a PhD recipient at the University of Chicago. The former holder of two endowed chairs at two premier institutions and still quoted frequently in essays and books relating to his field, Beauchamp was the English Department's prized hire of the late 1980s, when he was already at the top of his game. Twenty-eight more fruitful years followed at the prestigious university at which Nichols pal Doug Finneran taught but had no chance of being retained. A scholar with academic recognitions from seven countries—with civic awards from three New England states, Beauchamp was known to his colleagues and students as a man with a political conscience and an environmental commitment—regardless of the titillating rumors about his CIA affiliation that Finneran shared on the phone the night before.

After the server took their order, Nichols expressed his gratitude. "Sir, it's very kind of you invite me to have lunch with you. I mean, after having already talked with me on Saturday. Thank you."

"Come on, Jeremy. Call me Fred. I'm seventy-three but not all that venerable." Nichols wanted to argue the point but merely nodded as Beauchamp continued. "You know I was thinking about that talk we had regarding the murder of Jack Lawrence."

Nichols was startled by the abruptness and coincidence of Beauchamp's comment. "I have too,...Fred. In fact, I was giving it some thought both last night and this morning."

"Really?" Beauchamp nodded his head. "Jeremy, you know it's very possible you could follow your three-year appointment here with another one of the same duration. I could help make that happen."

To Nichols, it was both flattering and assuring that he had made an impression on the emeritus professor, but still Beauchamp's remark left him uneasy and suspicious. Vanity aside, Nichols knew the retired professor was still carefully evaluating the young scholar sitting across from him. Once more Doug Finneran's warning came to mind.

"You know, Jeremy, I'll never forget last winter when Jack was killed. It was a week, maybe ten days, later that I was heading up to Durham to give a paper and got caught in one of those rare cyclone weather effects you hear about but only rarely ever see. Twenty inches of snow over the next couple of days. Snowfall amounts in Philadelphia, Harrisburg, Hartford—all unusual. Anyway, when I was up in New Hampshire, I kept thinking how much Jack would have loved being stuck in all that snow. He was a pure romantic, you know. The only man I ever knew who quoted Chaucer, Shakespeare, and Dickens while skating on that little oval lake near where we once both had cottages."

By now, Nichols was eager to hear anything Beauchamp had to say about his former colleague, and he offered a smile as an inducement for the older man to continue.

"Tell me. Does your wife work, Jeremy?"

"I'm not married. Never have been, if truth be told."

Beauchamp frowned. "I shouldn't have asked that. Forgive me. I thought you had a daughter."

"I do. Belinda. The proverbial light of my life. But I've never...I mean, I'm not married."

"Now I'm not too old to appreciate that we live, excuse the cliché, in a complicated world, my boy."

Beauchamp turned his head and stared at a couple sitting in another booth. When he turned it back, Beauchamp's face wore a different expression. Nichols thought it impish. "Jeremy, you know you could make more money teaching elsewhere. The university knows it too, and they also know damn well they won't pay you what you're worth. They argue that you'll come away from here with a golden resume. With the university's imprimatur, as it were. Let another university pay you a decent wage after you've finished your time here. At any rate, that's their carefully considered and penurious opinion on the matter."

The men laughed, and Nichols realized he felt just as comfortable in Beauchamp's company as he believed the emeritus professor did in his.

"Jeremy, getting back on track, I have to tell you I've been thinking so often lately about the day Jack Lawrence was killed. I don't know. Maybe it's because we've just passed six months since the murder." Beauchamp paused while the food was placed before them. "Now I'm not boring you with the subject—am I?"

"Not at all. I'm of course interested to learn as much as I can about Professor Lawrence." Nichols was certain Beauchamp could tell he wasn't feigning interest in the slightest.

"That's good. Very good."

Still, Nichols remained perplexed by Beauchamp's confiding in him about Lawrence and his murder. Was this another test? Or was Beauchamp's mind beginning to show evidence of instability? Nichols knew he was otherwise razor sharp, especially for a man in his seventies, but recalling his own maternal grandfather and how quickly he fell into the dreaded abyss of Alzheimer's made Nichols cautious about Beauchamp's apparent affection for him.

"Well, my boy, let's pause for a second and have a bite of these sandwiches. I can guarantee you'll find that one to your liking."

• • •

After returning from the Hendley, Sandra Stark started gathering the desired snacks for the arrival of her step-sister Aubrey, who was driving down from New Hampshire to spend a couple of days with her. The periodic "Escape from Dartmouth," as her step-sister called it. Having left school for eighteen months after her sophomore year to "see the world," which consisted of a year in Sonoma and six months in Berkeley working while her then boyfriend finished his degree and began graduate school in California, Aubrey had returned to Hanover early to await the beginning of the summer term, spending leisure time with her roommates and with her latest romantic interest, a Dartmouth senior whom Sandra was most anxious to meet. Aubrey announced she would return to the Dartmouth swim team and—oh, by the way—that she also planned to gain admission to the medical school after completing her Bachelor's degree. The joke between them was that she would rock the medical community by making "poolside calls"—but only, Aubrey added alliteratively, if "the male pulchritude by poolside was promising enough."

Family. It had always been foremost on Sandra's mind from the time she could remember. The memories of family were her dolls and blankets, the memories she would caress and cover herself—or rather hide herself—in.

Her mother had two happy marriages. The first ended tragically when Sandra was barely two, when her father lost his life on a recreational flight to Western Massachusetts. Sandra's mother remained a widow for seven years until she fell in love with a newly retired NHL goalie. Recently divorced, Sandra's step-father brought to the marriage a seven-year-old boy, Will, and a five-year-old girl, Aubrey—who, owing to a highly satisfactory agreement between their biological parents, spent a considerable amount of time with their father's new family. The step-siblings also joined a rather large brood of Stark cousins, who in the fall would gather *en masse* for a campground spectacular in the Minutemen Region of Massachusetts. Sandra would never forget the songs, stories, potluck dishes, wine coolers, beer, and roaring campfires. And of course, the annual warnings to all the children to stand safely away from the fire when they were allowed to toss their half-eaten corn cobs into the blaze.

Sandra picked up the large framed photo of her then immediate family—her parents, the two step siblings and her—taken when she graduated from high school. With her finger, she gently touched each of the faces—even her own. At that moment, the breeze picked up and nudged the chimes on the deck loud enough to hear through the closed back door.

CHAPTER 9

I am well aware that far too many think a professional actress is, in essence, little more than a sibling of the prostitute who, in exchange for a paid role in a play, would in effect offer her chastity to an eager audience or to her fellow actors. How could I ever believe that at age eighteen Ellen Ternan is in any manner impure—in her actions, in her musings, or in her personal history?

Yet should I give life to my imaginings, Ellen's reputation would suffer, as well as and even more than my own. What I could survive following public scrutiny she most certainly could not.

The difficult truth is that I can no longer bear the thought of beginning another year living with my wife. When I first experienced contempt for Kate, I was horrified, even though I felt justified because of her utter lack of sparkle. How her energies sagged with the birth and burden of each child.

And such was the state of my spirits when first I saw Mrs. Ternan's youngest daughter. The fact that young Ellen was on the threshold, ready to step in and take up full residence in my heart, still has nothing to do with my decision that being in the same bedroom with my wife can no longer be endured. To leave the house and my wife must be an action taken and not merely a pathetic wish. Now there is a real and desirable young woman who finds me worthy of her attentions.

The reader of the diary entry visualized Dickens setting down his pen with the understanding that what he believed he couldn't have with Ellen he would experience by writing what no one would be permitted to see but himself. Secrets to be kept—for the rest of his life—and beyond.

• • •

"Jeremy, you really would have liked Jackson Lawrence, I'm quite sure of it."

"I'm sure I would have." Nichols dropped his eyes and surreptitiously checked his cell phone for any missed calls from his sister Janis, who had Belinda while he was away. He slipped the phone into his pocket without Beauchamp's noticing.

Beauchamp chuckled as he took a sip of the house Merlot. Nichols imagined that the retired professor ordered the same sandwich and the same wine each time he came to this establishment. Regardless, Nichols appreciated Beauchamp's utter lack of pretentiousness.

"Jack Lawrence was a first-class rascal. Attending conferences with him was memorable, to say the least."

Nichols noted the blithe expression on Beauchamp's face. He wondered exactly how close the two men were. He wanted to learn more about Lawrence and was eager to encourage Beauchamp to speak further of the murder and any possible motive for it. "How long did you and Professor Lawrence know each other?"

"We first met when I came here to teach, but we never really became friendly until we talked in the hallway after a rather difficult department meeting. We found we both had little use for the new department head, who demonstrated his intolerable Machiavellian side, which was little remarked upon by our department colleagues. Jack and I then sauntered over to what later became our favorite watering hole and did a full analysis of the new head."

"And you determined...?"

"That he was good at forwarding himself as a thoughtful and personable colleague, even though we could tell he didn't give a damn about whose feet he'd step on or into whose back he'd place the blade. It took a while, but Jack and I were proved right."

"And what happened to the department head?"

"He lasted only one year. He early on decided to play hard-ball with Jack. I was a bit offended that he left me alone, but I think my skin color had something to do with that. You see, the man understood the politics of university life very well."

Jeremy delighted in the tale. "And where did he go after that year?"

Beauchamp finished his Merlot. "Right where he belonged—and wanted to be. His punishment was to be named Dean of Arts and Sciences. Needless to say, he was in a position to continue his bombing runs on poor Jack. But..."

"What?"

"Never mind for now. I have to hold some things back so that you'll want to have lunch with me again."

Jeremy still couldn't believe his fortune. Fred Beauchamp felt him worthy of his old war stories and further lunches.

"Speaking of my late friend, Jack was a dynamic speaker."

"So I've learned from others in the profession. I truly regret being unable to hear him at two conferences I planned to attend but couldn't."

"Couldn't afford the travel?"

"That and some personal issues that came up."

"I understand, but as I was saying, Jack was simply brilliant. He had the complete attention of everyone he stood before—especially the female gender." Beauchamp flashed the smile of the knowing and ordered another glass of wine. "Let's just say that Professor Lawrence had this gift of communicating marvelously with his female undergraduate and graduate students. If he were a modern-day rock star, he would have had more than his share of groupies." Nichols laughed at the seeming incongruity of Beauchamp's using such a term. "Jack was the most popular teacher we had—at both graduate and undergraduate levels. He literally had to turn away students who wanted him to direct their theses or dissertations—even though,..." Beauchamp couldn't contain his smile.

"What?" Nichols felt like a schoolboy about to hear his first prurient tale.

"It's nothing. Just that now that I look back, I believe he only turned down male students." Nichols's face expressed his skepticism. "No, I'm serious, Jeremy. The man clearly adored women and the feeling was, more often than not, quite mutual."

"Any 'documented' relationships with his students?" What the hell, Nichols thought. He might as well be direct.

"Jack wasn't the 'kiss-and-tell' type. Nor was anyone he might have been involved with. On more than one occasion he said to me with that characteristic dramatic flair of his, 'I can neither confirm nor deny.' I know for certain that the wily son of a bitch had at least a few romantic liaisons with some of these younger women."

"Really?" Nichols wanted Beauchamp to be as specific as he could.

"You should have seen him at the conferences. We'd be in a bar having a couple of drinks after the day's sessions were over, and it never failed. Jack would be holding court with our female graduate students who attended the conference and with those from other schools who listened to his paper earlier in the day. The next thing I knew, our original plan to have dinner for two proliferated into a table of seven or eight. As I said, women simply loved him. He had this uncanny ability to make each one think he was interested only in her, even though he might be talking with five others at the same time."

Taking the second glass of Merlot from the server before it touched the table, Beauchamp's face erased its cheeriness and replaced it with a look more contemplative. Nichols knew he was about to bring up the matter on which he ended his conversation a few days earlier.

"Jack told me shortly before he died that he possessed two things he could be killed over."

Nichols's mind again ran through the possibilities. None of them made sense. "Did he tell you what they were, Fred?"

"He told me what one of them was but not the other."

The look on Beauchamp's face suggested to Nichols that he was most satisfied with the younger man's interest. Nichols had the uncomfortable feeling he was being gently shepherded into some kind of trap. Again, he thought of Doug Finneran's admonition.

Beauchamp's sustained silence prompted Nichols's follow-up question. "Could it have been some kind of matter relating to the government? And by 'government' I don't mean state or university."

Beauchamp threw up his hands in mock horror. "What are you saying, Jeremy? Something like the CIA?"

"Or a similar agency."

As Beauchamp stared at the glass of the inexpensive wine, prolonging his reply, Nichols concluded that the emeritus professor had picked up at least some of Jackson Lawrence's impishly teasing ways. Beauchamp moved the glass several inches on the table and looked both left and right before speaking. Nichols believed Beauchamp was deliberately putting him on with these little histrionics.

"So you think the CIA or a 'similar agency.' I see. Not sure you're aware, my boy, of the presence these organizations historically have had at this university and elsewhere in academia."

"I've heard tales. I also flipped through a decent book on the topic last summer." Nichols assumed Doug Finneran would feel vindicated, since his good friend warned Jeremy that he was being evaluated for some extra-curricular work by the venerable Fred Beauchamp. Still, Lawrence's murder in the Hendley kept getting in the way of unimpeded consideration of any direct discussion relating to intelligence agencies. But perhaps now Nichols was going to be informed of a connection between the two. He looked in Beauchamp's eyes for any sign that indeed there was one.

Beauchamp smiled and daubed his mouth with his napkin. "You know, Jeremy, some in the ivory tower slip out through the subterranean passages from time to time for all kinds of fun assignments both at home and abroad. Have any idea how many sabbaticals are spent in Washington or at Langley?"

Nichols frowned. He recalled that only two weeks ago he had laughed at a colleague's assertion that ninety percent of the faculty where Jeremy was heading off to teach would be willing to assist the FBI if so asked. Nichols thought the estimate ludicrous, conceding only to twenty percent, tops. And he made clear he would not be one of that twenty percent.

Beauchamp spoke next of the various recruitment techniques and the concerted effort on the part of the CIA to improve relations with academia. Now Nichols wondered if Beauchamp himself had been become disenchanted with the agency, for Nichols was convinced that the distinguished professor had indeed been in the CIA's employ. Instead of recruiting him, was Beauchamp planning on using him as a willing ear to his complaints and anecdotes from his more colorful past? And again, what did Lawrence's murder have to do with all this?

"Fred, I have to say that I've almost exclusively thought of the agencies and academia as the cobra and mongoose. The former hunting out and hounding whom they believed to have too dangerous a dissenting voice and the latter fighting back with indignation and lawsuits, maintaining active diligence as well as hostility for such trespassing."

Beauchamp's broad grin left Nichols uncomfortable. "Well put, my boy. Very well put. You *do* know, don't you, that several years ago the Senate created a scholarship for the training of analysts and intelligence operatives in our universities for careers in the CIA and related agencies? You do know that, *don't* you?"

"I'm embarrassed to say I wasn't aware of that fact."

"Oh yes, my young friend, the names of the participants are shrouded in secrecy by Senate decree."

Nichols wanted to ask him how he'd been tapped. He knew Beauchamp hadn't attended an Ivy League school. Was he approached before he graduated from Howard University, which was conveniently located in Washington? It made sense. Nichols's reading the previous summer informed him that Howard led all the historic black colleges and universities in the number of its graduates on the CIA's roll call. But what about in the late 1960s?

"Jeremy, many of my colleagues here and in the profession are greatly concerned about what seems to be the warming of relations between your mongoose and cobra. The standard line delivered by these colleagues is that the relationship was far too chummy back in the 50s and early 60s. They have of course generally conceded that the more hostile atmosphere of the late 60s, 70s, and 80s wasn't quite ideal for either the cobra or the mongoose, but they would still prefer to see the wariness remain more knee-jerk than carefully reasoned. They fear in the post-9/11 world another era of mutual trust and affability between the agencies and academia has begun." Beauchamp paused for another sip of Merlot. "Is that your feeling as well, Jeremy?"

Nichols realized his answer might well determine the nature of his future relationship with Beauchamp. Were he to say what his instincts encouraged, he assumed the kindly professor would cease all social communication between them. Then it hit him. Was the conversation about Jackson Lawrence's death meant, then, as a form of intimidation? Could it be that Beauchamp was suggesting a similar fate for the young untenured professor if he refused the offer Beauchamp had yet to present him? Nichols literally shook his head to knock such an absurd scenario out of his mind.

Beauchamp sighed as the server removed the plates and silverware from the table. After the young woman departed with Beauchamp's credit card, he reached over and touched the top of Nichols's wrist.

"The relationship, as you may also know, is also becoming less discreet. More students are showing interest in doing work for the CIA—even lining up at recruiting booths. The tragic blunders in the Middle East haven't dampened the enthusiasm any, I'm afraid. I'm just worried about the direction it's all going. Wide-eyed eagerness is not all it's cracked up to be. It suggests only an ephemeral commitment. High school stuff, really. And such youthful exuberance can lead to blindness and behavior of the worst kind."

Nichols desired the topic of their conversation to end—at least for the time being. He was ashamed of himself for initially seeing Fred Beauchamp simply as a brilliant and congenial scholar of a by-gone era. He moreover felt embarrassed at having even for a moment been vain enough to seek being courted by someone representing the CIA or FBI. But now he didn't want to hear any offer, regardless of how indirect. He kept thinking of Jackson Lawrence lying dead in the Hendley tower.

"Anyway, getting back to Jack Lawrence."

Beauchamp's transition unsettled Nichols, who found the only way he could regain his footing was to ask questions. "Professor Beauchamp..." His lunch companion tightened his face at the return to the formal address. "...did Lawrence travel much abroad?"

"On the average of once or twice a year—spending at least a full week in England and Europe during each trip. And as a noted scholar of Dickens, he of course spent a great deal of time in London at the British and the Victoria and Albert Libraries."

"Did he spend any time in university administration?"

"Oh, no. Don't you remember what I told you about his enemy—his cobra, the Dean of Arts and Sciences?"

"Right. Well, did he take frequent trips to Washington?"

Beauchamp took some time answering, almost as if he were trying to determine exactly on how many occasions Lawrence drove or flew down to the national's capital. Nichols had the feeling Beauchamp was again playacting.

"Let me see. He told me he went down to D.C. *at least* once every three or four months. Said he had a sister and her family down there. Though I don't recall ever having met them. He never married, you know."

"So, you believe he knew something that might have compromised national security and therefore believed himself in danger?"

Beauchamp's face radiated a mixture of surprise and delight. "What a fascinating hypothesis, Jeremy. There is no question about it. We've just hired ourselves a first-rate mind. May I have a moment to bask in some self-congratulations for having attempted to influence the faculty vote?"

Nichols was by now bewildered by Beauchamp's reaction and the direction he had taken their conversation. But he knew that something else was coming. Once more, he sought to direct the topic back to Lawrence's murder, but before he could pose another question, Beauchamp signed the credit slip and placed his wallet back in his pants pocket.

"Jeremy, I think it best to say no more about that unfortunate night—at least for right now. Never fear—we will return to the subject. Now then." Beauchamp wiped his mouth a final time and placed both hands on the table and folded them like a schoolboy.

Here it comes, Nichols thought.

"Jeremy, you're a talented young man in your field and in the classroom. You are well liked by your students and you have the support of the other junior members of this faculty whom you've met. And those of the tenured faculty who have given you a second thought have offered some praise as well."

"Thank you for saying so."

"But I think you know that I'm not sitting here having lunch with you merely because you're a fine scholar and teacher."

"I know that, sir. I understand."

"I'm sure you do. So let me get to the point. We think you would make an excellent..."

Nichols put up his hand, his palm toward Fred Beauchamp. "I've thought about this possibility, sir."

Beauchamp began to nod even before Nichols got to his answer. "I'm sure you have, Jeremy...but?"

"But I don't think the kind of life you're hinting at is for me. Please don't take offense at that, Fred."

"Do you know how many who are in the employ of their country begin by saying the same thing, Jeremy?" Beauchamp paused only briefly. "You can put down your hand now." A flustered Nichols folded his hand into a fist before he put it back on the table.

"Sir, I'm not political. I'm not very adventurous. I don't like to take chances. So I..."

"Really? You sure about that, Jeremy? You're really sure about that? Beauchamp raised his thick salt and pepper eyebrows.

Nichols froze. "I...I..."

"Pretty big chance you've taken in your private life. Excuse me. *Are* taking, wouldn't you say?"

Stunned, Nichols realized Beauchamp was alluding to his relationship with Elizabeth Ellertson.

"Wondering how I would know about that, Jeremy?" Nichols remained impassive yet aghast. "Think about it. What's the cliché of the day? *Vetted?* I know all about you. Your past as well as your present. And I have a good idea about your future."

The server interrupted and asked if there would be anything else. But it didn't matter, Beauchamp was through talking.

"I think we're going to have a splendid relationship, Jeremy. There is so much you'll be able to do for your country. In fact, you may be the only one who can do what we need done." His face lit up with a chuckle and massive grin. "I'm sure you'll agree to take on the assignment." Beauchamp didn't wait for an answer he wouldn't be getting anyway. "We'll talk again soon. Have a nice drive back, my boy."

As he watched Beauchamp exit through the door, Nichols tried to take the last swallow of his draught beer. He put down the pint glass as soon as he looked at his hands. They were shaking too violently to lift the glass to his mouth.

CHAPTER 10

Belinda Nichols paid no attention to the blue sedan slowly passing by. Tossing a clump of pine straw over her head and then scampering out of the way before it fell demanded too much concentration to allow for any scanning of the street in front of her house.

"Aunt Janis, watch me!"

Janis had just come around the house with rake in hand. "Okay, show me your speed, Belinda Bug."

Belinda tossed up another clump, but not high enough this time. She scowled as she felt the moist pine straw clinging to her hair. She approached her aunt, stoic in defeat. "Can we go inside now? I want to paint another picture for Daddy before he gets home." What a face, Janis thought to herself. She looked toward the street just in time to see a blue car stopped several houses down the block.

• • •

Stuart Dryden had long ago left the life of an active publishing scholar, but he still liked to keep up with whom his old department hired over the years. Since Dryden learned that Jeremy Nichols was about to begin a three-year stint, he asked for and received background on the young man. His interest turned to concern when he saw that Nichols was a Dickensian. The young scholar was evidently qualified and talented; he might well in a few years crack into the selected circle of outstanding scholars currently writing on the famous Victorian novelist. Nichols had a book in press and had already published two particularly fine articles, as well as delivered several papers at regional and national conferences.

Now fifty-eight, Dryden was on the threshold of an incredible achievement, especially for someone of his background. Given that his last name was the same as the greatest English writer of the late seventeenth century, John Dryden, it seemed fated that the highly intelligent Stuart Dryden would do a PhD in literary studies. But what wasn't imagined was that he would publish several important books and essays on another famous Victorian novelist—William Makepeace Thackeray, the author of *Vanity Fair*. Son of an acclaimed Boston attorney, Dryden came from solid Puritan stock, on both paternal and maternal sides, all of whom believed discretion always trumped valor along with most of the other virtues. They expected their son to have a long career publishing scholarship and criticism on Dickens's rival, work emphasizing Victorian morality and propriety, but they couldn't have imagined their boy would toss his scholarly career aside for the dirtier business of politics—first as Dean of Arts and Sciences at the university, followed with three terms in the state Senate, and finally as a member of the U. S. House of Representatives. And now he was positioned to run for and win his party's nomination for an expiring U.S. Senate seat in the election a little over a year away.

Dryden began to type his congratulations to Nichols after double-checking the younger man's current email address. He only finished the "Dear Professor Nichols" salutation when he quickly lifted his hands from the keyboard. The same intruder crept up once again: Jackson Lawrence. Just the brief conscious memory of the man—that was all it took. Yet his thoughts of the deceased scholar were hardly ever brief. Dryden rolled his chair away from his desk and took a deep breath. The difficult moment brought back the memory of events at the Hendley Library. Through connections, he had influenced his old department to avoid hiring a senior Dickensian to take Jack Lawrence's place—and they did not, giving the full professorship to a noted scholar of Victorian women novelists. But they had signed on for a three-year position a young and probably highly curious and tireless Dickens specialist in Jeremy Nichols. Dryden decided against sending the congratulatory note to the new hire. No need to make the lad wonder why the present congressman and likely future senator would attempt to strike up a relationship with him. Dryden would have to keep tabs on the young scholar in other ways.

• • •

Driving back home late Tuesday afternoon, Nichols fought the constant urge to replay and decipher all Beauchamp had said to him, especially moments before they parted. He was certain the emeritus professor would make his intentions clear enough in the days ahead. Besides, Jeremy was looking forward to the rest of the day in large part because he would be able to see Elizabeth. She would drop by after 8:00 p.m. for an hour or two. Steve Ellertson would be taking an afternoon flight to attend a musical symposium at the University of Maryland, which was scheduled to begin Wednesday afternoon. Ellertson wouldn't call his wife while he was away; he had stopped extending that courtesy months ago.

Accordingly, Nichols understood he'd once more be wrestling with the thought of convincing Elizabeth to spend the night in his bed. He assumed she'd balk and ask what would happen "if Steve for some reason did call home," and then she would remind Jeremy that his daughter was sleeping only a few feet down the hall. He was genuinely sensitive to her concerns and was grateful both for her conscience and prudence, as well as her refusal to say that making love and sleeping in his bed would be in any way "wrong." He just wanted her for a full night—to make love to and then caress as she lay asleep next to him.

With his and Elizabeth's flexible schedules—as well as with Steve Ellertson's own penchant for traveling to Manhattan or Boston and occasionally to the Baltimore-Washington area for musical events and conferences—being in each other's company wasn't difficult, although one or two hours was normally the longest they could spend together at any one time. Yet, during those days and early evenings, Elizabeth never felt comfortable enough to make love. She even had scruples about kissing and touching him too ardently, not wishing to add to the frustration they both felt when they were together. And of course, there was nagging guilt and fear of discovery. Nichols had already grown weary of only imagining how she would feel against his body as she moved under him.

Nichols turned off the car radio and reached for his cell phone. He realized he hadn't turned the phone's volume back up after parting from Fred Beauchamp at the coffee and sandwich shop. He had a voice message—probably Belinda or Janis wanting to know when he'd get home.

"Jeremy, it's me—Heather. Well, it all worked out, as Doug told you. So, I'm wondering whether you had a chance to...wait...hey!" Her voice suddenly become so soft that it was hardly discernible. After several moments of muffled sounds—as if the phone were beings rubbed against her clothing, her voice came back on the line. "I can't talk now," she whispered and the call was cut off.

Nichols's initial feeling of anxiety was eased when he recalled what she wrote in a brief email to him a week and half ago.

Jeremy, I don't know how it's going to go with Doug when we
take our trip to Canada for a week. But if things work out for us,
I want to plan a surprise birthday party for him at the Boathouse
in Central Park, and a Yankees game if they're home on the 24th.
I want you to join us. But it's a SECRET. Don't tell him anything,
okay? Check your schedule.
Love, Heather.

Nichols concluded that Doug surprised her just as she began leaving her message. He laughed. That bastard Finneran always had a knack of screwing up surprises. He couldn't keep a damn secret to save his life.

Nichols recollected how for almost two years after the day Meredith walked out of his and Belinda's lives, he had experienced palpable anxiety whenever the phone rang. It took him that long to stop believing Meredith was any day going to call him and ask about her daughter, whom she wouldn't be able to recognize if her life depended on it. Then she'd want to see Belinda. If he refused his permission, she would likely get an attorney, and he knew there was no judge in the state inclined to deny the birth mother the right to see her daughter, even if she had abandoned that child shortly after its birth. Perhaps Meredith had purged her personal demons, finding religion or whatever it might have been that finally stimulated a latent maternal instinct. Yet it was also possible she had deteriorated even further in the four years since he last saw her, even harboring a sadistic wish to hurt Jeremy in the one way she knew she could most effectively damage him—through their daughter.

He called Meredith's mother a week after her daughter left and again three weeks after that. Greta Jamison didn't know where her daughter was and had only spoken with her by phone. In fact, she hadn't seen her "in about a year." She moreover made clear she wished to honor Meredith's request that she keep from Nichols her whereabouts, but added that her runaway daughter would contact him "when she felt the time was right." When he hung up, Nichols was already convinced Mrs. Jamison had no idea her daughter was even pregnant, let alone that she had given birth to a beautiful baby girl. He understood he could have called back and at least informed the woman she was a grandmother—but he never did.

Nichols shifted his thoughts to the murder of Jackson Lawrence, and by the time he drove into his neighborhood, he decided to make another trip up to the Hendley—probably on Thursday or Friday. Besides, he needed to go back and sign the papers on the house he had chosen for him and Belinda and to look at other homes nearby for Janis and the girls. He smiled. His sister certainly wouldn't have accepted anything he was shown today. Once he was satisfied with the price and narrowed the choices down to those he thought she would like, he would make another visit with her and his nieces. But for now, he wanted to limit the visit to the realtor's office, the bank, and the Hendley. This wouldn't be the time to bring Belinda with him; she could make the trip with her aunt and cousins in a week or so.

No, Belinda would not accompany him. But perhaps Elizabeth might.

CHAPTER 11

While observing one of his many early evening rituals—enjoying a brandy cocktail dubbed a "Mikado"—Beauchamp picked up another of his favorite photographs. This one captured him and Jack Lawrence standing outside a Manhattan theater in August 2018—some six months before Lawrence's murder. The photograph was taken as they emerged from a stage production of *Dracula,* both men full of critical observations about the play and the Stoker novel that spawned this and so many other stage depictions of the tale since its initial publication in 1897.

But Beauchamp remembered being most intrigued by Lawrence's conflicting reactions to the two persons with whom he had discussed Stoker's book. Lawrence spoke of debating the merits of the novel with a fellow Victorian scholar at a scholarly conference a dozen years earlier. The man had dismissed the literary value *Dracula,* calling it little more than vivacious hack writing, while Lawrence argued for Stoker's superb literary craftsmanship in the novel.

"Do I know this Victorian scholar, Jack?"

"You might. His name was—and still is—Stuart Dryden. You know, the same Stuart Dryden who served miserably as a Dean of Arts and Sciences and then, when he realized he'd be replaced, jumped into the fetid pool of politics."

Beauchamp laughed. "And came out smelling like a rose." Beauchamp was well aware that Dryden brought out the worst in Lawrence—and vice versa.

Beauchamp also recollected that as the two men continued their walk from the theatre in Kent, Lawrence told him he just recently had a splendid conversation about the book with a young beauty, and former student, newly hired for duty at the Hendley's circulation desk. Apparently, a copy of Stoker's novel had just been checked out, and the ever-perceptive Lawrence used that as an invitation to speak with the woman, who Beauchamp only later learned was named Sandra Stark. Lawrence waxed poetically about her loveliness and how much he was going to enjoy his visits to the Hendley throughout the rest of the fall term "and beyond." At the time, Beauchamp playfully inquired if his friend was planning a seduction, to which Lawrence answered with a naughty paraphrase of Dickens, "It will be a far, far better thing that I will then do, than I have ever done."

An exuberant Lawrence added that the lovely Sandra Stark had uncommon literary tastes. She impressed him by speaking intelligently about works not on the usual reading lists, such as Nabokov's *Ada or Ador: A Family Chronicle,* John Irving's *The Hotel New Hampshire,* and Lawrence Durrell's *The Alexandria Quartet.* Lawrence told Beauchamp he was charmed by her knowing three books he had never read and vowed to read them in order to have further excuses to spend time in her company. Lawrence ended his discussion on that day by offering an almost adolescent and "secretive" admission that at the same time he touched her as he reached "innocently" for her pen to write down the name of the three books. He wistfully asserted that she had "perfect" hands. Not long afterward, he informed her that he'd be happy to admire them for hours on end without desiring to do anything more.

Beauchamp smiled and replaced the photograph on the bookshelf. It was time to feed Usher.

• • •

Kissing the nape of Elizabeth's neck after they had finally gotten Belinda to bed, Nichols felt the moment right to ask if she would accompany him on his return visit to the Hendley Library. He would of course have to come up with something to explain to his daughter his *third* trip to "the new school" in five or six days, not to mention the repeated request to his sister that Belinda spend the night with her cousins.

Janis hadn't confronted him directly about Elizabeth, but Jeremy knew the interrogation could come at any moment, for his sister had begun wearing the familiar expression he had known since his teenage years—the one that said, "Well? Isn't it about time you filled me in, dear brother?" He wanted to confide in her, but he knew he'd have no patience with her argument that he was out of his mind to be in love with a married woman, particularly with his impressionable daughter's delay in posing pointed questions about the nice woman he called his "friend." For her part, Belinda liked Elizabeth and showed no evidence of even a casual curiosity regarding her missing mother. Only her drawings spoke to the complexities within her developing mind. Jeremy once more recalled Belinda's drawing of the prone man with a book in his hand, but he was diverted by Elizabeth's softly rubbing his arm. It was now time to ask. He explained that neither Belinda nor Janis would be going with him this time. "I really want you to come with me. What do you think?"

Elizabeth listened without protest but didn't respond until his face sagged in disappointment.

"If you make it Thursday, I think I can go. If you really want me to."

Before he could express his delight, Nichols had to inquire. "And Steve?"

"Can you believe it? He phoned me. So unlike him. Anyway, he's not coming home until late Friday. He's accepted an invitation to speak at an opera workshop this Thursday at Rutgers in conjunction with a student performance of a short opera by Mozart. As luck would have it, I told him I might take a road trip to Saratoga this week to visit a couple of friends. But I can now change that to another location—that is, if you would deign to call yourself one of my friends. That is, just for the occasion."

Nichols wanted to laugh, but that too was stymied by another unhappy possibility. "What if he calls Saratoga?"

"He never asked where I was going exactly. He doesn't know who my friends are there. Besides, have you forgotten the century we're living in? It's the cell phone age, Jeremy. Nobody leaves a number where they'll be anymore. So if you want to go Thursday, I'm your girl."

Nichols took her left hand and kissed it. He felt her wedding band touch the edge of his lips. He wondered if she would remove it when she was with him. Did he even have a right to ask such a favor?

• • •

The man would never forget that he removed his winter gloves moments too soon on that frigid February night six months ago. When he touched the front door latch of the Hendley, he immediately lost all feeling in his left hand. What was wrong with him, he had wondered at that moment? He lived in a northern climate; he was well aware that cold metal glued fingers to its surface when the temperature was as low as it was that night.

Even so, he had done his homework. And he was attentive to what he heard and observed. He knew that Jackson Lawrence was at that time in the library, and he had learned enough about the professor's habits to guess where he would be. The man had himself been in the Hendley earlier that afternoon, and felt comfortable about getting out safely, without detection. He knew where he could position himself to remain hidden from view and where to walk so that he could escape the stare of those with aching backs and bleary eyes who remained at the Hendley right up until closing time.

The stacks would provide satisfactory cover and permit him natural movement, without any mad dashing or awkward stooping. He fancied the volumes as his accomplices to what he wished to accomplish that night. The stairwell on the opposite side from the stack level where he'd confront Lawrence would facilitate his retreat. It would all take very little time, of that he was certain. He and Lawrence alone among hundreds of mute witnesses. So many of the volumes coated with a veneer of dust for not having been pulled from their resting places for many years. That night, as he made his way to the seventh stack at the top of the Hendley Tower, his heart hammered incessantly against his chest, but not out of fear. Rather it was out of an exhilarating sense of justice.

Yes, just the two of them, he then assumed, in a sublime moment no one else could possibly understand.

CHAPTER 12

As she liked to do every Wednesday, Elizabeth sipped a *latte macchiato* and skimmed through a biography at her favorite book store. But today when she walked down each aisle, she felt the overwhelming sense of being incarcerated by books—row upon row of books. Just as she had some seventeen years ago at the Hendley Library. She was scared to death then, but only in part because she was still so impressionable. The uncharacteristic demeanor of her escort to the Hendley that day unnerved her as much as the intimidating volumes peering austerely from each row. After telling her of a professor's recent suicide there, the man pulled the reluctant middle-schooler along, hurting her arm without realizing it. But she never uttered a peep, for she had been taught by her mother never to make a sound when she was in a library. But her escort that day had been speaking, and he wasn't always whispering. She remembered it took six days before the bruise on her arm disappeared.

So after all these years, she was going to see the Hendley again. The man she was in love with would soon be doing his research there. Was this mere coincidence or some unidentified irony? Still, she'd said nothing to Jeremy about having visited there such a long time ago. Had it changed she wondered? And would she still dread seeing the ghost of the suicidal professor? That early spring evening, when she had her arm squeezed black and blue, she was terrified at the possibility that she might see among the stacks a gruesome specter of a man with a bloodied head blasted apart by a pistol shot. She was told then that the Hendley's old bell chimes ceased working when the first dead body lay on the grounds a century and a half earlier and that many believed other suicides and several murders occurred at the library in the dark hours after everyone left for the night. Her escort that evening was very knowledgeable of the library's frightening history and the suicide that occurred several weeks earlier—almost as though he'd been present when it happened.

Perhaps it was best if she went up to the higher stack levels alone. She could then face this dreadful and recurring memory and defeat it—on her own. Would she purge her fears if she went up during the day? Or did it have to be at night? Would it even count if Jeremy waited for her in the stairwell? Or even on the main floor? He had just informed her that a well-known professor was found murdered on the seventh stack level of the library and that he would tell her all about it when they drove up on Thursday. She wanted to say she'd been well aware of that fact for seventeen years and that it was suicide, not a murder, but she didn't want to preempt or contradict his story in any way. She loved him too much to do that. She placed her finger into the latte. She was surprised it was still warm.

• • •

The tower of the Hendley was partially shrouded by the mist and light rain on this late August afternoon. The tower invited the imaginative mind to ponder the several mysteries about the building and the surrounding area since the time of its initial construction in the nineteenth century.

The impressive and intimidating Hendley stood on the same spot as the original library, then a narrow two-story box-like structure that rose upon an empty field just as soon as the spring of 1842 settled in. At the time, many considered constructing anything on the site to be a bad omen—or rather a dangerous encouragement to something evil or catastrophic. It was there on the once bare field that a state legislator, Thomas Sims, took a bullet in the abdomen from Alexander Reynolds, the congressman who represented the district in Washington. The date was the twenty-fifth of March 1842.

The men had both traveled to Boston to take part in a formal New England welcome of the mother country's most popular young novelist, who had arrived with his wife on January 22. The young author's impassioned argument for some form of international copyright to protect the literary works on both sides of the Atlantic struck a chord with Sims, whose playwright father was twice the unfortunate victim of literary piracy. But copyright was not the issue over which Sims and Reynolds drew pistols later that March.

Back home on March 24, the men were discussing Mr. Dickens's recent sojourn to Washington D.C., which he concluded only three days earlier. Reynolds spoke derisively of the novelist, owing to Dickens's attitude toward the slavery question. Unlike Sims and most of his New England brethren, Congressman Reynolds believed the institution should be allowed to continue where it was needed and desired. He was particularly adamant that slavery shouldn't be criticized by "a long-haired English scribbler who didn't know his damned place."

When Sims asked what the novelist saw while in Washington, a still agitated Reynolds informed him that Dickens toured the White House and had an awkward meeting with the president. Now Sims felt his own indignation rise, and he offered without prompting a rather slanderous estimation of John Tyler. Reynolds grew angry and defensive at the estimation of the current president, whom Sims derided for his "hands off" attitude toward the slavery question. After finishing another short glass of whiskey, Sims cursed "that hawk-faced bastard" Tyler for being a slave owner and added that such a fact ought to disqualify anyone for national public office, especially the presidency.

Reynolds vigorously took the opposing view, and before long the men latched on to Dickens and dragged him back into the argument. The novelist had made clear while visiting Congress—and Reynolds was there to hear him—that he wanted to travel south to observe the cruelty of slavery first hand but that Henry Clay had talked him out of it.

Past the point of temperance and discretion, Sims lifted his glass to honor the Englishman's position, and within a minute both men hurled aspersions at each other as well as at Tyler and Dickens. Sims particularly enraged Reynolds by claiming that the congressman was the northern eyes and ears of the hated South Carolinian John Calhoun, Tyler's Secretary of State.

By this point, Reynolds had had enough and offered to meet Sims the following morning on the field across the wide road that ran by the west side of the college grounds. Sims got off the first shot, but missed his target. Reynolds's aim was truer. As the popular state legislator lay dying on the wet tamped-down grass, the students and citizens who witnessed the duel crowded around him, and all heard Sims's bitter and agonizing final words, which cursed Reynolds, Tyler, Calhoun and the rest of the "damned hellish crew" who would "soon destroy the United States of America."

The construction of the original library and its two major renovations in 1879 and 1921 caused many to predict misfortune and tragedy for the university and for those working in or visiting the building constructed on the spot where Thomas Sims cast his final, bitter, and painful aspersions. According to local history, the moment Sims died—at exactly 7:00 a.m.—the bell set in the original structure stopped after the sixth toll. The bell never rang again, and although it was later removed from the top of the building and stored in the basement of the renovated Hendley, many locals believed it would again chime when the evil spirit inhabiting the library was finally exorcised. Modern research proved that there had in fact been unusual and violent deaths of faculty, students, and staff personnel who spent at least some time in the university's library, and there were still those who were convinced that the Hendley and its immediate area had not yet purged the ghosts of that late March day in 1842.

CHAPTER 13

The rain shower having passed, the clouds parted enough to give her a taste of the lovely summer sunsets she so loved—the kind that always inspired contentment and memory. Sandra Stark rested alone on the elevated deck of her new house, reading a book recently sent to her by step-brother Will—Matthew Lewis's eighteenth-century Gothic thriller *The Monk*—a book, like so many others she read, that seemed particularly relevant to the course her life had taken. She let the heat from her freshly brewed tea caress her soft and unlined cheek. As was her way, she would in a few moments press the mug against each side of her face, warming her skin and her sensibilities even further. It was what she only half-jokingly called her erotic fix, seeing that sex with a man was put in abeyance until the memories of her last lover faded enough to permit sexual intimacy with another—although at this point, she wondered if time would ever lessen his effect on her emotions.

Sandra never sought physical affection from her current "boyfriend" beyond a warm hug and momentary kiss. She only required from him a steadiness and respect for her privacy. In this way, he was the perfect mate for this time in her life, and he never intruded on her imagination, as active as it was and had always been. More importantly, he never encroached upon her memory. In Sandra's mind, anything even approaching periodic sex with him was a betrayal of that memory, as well as a violation of her penance.

As she sipped her tea, she recalled the table for two situated by a cozy fireplace at an intimate restaurant fifteen miles from her first apartment. Hardly inviting on the outside, since it was nestled in a storefront complex alongside a busy highway, the restaurant's motif was reminiscent of the private library of a wealthy bibliophile. Suggesting her field of endeavor, the restaurant relaxed and charmed her—in part because of the large fireplace, in part because of the impeccable service, and in part because of the Steak Diane and Cherries Jubilee, both prepared table-side. But most enjoyable was the man sitting across from her on that warm September evening in 2018—the handsome, captivating, and most attentive Jackson Lawrence.

Hearing a slight rustle of her wind chimes, Sandra recalled further Lawrence's account story of the restaurant's history, the polite way he prevented another patron from lighting up—owing both to restaurant policy and to Sandra's stated sensitivity to cigarette smoke—and the manner in which he reached across the table to examine the ugly paper cut on her hand. She knew the moment he took her hand that she didn't want him to let go until he had softly touched every one of her delicate fingers.

She, once more, pressed the mug against both of her cheeks, closing her eyes for one last memory of that special night. It was the moment when Lawrence paid the check and unwrapped the chocolate mint for her—and her shaking her head "No thank you." He seemed almost wounded by her refusal of the mint—or was at least surprised, and all she could tell him was that she didn't want to spoil the wonderful taste of the Cherries Jubilee. He smiled and refused to open his own after-dinner treat, conceding that he had never been rejected by a more compelling argument. When she heard him say "rejected," she felt her stomach tighten and her face flush. If he asked anything more of her that night, she knew she wouldn't be able to reject him a second time.

• • •

"Excuse me for calling at supper time, but are you Professor Jeremy Nichols?"

Nichols was certain he'd never heard the voice before. "Yes, this is he. And you are...?"

"You are a Dickensian, is that right?"

Jeremy thought the voice gave the question a dismissive inflection—as if the caller already knew. "Yes. So, what can I do for you?" The

British voice defied any guess as to the age of the caller. It could be a student or the parent of one—Nichols wasn't sure.

"Professor Nichols, might you do me the favor of listening to me for a moment?"

"Of course." Nichols assumed he'd be getting a sales pitch of some kind, although why the caller mentioned Dickens seemed especially peculiar.

"There exists in someone's possession a collection of papers you would find most significant for your research."

Nichols rolled his eyes at the apparent naiveté of the caller's remark. That this person would say such a thing to a scholar was of course laughable. There were in fact papers all over the world a literary researcher would find significant—in major research libraries and in personal collections.

"Okay." Nichols wished to remain polite, but he was losing patience. He was formulating how to ask the caller to get to the point, when the voice cut sharply through his annoyance.

"Professor Nichols, I mean something in Dickens' own hand—seen by only a few."

"I'm sorry. What...what do you mean, specifically? In Dickens' own hand? How...how do you know...?" His attention fully captured, Nichols sat at the dining room table.

"In Dickens' own hand and unseen by any scholar of Dickens from 1870 to the present day."

Nichols's jaw tensed. The caller had noted the year Dickens died. It wasn't much, but it served to give the person at least some credibility.

"Excuse me. I should have said every scholar of Dickens save one." The name formed in Nichols's mind only an instant before it was spoken by the caller. "Jackson Lawrence."

"I see." Jeremy rolled his left hand into a loose fist as he shaped his reply. "Can you tell me what Lawrence saw exactly? What was written in this...journal, was it? A bound journal of some kind?"

"No, the pages are loose. All sequentially numbered—but loose."

"Well, have *you* seen them recently? How do you know they're loose?"

The caller laughed softly. "I've not seen the pages since the first week of February. But I'm sure they are still loose. Perhaps in a folder or box of some kind—but still loose." Nichols groped for a pen and something to write on. He secured an unopened envelope on the table—his water bill.

"Can I have your number so I can get back to you?"

"You don't have caller identification?"

"Sorry, I don't. It's an old phone."

"Well, it wouldn't have mattered, since I'm calling you from a hotel. I've been traveling."

Nichols became desperate to extend the conversation. "Please, what is your name?"

He was startled by another soft laugh. "'To whom do you have the pleasure of addressing,' you mean? Professor Lawrence was fond of speaking that way, you know. My name isn't important. I am only calling you because I have learned you will be soon be spending time at the Hendley Library. Returning to it, I should say."

Then someone he knew had spoken with this person. Doug Finneran, perhaps? How else would the caller...? But the thought was shoved aside by the insistent need to know what was written on those journal pages, even though they were highly likely not in Dickens's hand. A forgery of some kind, then?

"Before you hang up, will you tell me what the pages contain, or at least what the subject matter is?" Nichols's voice sounded as gentle as he could make it. He didn't want to lose the caller through any hint of aggravation or aggression in his tone.

"The subject matter is...how shall I say?...most personal. Too personal, as it has turned out. Professor Nichols, more than a life was lost that February night at the Hendley Library. I have always believed that within a year the conditions would be right for the discovery of the one who took what was rightfully someone else's."

"Do you mean who murdered Professor Lawrence on that night?"

"No, I am referring to the manuscript of Dickens."

Nichols sighed in frustration, and the voice on the other end of the line ceased. "Hello? Hello?"

"I would suggest that a volume from an older edition of Dickens's Christmas books on the seventh stack level might be your place to start. Goodbye. My efforts so far have been in vain. But the mind and energy of a young Dickens scholar might find what I'm looking for. I mean *your* mind and *your* energy, Professor Nichols." The line went dead. Dickens's Christmas books? The person on the phone hinted that the conditions for discovery were now right. A manuscript in Dickens own hand. Was the murder of Lawrence related to those pages? Who was this caller? Suddenly, Nichols felt as though he had been grabbed violently by both wrists. Someone whose face he couldn't shape in his mind had looked intently into his eyes and told him he had to investigate two matters that must be related to each other in some way. But why call him? A young, curious, and energetic Dickens scholar? What was in that? Here it was, then. A purported hitherto unknown manuscript in Dickens's hand, the death of a noted Dickens scholar, and a young untenured Dickensian still not officially a part of the university where the murder took place.

Nichols made his way to the refrigerator for a cold beer. He tried for a moment to guess who the caller might be, but he had absolutely no idea. Again, he was positive he had never heard her voice before.

• • •

Another two pages of the manuscript were removed from the stack. *I am deeply in love with Ellen. I think constantly of how I want to talk with her and listen to her voice—as she speaks and as she sings. I wish to be no more away from her than a breath's distance for hours on end. To smell her hair, to place my lips gently on the side of her face, as often as I require. I want always to see in her eyes her admiration for me and her wish to please me through the smallest of services.*

Shall I admit these passionate feelings? I feel I can only make them known to my dear friend Forster. I can tell him that poor Catherine and I are not made for each other, and there is no help for it—yet he would see that as superfluous. He would surely understand that my falling in love with Ellen could have nothing to do with my decision to separate from Kate. He knows that a severing has been coming for years, steadily advancing in its implacable inevitability.

Can it be that I spoke my vows to Kate three years before my beautiful Ellen was born?

But there can be no divorce in this case. On what grounds could I assert Catherine's unfitness as a wife? That I have ceased to love her? That she has annoyed me to no end? That her awkward manner, literal clumsiness, and inability to complete with competence even simple tasks have rubbed my sensibilities beyond rawness? No, I may not divorce Kate. But may I indulge the thought of adultery? Only a thought permitted now. Forgive me, dear God, for making the thought a steady companion as I lie otherwise alone. Forgive also my determination that I will from this point on do all I can to make an unthinkable wish become a most palpable sin.

I must continue writing these indefensible thoughts. I cannot merely submerge them into an episode of fiction as I have done before, complete with substitute names and restrained candor. If and when my passionate desire abates or concludes, I will re-read what I have written, perhaps smile over my temporary lunacy, and then burn the pages, however many there happen to be.

The reader placed the two pages under the others in the shallow box, never once considering the price these entries would command on the open market.

CHAPTER 14

Stuart Dryden sent his staff out of his congressional office and leaned back at his desk with his hands interlocked behind his head, as he did when he was making his name as a specialist in Victorian prose. Yet, no one knew that instead of William Makepeace Thackeray and aspects of Victorian morality, Dryden would rather have devoted his energies to the small literary period he believed inspired and satisfied him most—the decade of the 1890s in England and Ireland. The work of Shaw and Wilde, especially, had amused and intrigued him ever since his undergraduate days at Williams College. But rather than Shaw's and Wilde's comic plays, he found most meaning in Wilde's prose masterpiece, the psychological horror tale *The Picture of Dorian Gray*. And from this book it was a very short step to Bram Stoker's *Dracula.*

Dryden read an abridged version of the famous horror novel as a boy, but he came to know the tale primarily through the film adaptations—or "desecrations" as he would later come to call them—and the one or two stage pieces he saw. It was not until he read the book carefully in the late-1960s, then immediately re-read it, that he succumbed to its intoxicating appeal. The richly sexual aspects of the book—in their literal, figurative, archetypal, and psychological manifestations—stimulated in ways that at first frightened him. He quickly accepted that he wouldn't be permitted to admit his fascination with the novel, surely not to his family, who prided themselves on their long-standing Puritan lineage.

What the novel touched in him he found disturbing and impossible to reconcile with his outward defense of and commitment to what was morally orthodox, in his life and in his scholarly concentrations.

Whereas in public, he talked censoriously of the novel in highly intelligent, though dry and aloof terms, in private he allowed the tale—with its lush sensuality and violence— to fill that part of his imagination that since boyhood he desperately tried to suppress. Dryden often took some relief in the knowledge that some of his colleagues and others in the profession had their literary "mistresses" as well. He learned in graduate school that even some of the most productive scholars develop passionate interests outside the field in which they were hired to teach and publish. But they could boldly announce theirs. He could not.

When Dryden reached into his desk drawer to retrieve a binding clip for the short stack of correspondence he wished to peruse, he felt a small unframed photograph. He'd been searching for this item for several days and had failed to look in such an obvious place. It was an artifact he periodically retrieved from its hiding place, in order to recall the most humiliating day of his life and the most satisfying event that eventually followed.

It was a vintage photograph from the nineteenth century. He had inadvertently dropped it to the floor while in the Hendley Library, during the Thanksgiving break in 2006. This photograph was the only one Dryden still kept from the cache of similar ones he possessed at the time. As he did whenever he viewed it, he squeezed hard on the edges between his thumb and index fingers of both hands. He would never handle anything else printed in the nineteenth century in such a manner, but this artifact was different.

The photograph—dating from the mid-1860s—was of a young female of remarkable beauty, looking between fifteen and seventeen years of age. She seemed to be sitting in a private library, completely engrossed in the book she was reading. Although there was no way to tell, Dryden had always wondered if the book might have been a Dickens title. The girl's face evinced undeniable bliss. Her neck was appropriately covered in a white period blouse—suggesting that she lived in comfort if not in wealth. She was nude from the waist down.

In the photograph, an older man was servicing her with his mouth, with both his open palms resting on her open thighs. Her feet were bare and her toes visibly splayed.

Dryden never informed a soul he had done research in Victorian pornography. As he soon learned, the word itself was popularized during the period, and the center of erotica had generally made its move from France and the legacy of de Sade across the channel to England. Dryden was captivated by the images he viewed and quietly collected—beginning while in graduate school and continuing until that fall day in 2006. So much he had seen depicted the deflowering of young virgins, some of whom then turned to lives of promiscuity. He knew that part of the period's interest in erotica was a reaction against the public pose of strict decorum and complete intolerance for any deviation from rigid norms. That, of course, was a historical and literary commonplace. But he moreover understood that pornography was a weapon—the social anarchist's favorite device to expose the hypocrisy of the age.

Dryden discovered that in 1834, three years before Victoria's reign commenced, some fifty-seven shops in whole or in part traded in pornography on one London street. By the time Big Ben first chimed in the middle of the century, London had, according to one tally, exactly 7,194 prostitutes plying their trade. Some had written that the number of prostitutes, as large as it was, wasn't enough to keep satisfied the voracious appetites of Victorian men, and that throughout the century younger girls swelled the growth of involuntary prostitution, replete with its unsavory and sadistic activities. Dryden felt revulsion for the worst of underground Victorian sexuality but utter fascination for its more "conventional" side.

In addition, Dryden became willingly caught up in one of the colorful legends of the Hendley Tower, which told of a massive stash of Victorian pornography hiding on one of the upper stack levels that only a few had seen in the past century. It was in an attempt to ascertain discreetly more information about this rumored treasure-trove of erotica that prompted Dryden to enter the Hendley during the Thanksgiving break of 2006. And it was while sitting by himself at a table skimming through one of the library's old card-file drawers that he looked up and saw the scholarly *wunderkind* Jackson Lawrence smiling at him. The same Jackson Lawrence who had earlier engaged him in a spirited debate about Bram Stoker's *Dracula*. The same Jackson Lawrence who had so far shown him little deference, seeing that

Dryden had twenty years seniority on him and was considered a shoo-in for an administrative position.

Lawrence began pleasantly but also formally. "Professor Dryden, what brings you here during the holiday break?"

"Standard answer, Jack. Research."

"But not on Thackeray, right?"

Dryden was shoved off balance by Lawrence's point-on assessment. "I...well, not directly, no. Still Victorian, however." He remembered feeling justified in his hatred of the handsome and glib young Dickensian, whose career he would do anything to ruin.

"Anything I can help you with, Stuart? Need directions to a particular volume?"

"No, but thank you anyway. I think I'm done here now." Dryden wanted out of the Hendley immediately. But when reached for a book resting on the table, the edge of the volume knocked to the floor his thin leather folder, which included pages of unlined white paper, two pens, and half a dozen Victorian photographs.

"Here, let me." Lawrence bent down to retrieve the handsome folder before Dryden could stop him. Giving in to a puckish impulse, Lawrence slipped one of the pens into his pocket. He stood back up and handed everything else to Dryden. That is, everything but the pen in his pocket and one of the photographs, which he held out at arm's length. "Well, well. This isn't exactly reflective of your publications on Thackery and Victorian morality, *is it,* Stuart?" Lawrence's emphasis was reminiscent of a disappointed Victorian schoolmaster chiding one of his pupils.

Enjoying that Dryden was shaken and unable to respond, Lawrence chuckled audibly. "So, you serve two taskmasters, it seems. Can I assume you're here at the Hendley to locate once and for all the hidden treasures of Victorian pornography that according to legend are somewhere hiding in shame on one of the upper stack levels?" Completely mortified, Dryden dropped his head slightly, welding his eyes shut. Lawrence stepped closer to the table and leaned down. "Come on, Stuart,..." Lawrence's tone was now more school bully than school master. "Don't you think that if such treasures really existed, I would have found them by now?" He wiggled the photograph in his hand. "Here you go. Try to be more careful next time. It wouldn't do your career any good if word got out about this pretty little picture. I mean, given your heritage and your father's influence around these parts, it just wouldn't do to publicize your true *scholarly* inclinations, would it?"

Dryden held out his hand for the photograph; Lawrence kept wiggling it. "Well, at least the girl in the photograph is reading. Perhaps she's fantasizing about young David Copperfield while her Uriah Heep is worshipping at the altar, as it were." Lawrence tossed the photograph on the table and watched Dryden's awkward groping to retrieve it. "Again, try to be more discreet next time. You don't want anyone finding out about this little sidelight of your scholarly interests. I mean, you can't afford to give credence to a rumor that's beginning to make the rounds in the halls of academe. But no need to bring that up now. Have a nice trip back home, Professor Dryden. Say hello to your wife for me."

After Lawrence left the area, Dryden sat immobile, with both open palms covering the photograph of the young girl reading. What rumor had Lawrence alluded to? What had that son of a bitch found out about him? Was Lawrence having him followed? At the time, Dryden could only take comfort in the meeting he just had with a member of the Dean's office. It seemed they were interested in Dryden for the soon-to-be vacant deanship of Arts and Sciences—the job to begin after the New Year. On that November day at the Hendley, Dryden made up his mind to transition into the political end of the academic life and sacrifice his scholarly advancement, at least for the time being. He had to escape the English Department, where that bastard Lawrence would daily hound and humiliate him. Then Dryden smiled. There was no telling what damage he could do to Jack Lawrence from the Dean's office.

After he assumed the deanship, he impressed the administration with his political acumen and skill in public speaking. He began to give Lawrence as much of a hard time as he could—often disguising his role—but still he feared Lawrence's knowledge of something that could ruin him, besides the new dean's interest in Victorian erotica. But Lawrence said nothing, and after a time, Dryden began to relax. After another year passed, he became convinced that his nemesis had either forgotten about the incident in the Hendley or decided it wasn't worth running the risk of upsetting his own comfortable academic career. But Dryden overplayed his hand after he left academia and used his influence as a U.S. congressman to make sure Lawrence was denied the newly created endowed professorship the accomplished Dickensian sought—for both its added prestige and salary. When he learned of who was behind the decision, Lawrence sent Representative Dryden a Restricted Delivery letter—for Dryden's eyes only—which informed him exactly what he had on the congressman and what he'd soon reveal. That was in the first week of February 2019.

Dryden's thoughts were interrupted by one of his staff. "Yes, Tara?"

"I'm sorry to interrupt, Congressman, but I just want you to know I'm ready to help with your senate campaign in any way you need me to. And I shouldn't say this yet—but what the heck. I'd also hope you'll take me with you when you go to the White House."

Dryden grinned broadly. "Tara, you'll be with me, no matter what."

CHAPTER 15

After he was done helping his sister with the dinner dishes, Nichols meandered to the bookshelves for his periodic examination of Janis's titles. His sister had eclectic taste in fiction—from the classics to the fluffiest read. Taking only a quick glance at the classical section on her bookcase, which mainly consisted of his own hand-me-downs, Nichols discovered two new paperback Hemingway titles, *The Sun Also Rises* and *For Whom the Bell Tolls.* Nichols took some comfort from the first title. Perhaps the sun would soon rise for both him and Elizabeth. But that couldn't happen unless she divorced Steve Ellertson.

But the latter title reminded him once again of Jackson Lawrence's murder—particularly the fact that Lawrence's finger was resting between two pages of Dickens Christmas book *The Chimes*. The woman on the phone encouraged him to begin his search with the Christmas books. His search? What the hell was he doing thinking he could find a clue leading to the solving of Jackson Lawrence's murder in the Hendley Library tower? It was completely absurd. Surely the local police were continuing to follow up leads or trying to find new ones. Yet Nichols realized that for whatever reason, he'd inherited the responsibility for considering further the events of February 7, 2019. And he was going back to the Hendley on Thursday to do just that. If nothing else, pondering the matter would take his mind off his seemingly impossible situation with Elizabeth.

• • •

On the way home, Belinda promised to present her father with another of her paintings before she went to bed. Nichols recalled the one she'd made of the man lying prone with his arm outstretched holding a book. He hadn't asked her why she had drawn such a scene. But he always resisted the urge to have her explain what she drew or painted, because of that conspicuous oval she invariably included in her work. He disliked being so reticent, but he feared hearing her say that the oval was the shape of her mother's face—the mother she had never seen and never spoken about but now perhaps wanted in her life. Nichols wondered if his sister ever talked to Belinda about Meredith. Had she satisfied his daughter's curiosity on that score? No, Belinda would have said something to him. When would his daughter stare into his eyes and demand to know what happened to her mother? When she was five? Seven? Thirteen? Would she blame him for keeping the truth from her for so long?

Making the final turn toward home, Nichols saw that his beautiful child had fallen asleep. He wanted to concentrate now on Elizabeth and the joy of being with her for an entire night, but the way he and Fred Beauchamp parted continued to bother him. Nichols couldn't help regretting that he reacted too quickly or dismissively to the emeritus professor's recruitment of him—if that in fact was what it was. Nichols had never responded automatically to a well-delivered appeal to patriotism or national security, and he held very firm views against wholesale domestic spying even during a time of war or fear of terrorist attack. He was moreover what he called a "staunch First-Amendment kind of guy." At the very least, Beauchamp would ask him to keep an ear open when he joined the junior faculty, if not an eye on someone perhaps legitimately under suspicion. Nichols questioned whether he could modify some of his principles and do that much for his country, if not for himself and his academic future.

Still, he was most uneasy about the possibility that he might have ruptured his relationship with Beauchamp. He genuinely liked the man and wanted him in his corner during his three-year stint on the junior faculty. Approaching the house, Nichols made up his mind to contact the retired professor and try to salvage what he could without committing to any formal agreement to assist in any intelligence work. Perhaps he could tell Beauchamp that he'd keep an ear open for any form of subversive talk and then say that he hadn't heard anything. But Nichols knew that once he made such a casual agreement to serve, he might well be caught up in something he would deeply regret. He'd read enough to understand that even the slightest acceptance of such work inevitably becomes a Faustian bargain. Then again, he might be grossly exaggerating the whole matter. Regardless, he at least had to call Beauchamp and attempt to make things right.

As he turned into his driveway, Nichols caught sight of a car oddly parked in the area. His neighbors were in California for a week, and therefore no one should have been parked at the bottom of their driveway. Nichols checked his rear-view mirror before making the left into his garage. There was no one in the car which was dark blue, dark green, or black—there wasn't enough lighting to be sure. He unbuckled Belinda, who was still asleep. After failing to wake her with his first shake, he decided to leave her in the front seat while he again glanced across the street. Nichols locked the car, stepped out of his garage, and began to move down his driveway for a better look. The dark sedan was gone.

• • •

The photo album was the only family possession to have survived the many changes of hands since the mid-1860s. The photographs, dating from the five-year period of 1866 to 1871, included not only family members but also some of the most important names in contemporary London society. Among the most distinguished photographic captures were those of the great political figures Gladstone and Disraeli, the writer Wilkie Collins, the actor William Macready, the painter Daniel Maclise, the biographer and critic John Forster, and the physician Frank Beard.

Centered inside the album was another photograph—this one of a mature man and a young woman. The man looked more serene and content than in any other photograph of him in existence—the woman appeared half bemused and half resigned, at least so it always seemed to the present owner of the album. This photograph of Charles Dickens and Ellen Ternan had never been seen by any scholar or biographer of the great Victorian novelist. It had remained cloistered in the photo album, with a mere handful of family members privileged to examine it. And the same should have been true of the private journal in Dickens's hand. But it was not. Someone else had seen it. Jackson Lawrence.

Helena Allingham knew it was too late for regret; she had made the call to Jeremy Nichols and had begun unraveling the tightly bound secrets she swore to her mother she would keep her entire life. Secrets she was to pass on to her daughter, so that the women in the family would have something significant in their possession for as long as there were descendants of Mary Bertram—the woman who was in possession of the Dickens manuscript pages at the time of the novelist's death and who had passed them on to her daughter Caroline. She had given Caroline the impassioned charge to keep safe the unbound journal, to tell absolutely no one about it, and to bequeath it to her older daughter with the same plea and implied command. To the best of her knowledge, Helena Allingham knew of no violation of the promise made by all the eldest daughters up to the time she herself dishonored it in a way that would have disgraced her in the eyes of her mother, grandmother, and all the way back to her great-great-great grandmother Mary Bertram.

Helena often wondered what would happen to the journal if a female child wasn't born into the family. Helena's mother was a sixth child, following five male siblings. Did her grandmother insist on yet another pregnancy because she felt duty bound to have a daughter to inherit the family's literary secret—the manuscript in Dickens's own hand? Again, what if there were only sons? What if the recipient of the literary treasure died before informing her daughter about the inherited responsibility? Helena thought she was pregnant in the fall of 2018, but to her relief the pregnancy wasn't confirmed. But her calm was short-lived, as she reminded herself that she was obligated by her family's and literary history to produce a female child. And then, soon afterward, she lost the Dickens journal. Helena had inherited the pages at the youngest age of any woman who had previously received them. She was but seventeen when her mother died and twenty-one when the pages disappeared from her life.

Now twenty-two, Helena long ago determined that the metaphor of her life—its very dynamic—was flight and escape. It was the subject of her one major recurring dream. She adored books that featured heroines fleeing physical danger or emotional difficulties. Her favorite novel was, not surprisingly, Charlotte Brontë's *Jane Eyre*. As an adolescent, Helena longed for the kind of traumatic love that would force her to run away, preferably to Yorkshire and Brontë country, escaping her home in Suffolk, England. But as it was, she had no romance passionate and turbulent enough from which to flee and instead made her way to the United States to attend college, dismissing her father's insistence that she matriculate at Cambridge. As she rationalized, perhaps she ran away after all—not from a lover but from a father who thoroughly disgusted her.

She first saw Professor Jackson Lawrence at the Hendley Library at the end of her junior year, when one of her friends pointed him out, suggesting that Helena really needed to take a class with the charismatic and popular teacher. Accordingly, Helena signed up in the fall term for an undergraduate seminar on the early novels of Dickens. She believed it would be all the more amusing to enroll in it, seeing what she had in her possession, brought with her from England and locked tightly away in her apartment. Still, she was certain she would never mention it. She would never drop, as her American friends liked to say, such a veritable "bombshell" in the middle of the undergraduate seminar, although she took frequent pleasure in imagining the reaction if she did. At the time, Helena had long golden hair, which did much to balance some of the more irregular features of her face: a nose a bit off center, an unpleasant scar running a full inch above her right eyebrow from a rock hurled by a demonic male schoolmate, and rather unattractive ear lobes—the most telling indication that her father was indeed her biological parent.

Helena knew early in adolescence that she leaned more to the plain than the attractive, but then so did Jane Eyre. But she also concluded by the time she was fifteen that she possessed an undeniably aura of sexuality that moreover neutralized the plainness of her features. And when she came to America, her accent didn't hurt her chances for social interaction either. Some of the young men she dated admitted that they wanted to take her out just to hear her talk. Yet it was when they opened their mouths that her interest in them waned. Her sensibilities demanded kindred with a similarly imaginative mind, one that could translate stimulating images and fantasies into alluring speech. Less than three weeks into the Dickens seminar, Helena finally found that kinship—in the intoxicating voice and manner of Jackson Lawrence.

It was during the fifth week of the seminar that Helena began entertaining thoughts of sharing her family's secret. Simply put, she dearly wanted Professor Lawrence's attention. Something more than the recognition he gave when she raised her hand and offered answers to his questions or proffered general commentary about *The Pickwick Papers.* She fought her growing jealousy whenever one of the four other women in the seminar engaged with him in conversation. With them, he seemed easily playful, whereas his interaction with her was much more professional in tone. But her jealousy was directed primarily at the young woman working in the Hendley whom Helena and others in her class knew Lawrence was more than sweet on, with Helena believing the two were romantically involved.

Helena learned the young woman's name and asked others in the library about her, disguising her desire to know enough to dispatch whom she saw as her rival for Lawrence's time and affection. Yet, Helena was encouraged by the fact that, for this man especially, she had even a greater inducement than sex—a never-before-seen manuscript in Dickens's hand. On the night of her sixteenth birthday, her mother emphasized why such a literary treasure had to be kept within the family and fervently insisted that her daughter understand why ownership of the pages had to be exclusive and access completely unallowable, even to husbands. Soon, when it was apparent that cancer would soon take her life, Helena's mother showed her the letter in Mary Bertram's hand explaining how the manuscript had come into her possession and how vital it was to keep the promise she had made to Dickens himself.

I expect that all who read this will honor my wishes and those of the greatest writer in our language since our beloved Shakespeare. Mr. Dickens handed this journal to me in the late winter of 1870. He furthermore sent me the enclosed letter only three weeks before his death. This letter and these pages must never be given to anyone—nor ever shown to anyone other than the eldest daughter of each succeeding family. This is a sacred responsibility, as you can see from his plea. We moreover keep this journal because of all the women in England—even in the civilized world—we possess something more important than land, jewels, or money. It is the request of a great man who trusts us. Let no woman of our family ever violate that trust. We are of significance in no greater way than this.

Helena was often the iconoclast during her youth. Therefore, coming to the epistolary inheritance at such a young age made her more vulnerable to the financial enticements tempting her in the immediate months following her mother's death, even though her family was fairly well off and her expenses were never a major concern. She could at least take solace in the fact that she had so far resisted the temptation. Yet turning twenty-one and owing to her active infatuation with a handsome professor much older than she, Helena considered using the journal as a crass bargaining chip so she might further nourish that infatuation and growing desire for the attentions of Jackson Lawrence.

Smiling wearily at the memories of that time in her life not so long ago, Helena moved to the chest of drawers in her bedroom that held a large and ornate jewelry box. Taking it from the top drawer, she opened it and ran her fingers through the inexpensive baubles and the few coins from her foreign travels. No thief would have bothered to grab them, nor the box that had no clasp, let alone a lock. Her fingernails burrowed beneath the trinkets and touched a single sheet of stationary dating back over one hundred and thirty years. A piece of stationary containing the letter from Mary Bertram, written in the middle of May of the year 1870—three weeks before its famous sender passed away from a stroke.

CHAPTER 16

What can I do? I cannot think of a new story to write. More public readings, perhaps? But I must do something.

Thoughts of embracing Ellen console me. They are the only thoughts that can. To come to her and feel the tender warmth of her touch. To place my hands on her shoulders and caress her arms as she looks at me with those captivating eyes. I cannot bear it, for each night I have seen in my mind there.

The reader saw that this unfinished page was mostly stained. Perhaps the great novelist had spilled a beverage of some kind, therefore interrupting his thought, to which he apparently never returned. Was it possible Dickens was drinking heavily the night he wrote this entry—or might it have been morning coffee or afternoon tea? The reader knew the blemish would make the document no less valuable to a collector, although the reader had vowed many times that the journal entries would never be seen by anyone else.

• • •

"Steve?"

Elizabeth was transfused with nervousness and disdain. Why did her husband call? He'd long ago ceased checking in whenever he was away like this. And she was surprised by her anger at his having interrupted her while she was deciding what clothes to bring when she left with Jeremy on Thursday? Shouldn't guilt have been her dominant emotion?

"Steve? Everything is fine, isn't it?" Hearing no reply, she took a full breath and proceeded. "Why did you call me?"

"You know something, Elizabeth. I've noticed that you don't freshen your makeup in front of me anymore. Remember what I told you when we first started getting serious?"

"Please, Steve." Did he want her admission that she no longer cared enough to look her best in his presence? She knew it was more than reflective of the distance between them; it was also an indication that she wanted to preserve that distance. She was very careful about what she put on when he was around her. Avoiding short dresses and keeping her feet hidden in her shoes, she frequently pinned her hair up in his company.

"I told you how much I liked it when you put on fresh lipstick after we ate or came out of the movies." Now it was her turn to remain silent. "Anyway, I called because I just wanted to hear your voice, Double E. I'll see you later in the week—late Friday, although it might have to be Saturday." His pause frightened her. "Perhaps things will be different when I get back. Goodbye."

• • •

Jackson Lawrence decided to change shoes before walking to the Hendley Library from his office in Myers Hall. He checked the large calendar in his office and noted his cryptic marking "HA7H." It was the third of February 2019 and yesterday in Pennsylvania, Punxsutawney Phil didn't see his shadow. If the celebrity rodent was correct, an amused Lawrence reasoned, it would be an early spring. Lawrence looked forward to a four-day getaway to the southeast in early April to enjoy the copious and breathtaking azalea blossoms. Azaleas reigned as his favorite springtime bloom, as they were of the woman who at present ruled his heart and who would be accompanying him—Sandra Stark. But before that would come February 14th and the opportunity to present her with something impressive and creative. Candy and flowers simply wouldn't do.

But there was another meeting pending on this frigid February night. The sidewalks were relatively clear and well enough lit to avoid slipping on any treacherous ice patches. The shoes he'd been wearing all day were recent purchases and hadn't yet lost their annoying squeak.

Because he wished to avoid calling attention to himself inside the Hendley, he opened the door of his office closet and drew forth the shoes he kept for such sartorial emergencies as the one he faced with the squeaky shoes.

Rapidly tapping his fingers on his desk as he leaned back in his office chair, Lawrence believed he had just experienced a most gratifying stretch of several months. Everything had gone according to plan. He had successfully regained the upper hand over Coy Mallory. Their relationship had been damaged, surely, but it had been worth it. And Fred Beauchamp had no idea what he'd done. Perhaps he would never find out—that is unless Mallory told him. And that would mean that Mallory would place himself and his reputation in jeopardy.

On the academic front, a new edition of Dickens Christmas stories was met with nearly universal approval, and Lawrence had already outlined his next book-length study concentrating on Dickens's early novels, from *Pickwick Papers* (1837) through *Dombey and Son* (1848). But now there was a bold claim by one of his students that she possessed previously unexamined journal pages in Dickens's own hand. Playing hard to get the entire month of January, or at least he thought so, she finally agreed to show the pages to him. She was quite eager in December when the seminar concluded, but he apparently didn't show enough enthusiasm. Therefore, she forced a now more curious Lawrence to call her after classes began following the Christmas and New Year break. On the phone, she told him she still detected skepticism in his voice and therefore didn't want to show him the manuscript merely to have him laugh at her.

Lawrence hung up that night believing that she was quite possibly disturbed, and he cautioned himself about what she might accuse him of doing if he persisted in his attempt to see the pages. But on the last day of January, she came by his office and couldn't have been sweeter. She apologized if he thought she was playing games with him. The journal was very important to her and her family, she stressed, and she really did want him to see it—just to tell her once and for all if it was genuine. When Lawrence suggested they meet in the safe confines of the Hendley, she made him promise not to ridicule her if the journal pages turned out to be forgeries.

When he agreed, she rose from the chair in his office and headed to the door. She looked back and smiled before leaving. But it wasn't the same shy smile she had greeted him with ten minutes earlier. At least he had the consolation of knowing that whatever she was teasing him with had nothing to do with her grade. He had already awarded her an *A* in the seminar the previous term. Lawrence entered on his cell phone calendar for Saturday February 2nd "HA7H." Helena Allingham, 7:00 p.m. at the Hendley.

Lawrence found the Hendley Library as the best choice for the meeting for several reasons. Only a few patrons ever sat in one of the reading rooms at this time on a Saturday early in the term; therefore Ms. Allingham could lay out the purported Dickens pages on one of the larger tables. She would feel safe. He would feel even safer. Lawrence reassured himself. She might not in any way be calculating or emotionally disturbed; she might just be naïve.

Lawrence delayed his walk from his car by five minutes so that Helena would arrive before he did and go directly to an empty table in the reading room, as he had instructed her to do. He didn't want to be sitting there waiting for her. But more than that, he preferred not to see her at the door which would then require his escorting her to the assigned meeting place before the watchful eyes of the beautiful Hendley employee Sandra Stark, who, as he knew, was scheduled to work at the circulation desk that evening.

Fortunately, there were three persons waiting to get information from Sandra when he passed her station. He made sure she saw him, and he waved and pointed upward to suggest that he was going to the stacks to do some research. He feared that if he pointed to the reading room, she would break free from her duties and discover him with his student. Lawrence hadn't been successful in winning the affections of women, without understanding the need to make each one feel she was not merely one of several. Sandra smiled and lifted her hand to her shoulder and wiggled her fingers in a casual wave. When he observed she was again completely preoccupied with a questioning patron, Lawrence went up to the stairs to the second stack level, walked all the way across to the other side, came down the other stairwell, and slipped into the reading room unseen by the library's most attractive employee.

He rolled his eyes at what he thought was nothing less than juvenile cloak-and-dagger high jinx in a major research library. Still, it was how he occasionally conducted himself in his adult social life.

Lawrence made his way to where Helena was waiting. It was as if he had walked unannounced into her bedroom. Her face was flushed as she stood behind the chair pushed under the broad table in the reading room. A rust-colored file jacket was open and the manuscript pages peered out from the folder, seeming to entice by revealing the barest of glimpses at what Lawrence could only pray were indeed the forbidden delights. He felt oddly virginal—since no one else had seen the manuscript but the woman's mother, grandmother, and so-on back several generations, at least according to what she had told him earlier. Lawrence wondered if his eyes registered any leering qualities as he gazed upon the object on the table. His former student placed one hand on the file jacket, running her index finger, with its impressively manicured and polished nail across the rust colored surface. Her face almost matched the color of the folder. And she was sitting at the same table under which Stuart Dryden had in November dropped the Victorian erotica resting in his own folder.

He smiled warmly. "May I sit?" She nodded and Lawrence took his place at the table, looking up at her to receive the added affirmation. It was only then that she lowered herself into a chair.

Barely a minute into his examination, Lawrence sighed with a mixture of trepidation, fear, and longing. "Helena, I have examined Dickens's handwriting often in my career, and I see on each of these pages of the manuscript what appear to be unmistakable signs of authenticity."

"Yes, they are authentic, Dr. Lawrence. Regardless of what I said to you earlier, I really have no doubts about that." She hesitated. "Still, can you...can you tell me why you think they are genuine?"

"Of course." He beckoned her to sit next to him. When she moved her chair, she found it difficult resisting the urge to touch his arm. "See here? The telltale signs of a heavy pressure, the right slant to the writing, the ovals filled in, the longish T-crossings, and the variable spacing between words. All evidence of Dickens's hand."

Her finger traced over the words, coming less than in inch from touching his hand. "Then you are convinced, Dr. Lawrence?"

"I would at least want to compare one of these sheets with the facsimile pages of the novelist's handwriting I have in my office, but clearly everything suggests..." He trailed off, seemingly unconscious that he didn't complete his thought. This was exactly what she said it was—an undiscovered manuscript written by Charles Dickens. Lawrence continued to stare at the document in amazement.

She noticed his hand shake as he held one of the pages, and she sensed his fear. His involuntary reaction made her feel triumphant, and she began to formulate what she would say when he asked to take a page or two of the manuscript for closer examination and what she would say when he indicated—whether through words or mere looks—that he would do anything to have possession of what rested inside the rust colored file jacket.

"Helena, may I walk over there with one of the sheets and place it more directly under the light so I can look for other important marks on the page?"

She nodded her approval, but as he rose and turned his back to the young woman, he failed to see what transpired next. Her face registering the exhilaration she felt at the moment, Helena glanced up from the table and saw standing in the entrance to the reading room the beautiful young woman she failed to see when she entered the library five minutes before Jackson Lawrence appeared. The woman was staring at her with an indefinable expression. Helena only knew that the look unnerved her completely.

CHAPTER 17

"So who's the young man with Fred Beauchamp?" The two men examined the four photographs.

"Jeremy Nichols. He's coming aboard for a three-year appointment in the English department. His office will be on the second floor of Myers Hall. Everything checks out."

"Checks out? Now why in hell would Beauchamp be serving as tour guide and welcome wagon for new junior faculty? Use your head, son."

"Sorry, sir."

Coy Mallory winced at the young man's naiveté. It was understandable. The kid was only in his first year of PhD work in history—the department housed in the building right behind Myers Hall—but he had already made it known that he wanted a career in intelligence work. Mallory let him believe that this little assignment was in essence his audition.

"Let me know if they meet again, all right?"

"Yes, sir." With that, the young man headed to the Hendley for some deferred research on post-World War II German history.

Mallory thought it absurd. Nichols was a young scholar of Dickens of no renown when Jackson Lawrence was murdered inside the Hendley Library. Yet this person, soon to begin teaching at this august university, might well unravel all that remained hidden for years. Or was it that it had only lain dormant, awaiting the right person to stick his nose where it didn't belong and therefore jeopardize a life's work—a career of commitment, sacrifice, and compromise. Yes, it was still an incontrovertible fact that Lawrence was discovered on the floor of the seventh stack level under the older volumes relating to Charles Dickens.

But with this young scholar coming aboard—even if only for a single three-year term—something could happen. And why the hell did Nichols return to the university for that lunch with Beauchamp? Hadn't he taken the grand tour two days earlier? Mallory knew that if Nichols's curiosity was properly aroused, he might make another visit before his scheduled move in the next one or two weeks. And if he did so, he'd be going to the Hendley.

Two hours later, Mallory squeezed his bottle of beer as he sat at a quiet tavern not far from the Connecticut-Massachusetts border, recalling the time-line of events. The deceased Jack Lawrence was to be replaced this fall by a senior Victorian specialist, and English department had enticed Jeralyn McBride, a first-rate scholar/critic to come aboard, but she had just begun a fellowship in England and would take another fifteen months to make it back to the States. The department had a spirited debate over whether this woman or another highly respected scholar, ready to begin his duties immediately, ought to get the nod. Congressman Dryden's preferred choice for the tenured position lost out by three votes. Therefore, to hold the fort, as it were, while McBride was away, Jeremy Nichols was hired to teach the Victorian novel course, along with a promise that he'd be assigned a seminar on Dickens.

Mallory knew that the groundwork had been done to influence Nichols to head up to the seventh stack level and start looking around. As Mallory was also aware, the amateur sleuth sometimes gets lucky in real life.

Mallory stood up, dropped a five on the table, and drank the last of his beer. "That son of a bitch Beauchamp."

Stepping outside the tavern, Mallory rubbed his knee and dug into his pocket for some over-the-counter pain relief. Two arthroscopic procedures in the past two years had done him absolutely no good. He'd need major surgery on the knee if he ever hoped to walk without pain. It was so damned ironic. Mallory was a track star in high school—for three years his time in the eight-hundred meters remained a state record. And then there was all the sprinting and distance running he did for the government in such exotic locales as Beirut, Damascus, and Mosul—not to mention performing many of his own stunts on movie sets and locations. And here he was now just passing forty, barely able to walk thirty yards without desiring to rest his knee or pop another couple of pills.

Coy Mallory, Fred Beauchamp, and Jack Lawrence used to laugh at the prospects of one day being superannuated. Lawrence had made the inevitable "put out to stud" joke, and, being the eldest of the three, Beauchamp waxed philosophically about being effective in one's sixties and seventies, as were Supreme Court justices—some notable exceptions to the contrary. Mallory, however, never thought he'd care once his physical skills and his looks deteriorated. It would have been unfair to label him merely a man of action and little thought. He would never have received the assignments he did had he been nothing more than speed and brawn, but he clearly lacked the patience for thought and subtlety shared by Beauchamp and Lawrence. But their worlds were so different than his. Both men were recruiters—indeed Beauchamp had plucked Mallory from the classroom and shepherded his career in intelligence work. Lawrence provided secondary impetus, amusing Mallory with stories of his occasional academic spying assignments guided his senior colleague, Fred Beauchamp. Yes, Jack Lawrence with his tall tales and infuriating riddles and games.

Mallory recalled when the three of them were in Washington and had their photograph taken on the steps of the Supreme Court. Mallory believed Beauchamp would outlast them all, and that Lawrence would fuck something up that others would have to straighten out for him. Mallory just never thought that Lawrence would have held a knife to his throat for so long.

• • •

Toying with his lunch, Nichols pondered further Lawrence's reason for being on the seventh stack level that night, after the Hendley had closed up shop, spending his last seconds on earth groping on the floor, his finger placed inside a volume of Dickens Christmas stories. Nichols knew Lawrence had recently published his own edition of the stories. What on earth could he have been checking? If he was specifically looking at a section of Dickens's story *The Chimes*, then why? Surely his recent edition couldn't have omitted a passage or even a single line of text.

"Daddy!"

Nichols was startled by his daughter's exuberant shout.

"Here's a present for my Daddy."

Nichols took the sheet of white drawing paper and examined her latest painting. He found the grayish cloud she had added to her scene quite striking, since she had never placed anything next to her sun. But he felt immediate concern over what this cloud meant to his daughter. Was it a suggestion of what she was feeling as her father's life was becoming more and more complicated? Or was it merely her own anxiety over making the move from the only home she had known in her young life? At the bottom was the familiar empty oval, but for the first time she had added what looked like strings of hair to the shape. The hair was long enough to know she'd been imagining a woman.

Nichols felt the pressure increase in his forehead. Was this the day he long dreaded—when she would ask about her mother?

"I painted two, Daddy. Look."

"Wow." He smiled and pulled out the second sheet from under the first. Once more she had drawn the man lying prone with the book in his hand. Again to his mind, she depicted a scene she couldn't possibly have known about. The murder of Jackson Lawrence the previous February.

"Belinda, why did you draw this man like that?" He didn't sense how angry the questions sounded to his daughter. Immediately, the tears came. "No, no, baby, don't cry. I'm sorry. I'm not mad at you. I'm not. It's a really good painting. It's even better than the first one you did showing...the man. Can you tell me who he is? Or who you think he is?" Nichols couldn't believe how agitated the drawing had made him.

Belinda's expression shifted from confusion and hurt to childlike incredulity. "Daddy, don't you know who this is?"

"Yes—I mean, I'm not sure. Will you tell me?"

"Silly Daddy. It's you."

CHAPTER 18

"Don't you dare tell anyone, my lovely darling, but during one summer I ate several of my dinners on the seventh stack level of the Hendley." Lawrence gently ran the back of his finger across Sandra Stark's lips, ostensibly to silence her mock-horror at his admission but really to feel the warmth of her mouth in the aftermath of their lovemaking. He hadn't kissed her during their ardent intimacy, because he wished to keep his eyes continually on her incredible face until his passion was spent. Lawrence wondered if her lips would be warm or if they had begun to experience the cooling the rest of her body was now undergoing.

Lawrence preferred to keep his bedroom "invigoratingly brisk" as he termed it, and because she lay completely uncovered by any bed clothes, Sandra reacted to the cold air that seemed to be racing into her lover's bedroom. Lawrence rubbed his hand on her upper arm and then on her outer thigh, taking pleasure in her metamorphosis from a passionate lover to a woman on the verge of shivering. But still her lips were warm, a state he now verified with his own.

Five minutes later, Sandra sat up in Lawrence's bed, wrapped cocoon-like in his heaviest robe, waiting for him to heat up some tea. She noted the prints framed on his bedroom walls—Victorian depictions of medieval scenes. Most striking to her was the popular 1893 John William Waterhouse painting *"La Belle Dame Sans Merci"*—inspired by Keats's poem of the same name. The print depicted a knight leaning forward apparently to kiss and be otherwise enthralled by the beautiful barefooted enchantress, with her long-unpinned hair cascading down her back and across her covered breasts. Sandra had seen the print often enough but had never studied it as she did now. The lady's youthful yet enticing face presently alarmed her, for she realized it was eerily reminiscent of the way her own looked when she passed the first stages of puberty and became acutely aware of her attractiveness as a young woman. The Waterhouse lady without mercy had the same pale skin tone Sandra had in her middle teens—as well as the same lip color Sandra chose for herself in those years.

Stepping to the mirror attached to Lawrence's bureau, she picked up his expensive watch and looked for an inscription on the back. She smiled when she saw there was none. Turning it over again, she noted that the date on the watch corrected her misconception of the day. Today was December 27th, not the 26th. Standing before the mirror, Sandra examined her face, and was pleased that the color had remained on her lips. But then he had only kissed her once. She changed her favorite lip color the day she left for her freshman year of college. Her hair was below her shoulders now, some three or four inches longer than the length she wore it through her first two years at the university. Her skin was still the same tone, but her face had become even more beautiful and no longer looked exactly like the lady in the Waterhouse painting. The thought upset her. Did Professor Lawrence sense how much she had once looked like the lady in the print so prominently displayed in his bedroom—the print he likely caressed visually every night before falling asleep?

Without her realizing it, her lover stepped into the room as she continued to stare at the mirror. She turned suddenly when she smelled the aroma of chai tea. Lawrence's face was turned away from her and toward the framed Waterhouse print.

• • •

Beauchamp found the grade book. Apparently, it had long ago fallen behind some of the folio-sized tomes on the bottom shelf of his custom-made bookcase, the one he had constructed earlier this summer. He was determined finally to rearrange the volumes by subject and make some tough decisions as to which he would give away or trade at the used-book store flanking the north side of the university. He wasn't surprised at unearthing the grade book, for he found it was missing from the box that stored all the ones he used since commencing his teaching career over forty years earlier. This book included names and grades of his final three years of teaching, including the Winter term of 2018, his last before retiring in early August of that year.

Beauchamp opened the cover and gazed at the name at the top of the first page—"Allingham, Helena." The name had been circled with a red ballpoint pen. "His Helena," as he would come to call her. What had begun with a visit to his office to explain the unexpected family request to return home to England—forcing her to leave in early April—soon blossomed into a most special relationship between professor and student. He kindly allowed her an "Incomplete" in his American Literature class that term. She remained in England until the end of May and finished her class assignments during the summer. Throughout those weeks, Helena visited him often, and he easily understood she needed a mentor, an older confidant—someone she would later term "a father-friend." Beauchamp embraced the relationship in large part because he found her presence refreshing, owing to her active wit and vibrant intellectual curiosity. He moreover delighted in the fact that she showed no self-consciousness about either the age or the racial difference between them.

Although he'd just retired from teaching, Helena visited him often in the fall as she finished her last term before graduation. They met for lunch and a few dinners during this time, and their mutual affections grew. She told Beauchamp she loved him more than her own father and that she would never be out of his life, whether he "liked it or not." Following her graduation after the Fall term of 2018, Beauchamp pulled a few strings and secured Helena an interview in the nation's capital as an assistant in a congressional office, which led to a position at the beginning of March 2019. During her initial months on Capitol Hill, she drove to the university to visit him every other week, and occasionally he would travel to Washington and take her to lunch or to dinner. She never felt at all hesitant about providing him with information she had gleaned in the congressman's office about what was being planned, debated, rejected, or considered.

Helena was honored that Beauchamp trusted her to form her own opinions of what she saw and heard and even to share uncorroborated rumors. He simply asked her to tell him everything and to trust her own instincts when it came to discussing matters of others' loyalties and ambitions. What was most important to her was pleasing him; she never asked why he was interested in the coming and goings in Representative Stuart Dryden's office, which was located down the hall from where she worked in the Rayburn Building. There was nothing she wouldn't do to learn from others what Beauchamp wished to know.

Over their pleasurable lunches and occasional dinners, Helena shared details of her life in England and her many flights of fancy. But she also listened intently to all her mentor related about his colorful and sterling career and what he had missed in spite of his many accomplishments. He confided that he never had a daughter to shower with love and gifts and made clear that she was filling that void "admirably." He refused to act on any sexual desire he had for her, but he understood early in their relationship that he was falling in love with her nonetheless, needing frequent communication with this young woman to fill another void, the nature of which he never fully understood. It was far more than having someone there to replace his late wife. Perhaps it was nothing more than the need for a youthful feminine voice to sooth his conflicted sensibilities.

Still, Helena's confession that she had slept with "a few" men saddened him, but soon he began to take solace from the fact that she claimed never to have been in love with any of them. She plainly admitted that she eventually wanted a child, especially a daughter, and he was disappointed that she didn't suggest she'd want him to father it. He well knew such an arrangement would be impossible, even if he were physically capable of siring a child. A prostatectomy eight years earlier had rendered him unable to adequately perform the sex act. Still, should she become pregnant, he said, he would assist her financially, regardless of whether her family could or would not.

On his late wife Janette's birthday in early June—when she would have been sixty-seven—Beauchamp wrestled painfully with the desire to ask Helena to marry him, even formulating a verbal contract that would have spared her all forms of sexual interaction, even having to sleep in the same room with her older husband. But he knew that would also be impossible. If she said no, which he knew was almost certain, he might lose her from his life entirely, and the very thought was intolerable. Therefore, their relationship remained uniquely intimate over the months, and three days earlier, he called and left a voice message he thought would interest her.

As he petted Usher, Beauchamp recalled that Helena had taken Lawrence's undergraduate Dickens seminar, and that she was deeply affected by his death. At times her insistence over the intervening time that they talk about Lawrence deeply disturbed Beauchamp. She wished to know too much about his late colleague, he believed—especially about Lawrence's habits and idiosyncrasies. Beauchamp's immediate assumption was that his old friend had a brief affair with Helena or was on the verge of having one, and the thought wounded and infuriated him. His conversation when he was with Helena earlier this summer still perched forward in his memory.

"Helena, I fear that you became too close—too intimate—with Jack Lawrence."

Her reaction suggested a young woman close to panic. She took his hands and lifted them to her face. "Please, please, don't think that, Fred."

He believed she was making a concerted effort to cry. "It's just a question, Helena."

"You have to believe me. I was never involved with him like that."

Beauchamp wasn't convinced, but unable to stem his deep affection, he hugged her tightly and temporarily dismissed his concern.

Beauchamp just hadn't expected Helena's frequent questions about Lawrence after his death, particularly when she pressed him about any gifts Lawrence might have given him over the years and whether Lawrence had "bequeathed" anything to Beauchamp in his will. When Beauchamp laughed at this inquiry, her features became uncharacteristically stern. For a moment, she was someone else, he thought. Again, Beauchamp rationalized his beloved Helena had never been able to reconcile herself to Lawrence's death because they had been sexually intimate. Accordingly, he promised her he would always be willing to talk about Lawrence—that is, all aspects of Lawrence's life, save one.

Remembering that vow, Beauchamp spoke recently with Helena to say that he and the newly hired Jeremy Nichols had been talking about Lawrence's murder while up on the seventh stack level of the Hendley and that Nichols was coming back later in the week to continue his search for housing for himself and for his sister and her two daughters. Helena probed him about the young scholar and seemed startled when Beauchamp told her that Nichols was a Dickensian. Beauchamp couldn't understand her reaction.

CHAPTER 19

"You mean it's me in the picture, Belinda? I'm the man with the book in his hand?" His daughter nodded, the puddles of tears still in her eyes. "I don't understand. Do you think something is going to happen to me?"

She shook her head, causing the tears to spill down her cheeks.

"Baby, I don't understand why I'm lying on the ground like that."

Belinda sniffled. "You're playing with me in the picture. See, Daddy?"

"Playing with you?" Nichols was desperate for his daughter to explain what she meant.

"The other night. Remember? I was watching my movie and you were on the floor like a sea-snake?"

"Oh, God. I do. I do! Oh, I love you, Belinda Bug." He picked up his daughter and embraced her as powerfully as her delicate frame would allow. The other night he had snuck up behind her while she was engrossed in her movie, crawling on the carpet, which he called the ocean, like a sea-snake. His objective was to snatch the book she had left on the floor while she was watching the movie. Now he easily remembered how he stretched his right arm out and grabbed the book just as she turned and saw him, squealing with delight and eventually jumping and driving her knees into his back.

"Do you have to go away again, Daddy?"

"Just for one night. I have to go back up to the new college and find a house for us and one for Aunt Janis. I'll be back on Friday."

"Why can't I go?"

"Because you're going to have so much more fun with your cousins, that's why."

"But I don't want you to be lonely in the car or in the hotel."

"I won't be lonely, my sweet love." He found it difficult to look at her. "I'll be thinking of you all the time." His daughter smiled and went back to her drawing. At least he could take comfort in the fact that what he had told her was true. He wouldn't be lonely and he'd definitely think of her. His sadness came from his inability to tell her everything. Neither Belinda nor his sister could know—nor anyone else—that Elizabeth Ellertson was going with him.

• • •

At 10:00 p.m., Beauchamp heard the scratching on the rear door of his house. Curiously, his dog preferred being let out at this time of night rather than earlier. Usher. The name he chose for his dog in spite of Coy Mallory's spirited objections. Beauchamp recalled being glad he broke the news to Mallory on the phone and not in person, for the younger man might have forgotten the professor's age and deteriorating physical condition and wrung his neck. Beauchamp's mind replayed that phone conversation.

"Jesus Christ, Fred, are you out of your fucking mind?"

"Coy, the name 'Usher' will only be connected to my teaching and scholarly interest in Poe. Don't you see?"

"Not everyone is a damn lit major, Fred."

Beauchamp knew the name appealed to the side of him that had always courted danger. "Living on the precipice," he liked to call it. Or the "Imp of the Perverse," as Poe famously put it. Often since his twenties, Beauchamp had walked along the narrowest of ledges—with only his impeccable sense of balance saving him. Those who hired him to work for both their university and their government had no idea how much Beauchamp liked gazing into chasms before leaping to the other side.

"Fred, you know how screwed I'd be if it all came out that I shared that information with you? Even now, after ten years?"

"And the name of my dog is going to make that more likely to occur?" Beauchamp remembered grinning broadly as he asked that question, imagining Coy Mallory on the other end of the line stalking around the room, yanking at his collar and gnawing incessantly on the edge of his thumb.

As for Mallory, he utterly despised loose ends of any kind. His impressive talent was in gathering them up—if not cutting them off. But this one had continued to elude him—all because of Jack Lawrence.

By the fall of 2009, Coy Mallory was a player in an operation he informed his older friend was given the code-name Usher. Beauchamp was at the time reporting on activities and university personnel worth watching—one such person being his friend and colleague Jackson Lawrence, who had triggered the interest of someone higher up the intelligence food chain, Walt Rosenberry, officially for both Lawrence's iconoclastic remarks about the CIA and FBI but actually for his seduction of Rosenberry's twenty-three-year-old daughter, a graduate student in Film and Media Studies, whom Lawrence had met when he addressed her class on the topic of effective oral presentation. Cara Rosenberry wanted a more serious relationship after they made love, but Lawrence thought better of it. Lawrence never knew that Beauchamp was reporting on him—although his reports were incomplete and innocuous. Coy Mallory had been half a world away—having been chipped away from his assignment in Riyadh and sent with a small group to Damascus—ostensibly as part of an unofficial diplomatic splinter team charged with assuring the Syrians that U.S. intentions in the area were both peaceful and honorable. But Mallory wasn't aware going in of what others in his group believed was the real reason for the visit—something that involved U.S. suspicions that the Syrians were seeking WMDs and were providing Lebanon's Hezbollah with Scud missiles. Something of which Mallory would later and inappropriately inform Fred Beauchamp was code-named Operation Usher.

Beauchamp held the door open for Usher after the dog did his business. He looked out toward the tree line in the shadowed area just beyond the illumination of his backyard flood lights. The trees beyond his property were of varying heights. In the darkness, the tree tops reminded him of books on library shelves—all in neat rows. But the tallest ones were very difficult to see owing to their distance from the lighted backyard. Mysteries still deeply in the shadows, he thought. Yes, the name of Jack Lawrence's killer and what Lawrence possessed at the time of his death and where it was at present. And now soon to arrive at the university was Jeremy Nichols, an eager cub scout with a flashlight. Beauchamp laughed at the thought as Usher bounded back through the door into the house.

• • •

The leisurely drive up had at least given them the opportunity to purge feelings of discomfort by the time they arrived at the hotel which was situated less than a mile from the university. When Nichols picked up Elizabeth at her friend's apartment, she was visibly nervous. Since Caitlin had already left for work, there was no one there, but Elizabeth was waiting outside when Jeremy pulled up. He could tell as he placed her bag in his trunk that she was impatient to leave. She asked him to take an alternate route out of town, for fear of driving too near where she and Steve lived. It took her ten miles before she apologized for her request.

Nichols was glad Belinda would be spending the night with Janis. The strange car parked across the street from his house still worried him, although he chided himself for overreacting. He didn't share the incident with Elizabeth for fear she would think it was her husband behind the wheel. Then again, Nichols wondered if such an assumption might indeed be correct, in spite of the belief that Ellertson was still many miles away.

What would the beguiled husband say when he learned of his wife's extra-marital relationship? Elizabeth's assurances to Jeremy that the marriage was for all intents and purposes over didn't make the prospect of confrontation any less troublesome. And it was more than a fear that, given Ellertson's linebacker physique, he would channel his humiliation into violence, for Nichols hated the thought—given his own history with Meredith—that he'd be part of someone else's marital breakup.

"Jeremy, I'm sorry I wasn't the best company on the ride up here. I was just doing a lot of thinking." They had just gotten the room keys and were headed to the elevator.

Nichols didn't want her to share those thoughts now. He worried she might then talk herself out of seeing him after today. "Elizabeth, it's all right. I was thinking a lot too. Look, let's have lunch here in the hotel and talk about how you got started playing piano, and I'll tell you all about how I became enamored of Charles Dickens." She laughed, and for the first time since he picked her up, she seemed herself.

Entering the elevator, she questioned whether she'd tell Jeremy about her first visit to the Hendley Library, when she was in middle school. Her uncle insisted at the time that she should never say anything about being there, but that was seventeen years ago. Was he merely curious to see her reaction being up there among all those books? At her age, she was too disinterested to care about what kinds of volumes were on the shelves. Her uncle checked the rows of book in one aisle and even adjusted a few that were either pushed too far forward or too far back, behavior that struck her as particularly odd, seeing that her uncle was often guilty of being slovenly.

She saw him infrequently in the years that followed—he didn't attend her wedding—but they were still very close, talking periodically by phone. Still, she hadn't told him or anyone else in her family that she wanted out of her marriage and was in love with another man.

Nor had she ever mentioned to her uncle how he bruised her arm when he was through looking at those books in the Hendley and was pulling her in another direction from the one she wished to go. Even as a middle-schooler, she understood that he was upset and didn't mean to hurt her. After all, an hour later he was buying her a CD and ice-cream.

• • •

Ellertson knocked on the apartment door. He wasn't really surprised that no one answered. He knew his wife's friend Caitlin worked until 6:00 on Thursdays. He also guessed that Elizabeth was likely off somewhere with Jeremy Nichols. Ellertson had never bought for a moment her "going to Saratoga to visit friends." He simply wondered whether she had slipped up and in fact told him where the two of them were going. Now that he looked back over the past several months, he could see how she had given him clues that she was meeting someone on the sly. He fought off the temptation to view some of those clues as more deliberate than inadvertent.

Ellertson used his key and gained entry into his wife's car. He checked the glove compartment and the cup holders. There was nothing incriminating. The glove compartment was as neat as always, and there was only a single coffee cup with evidence of her lipstick on the edge. He rubbed at the residue. For him, she would no longer freshen up her lips after a meal, but she likely had them all neat and pretty when she went to meet her lover.

He was about to shut the car door when something lying on the rear floor caught his eye. It was a small section of a sugar cone and a dollop of strawberry ice-cream. Ellertson was certain it had been dropped by Nichols's kid. "So Double E is playing mommy as well as adulteress," he muttered. "How touching." He left the incriminating evidence undisturbed, locked his wife's car, and got behind the wheel of his own. He snatched the folded typed note resting on his front seat. The note he had looked at innumerable times since he found it several days earlier in his Music Department cubby hole. It read, "Your wife's seeing another man. Look no further than the Department of English."

When he first read it, he knew at once whom the anonymous correspondent was fingering—Jeremy Nichols. When he met him at the fall convocation, he observed the interest the handsome untenured professor had in his wife. It was at that moment he decided to hold off calling a lawyer. All of a sudden he wasn't as keen on getting a divorce as he had been over the summer, but he wasn't any more committed to working on his marriage either. Therefore, he decided to go about his business and let Elizabeth go about hers. Now, as he began driving away from Caitlin's apartment, Ellertson was furious for having been so damned naïve about what his wife had been up to these past nine or ten months.

Since he received the note the previous Friday, Ellertson had followed Elizabeth and lost her in traffic on two occasions as she headed out supposedly to do errands or make a recital practice. In any event, he hadn't seen her with Nichols. He wanted to think it was some sick joke played by a university colleague, but the thought of being a cuckold and having others know and talk about him chewed at his sensibilities. He was hell bent on finding out for sure, so he lied to his wife about being out of town and planned on coming over at 6:15 to catch Caitlin as soon as she got off work. She surely knew where his wife was, and he was confident he'd get her to tell him. But he was still in the dark as to who placed that note in his box. A discreet colleague or a malicious one? Or was it Elizabeth's own doing?

• • •

Sandra Stark finished editing the thirty-minute paper she was scheduled to deliver the following week at one of the state's smaller college libraries. She was flattered and surprised by the invitation to speak this early in her career about the joys and trials of library work. In the realm of academic research libraries, her goal was to be a superstar, one frequently in demand for presentations such as this one and for Q&A sessions that invariably and arbitrarily had to be halted owing to the number of questions asked.

She also loved sitting behind the small desk in her office at the Hendley. Yet it was spacious enough for her various piles, pen and pencil cups, and framed photographs of her family. On her book shelf between two recently published volumes reflecting one of Sandra's favorite literary genres—Cassandra Clare's young adult fantasy *City of Bones* and Tolkien's epic fantasy *The Children of Húrin*—were separate photographs. One was of her mother and late father; the other of her mother, step-father, step-sister, and step-brother at one of young Will's high-school baseball games, taken when Sandra was seventeen. After his death, she planned to place a framed photo of Jackson Lawrence on the bookshelf in her apartment, but she couldn't bear to look at any photographic representation of the man she still loved.

Locking her office at 3:45, Sandra headed to the circulation desk to speak with a new employee. Following their conversation, Sandra noticed a man moving rapidly toward the west-side stairwell heading up to the stack levels. Carrying a yellow legal pad, he looked about thirty and for all the world like faculty, although she was sure she had never seen him before. The serious expression on his handsome face made her curious enough to walk to the stairwell and look up. He was bounding two steps at a time. She closed her eyes and listened. She could still hear his steps as he climbed the stairs. Guessing he'd reached level six by the time she left the stairwell, she didn't like what she was feeling. Or what she was assuming.

• • •

Nichols reached the seventh stack level and made his way to the aisle Beauchamp pointed out to him as the site of Lawrence's murder. Nichols moved down to the exact spot where Beauchamp said Lawrence fell. The atmosphere of the place was a bit eerie, as Nichols expected it had always been. It was 3:55 p.m. on an early August afternoon, but it might as well have been midnight at the end of November. For a moment he reflected on the anxiety he experienced when he was in Memphis as a teenager visiting the National Civil Rights Museum and looking up at the balcony of the old Lorraine Motel where MLK had been assassinated. Now the intensity of that feeling had been easily eclipsed by being among the stacks where a noted Dickensian had been slain.

Nichols raised his head and saw the antiquated Dickens editions on the top row. Based on the anonymous phone call he received, Nichols assumed Lawrence grabbed the Christmas Books volume before he fell dying. Nichols reached up, but his fingers couldn't touch those on the highest row. He would need one of the rolling steps to grab one of those books. Seeing that the multi-volume edition began on the top row and continued on the one below, he spotted the book he was looking for. This one he could reach. He felt a rush of excitement as he began thumbing through it. Looking for traces of blood—and especially a relatively large blood smear on two open pages, he saw evidence of age and wear and some kind of spilled liquid in the book, but nothing that could have passed for blood. Nichols couldn't help grinning as he considered what the liquid stain might be. Coffee from a late-night visitor to the seventh stack level? Perhaps some scatological souvenir from a creative and disgruntled undergraduate in 1923?

Replacing the volume, Nichols jotted down its bibliographical information on his legal pad. Assuming he might have to come back to continue the search, he wanted to avoid thumbing through the same book twice. Nichols saw that another superannuated edition of the completed works rested to the right of the one from which he had drawn the Christmas Books volume. He pulled down the corresponding book from this edition, but it too lacked evidence of blood. He saw yet another edition farther down the row, but it was far from where Beauchamp said Lawrence had fallen. Nichols thought for a moment. Had he been pulling from the wrong shelf?

He tried to imagine the night of the murder. Lawrence had already been attacked before he reached up for the book and was therefore very likely hunched over somewhat from the surprise and the rushing pain in his neck. And Beauchamp told Nichols as they left the library that a number of volumes had fallen to the floor and others were knocked through the shelf to the section on the other aisle, also thrusting several volumes to the floor there. Accordingly, Nichols looked on the third row from the top and found resting there another old edition of Dickens. The volume of Christmas Stories was right above the area where Lawrence fell. Nichols opened to the title page and saw that the book contained the five Christmas tales—the famous *Christmas Carol* and four of the lesser known efforts, including *The Cricket on the Hearth* and *The Chimes*.

He thumbed through over one hundred pages before he saw the only partially faded smear of Jack Lawrence's blood effacing two pages of *The Chimes*. Why hadn't Fred Beauchamp pointed this specific volume out to him?

Before Nichols could ponder the matter further, the elevator arrived at the seventh floor. He shut the book and quickly place it back on the shelf, as he heard the elevator door open and then the sound of footsteps moving quickly to the aisle where he stood. He remained facing the books on the shelves but turned his head to the left in the direction of the footsteps. The face of the person who stepped into his line of vision reflected both concern and a slight trace of anger.

CHAPTER 20

Stuart Dryden was too agitated to enjoy his evening scotch. He felt similarly six months earlier, when he realized that the death of Jackson Lawrence wouldn't be enough to prevent public knowledge of Dryden's sexual tastes—those which if exposed could put an end to his political ambitions, as well as his reputation and thirty-seven-year marriage. In the immediate aftermath of Lawrence's murder, Dryden was allowed entry to the professor's office on the pretense of locating scholarly notes Dryden had lent him and needed back. In truth, he searched unsuccessfully for any of the evidence against him that Lawrence possessed. As the weeks passed, Dryden began to nurture a confidence that Lawrence was too clever for his own good. If Lawrence left a clue in the book he was holding at his death or elsewhere in the row of books where his body was found, neither Dryden nor anyone he had employed could find it. And to make certain no one would, Dryden used his influence to prevent another senior Dickensian from being chosen to take the tenure line Lawrence held. But he never considered the likelihood that the department would hire a young specialist for a three-year position. Dryden would be sure Nichols was watched, especially if he again wandered up to the seventh stack level. After all, Dryden was a former scholar; he understood that finding the kind of labyrinthine clue Lawrence might have left behind might well take a more experienced mind to uncover. But then Nichols might have a natural affinity for literary detective work, and even if the odds were against it, the kid was still a Dickensian. Having daily access to the Hendley might, possibly, lead to a discovery that simply couldn't be permitted. Not now. Not ever.

Dryden carried the scotch into his den, the only room in the couple's private home that hadn't capitulated to his wife's preferred decorating style. On the north wall of the den was the oil painting of his grandfather and his family, including Dryden's father, then eight years of age. Dryden hated that his puritanical father's and grandfather's eyes seemed always to be locked on him—evaluating him, no matter where in the room he stood. He wanted to rid himself of the portrait on a number of occasions, but each time he reminded himself that he was one of those men who couldn't escape his ancestry. Everything he did had to be in homage to that lineage. Family was his albatross. But unlike the Ancient Mariner, Dryden's responsibility to his heritage was so tightly wrapped around his neck that it could never be pried free. He reached for another metaphor. All he did and planned to do was sifted through the fine and antique mesh of that ancestry. And he bitterly resented the fact that he had both the paternal and maternal sides to honor, satisfy, and protect. That he'd disgraced his family years earlier by his actions frightened him less than having his past suddenly revealed to them at a time when he was on the threshold of bringing further glory to the family name by being elected a United States Senator.

Since he was a boy in prep school, he spent as much time at the Hendley as he could, occasionally in the company of his father, a proud and influential alumnus, who received his degree in history in 1953 before going on to law school and a prominent legal career. The elder Dryden continued the tradition of financial beneficence begun by his family in the nineteenth century. Whenever young Stuart went to the Hendley, he saw the tangible evidence of his family's generosity and commitment to the august library. After the Civil War, the family contributed funds for the purchase of hundreds of volumes in order to make the Hendley competitive with what were then the best college and university libraries in the northeast. Later, his family would see to it that the Hendley's rare-book collection was equal or superior to that of almost any other academic library in the United States or Europe. The family always answered appeals for building funds as well as for acquisitions. And at his death, Dryden's father left a check for seven figures to cover computer upgrades and the purchase of indispensable software. And yet his son couldn't resist the danger of indulging his sexual impulses, which he tried to limit to Victorian erotic literature and pornographic images. But for a short time before Lawrence's death, he had gone beyond voyeurism of that restricted kind and became a participant. Why didn't he consider that he might have been set up by Lawrence, who would soon have photos and a handwritten account by the woman who allowed Dryden to perform the fantasies he had only looked at and read about?

Dryden still harbored a grudge against the university's senior and emeritus faculty who had first- and second-generation grudges with the congressman's father, who sought compensation for his generosity in the form of honorifics and deference to his suggestions as to how his money ought to be spent. The English Department never received what it deemed its fair share of the senior Dryden's financial gifts, leading many to assume that he was disappointed in his eldest son's choice of literary scholarship as a life's calling. Again, Stuart Dryden was expected to do everything he could for the family name, but his heritage seemingly couldn't do much for him.

Even after he left the English department for the dean's office and then for the political world beyond academe, Dryden had periodically returned to the Hendley for the stated purpose of doing research on Thackeray and later on the history of the university. But Dryden's need to be at the Hendley transcended anything scholarly. He felt compelled to check in from time to time, almost as if his regular presence could prevent the library from whispering its deepest secrets about him. And every time he made it to the Hendley since the previous winter, he always walked up the west stairwell to the seventh stack level, turning down the aisle that housed the older Dickens volumes.

• • •

"Hello? Can I help you?" Nichols didn't know what else to say to the very attractive young woman standing at the end of the aisle. He was completely nonplused by her appearance and the concerned expression she wore.

His question brought back her normal demeanor. "Oh, excuse me. I didn't mean to startle you. I'm Sandra Stark. I work here at the Hendley—so I should be asking you the same question." Her friendliness, modesty, and wit relaxed him.

"Oh, then I should introduce myself. My name is Jeremy Nichols. I'm in the process of joining the junior faculty—to begin teaching this coming term."

"Well, congratulations. Welcome to our never humble institution." They both laughed at her witticism. "So, I take it you're a Victorian specialist?" She gave a furtive look toward the section of the shelves that Nichols had disturbed.

"Yes, I am."

"Of ancient and little used volumes and editions?"

"Well, let's just say that I have a special affinity for volumes of forgotten lore, as it were."

"'Volumes of forgotten lore.' I take it you've been talking to Professor Beauchamp, one of this country's best Poe scholars."

"As a matter of fact I have. He brought me up here and showed me..." Nichols halted, thinking it best not to reveal his interest in Jackson Lawrence's death. "...where these books were located." This beautiful young woman was likely working the day Lawrence was murdered. Had she known him?

She lifted her hand to her lips after Nichols's aborted sentence. "So you'll be teaching Victorian lit?"

"I will."

It took her several seconds to reply. "With a specialty in...?"

"Dickens."

She took a long breath and closed her eyes. Nichols thought she was preoccupied by something work related or personal. He decided to leave the area. He'd return to the Christmas Stories volume at another time.

"It was very nice meeting you, Ms. Stark."

"Please, it's Sandra. That is as long as I don't have to call you Professor Nichols." What would have been a delightfully charming remark was lost in her blank expression and almost lifeless voice.

"No, please don't do that. It's Jeremy. I'll be looking forward to exploring further this incredible library." She merely nodded. Nichols offered a muted "Bye" and headed for the stairwell.

Sandra put her hand against the edge of the shelving unit to steady herself. She noticed the yellow legal pad the young professor had inadvertently left resting on several books on a lower shelf. She saw the names of two editions scribbled on the page. She raised her head. They were both resting on the shelf above the volume that bore evidence of her lover's macabre signature—the unusual check mark he made in blood. Perhaps the young man had a bit of the scholarly eccentric about him and was for some reason intrigued by the more ancient editions. Perhaps. But he was a Dickensian like Jack Lawrence. Was it this coincidence that troubled her? Jeremy Nichols couldn't draw any conclusions about the murder even if he eventually saw the evidence of blood in the Dickens volume. Surely, no one could.

She could never remove the book from its place on the shelves, because it was in essence a shrine to her lover. The blood dried upon two pages was reflective of so much. She believed he would have wanted that volume to remain where it was on that horrible night. After all, she was the one who had placed it back correctly after Lawrence's death. The police had just set it on the shelf without concern for its proper placement. Six months ago, she determined it would stay there for as long as she remained working at the Hendley, even though it might contain a clue about the murder that could reveal so much—too much. After she retired or before she died, she could always ask for the book to be given to her. Or steal it.

CHAPTER 21

My domestic unhappiness so oppresses me that I can write little more than these tortured thoughts. I must continue with my public readings, since they afford me a way to endure my frustration and disappointment in not being with Ellen as I would like. This past spring the response was excellent for my reading of ***A Christmas Carol****, and I see no reason at present why it would not be well received even though it is now summer. I will include another of my Christmas books,* ***The Chimes****, and some scenes from my recent effort* ***Dombey and Son****. Yet I fear that some of the sections from these works are so affecting that I won't be able to get through them without great difficulty. Regardless, I must do something, or I shall wear my heart away.*

The reader replaced this section of the journal in its proper place in the stack of manuscript pages, and after a few moments pulled out another sheet at random.

I have recently purchased a lovely bracelet for Ellen, but the jeweler sent it to my residence by mistake, and Catherine discovered it. So easy has it become for me to lie, that I vigorously protested my innocence and reminded Kate that I often send gifts to those who have joined me in theatrical projects. But Kate rejected my assurances. "The girl is only eighteen," she said. "You are old enough to be her father." I could only listen, for there is only so much I can protest without feeling utterly humiliated, although my anger over the aspersions Kate cast at Ellen has been almost impossible to suppress. I have a deep need to protect and honor the young woman I love. May God forgive me, but I feel contempt for my wife for having spoken against the girl. Will I soon have with Ellen what my wife is suspecting and I am so dearly coveting? What I am risking the displeasure of God to obtain?

• • •

Nichols walked fifty yards on the sidewalk away from the Hendley by the time he realized he left his legal pad among the Dickens volumes on level seven. He muttered a mild profanity and began retracing his steps. When he reached stack level five, he heard steps coming down the stairwell. Between levels five and six they met.

"Jeremy?"

"Elizabeth? What are you doing up here?" He was troubled by the frozen look on her face.

"I...I just thought that you would..." She lowered her head.

Utterly confused, Nichols was gallant enough to assist her in an explanation. "Were you looking for me?" He told her he had a meeting with Fred Beauchamp, after which he would return to the hotel, but said nothing about visiting the Hendley. He fudged on the truth because he didn't wish to explain to her about his growing fascination for Jackson Lawrence and the details of his death.

"No,...Jeremy, I thought you were meeting with Professor Beauchamp. Are you looking up something or...?"

"Elizabeth, did you follow me because you thought I was meeting someone else?" He immediately regretted his question. The idea was ludicrous and he knew it, but perhaps she had seen Sandra Stark emerging from the stairwell.

"Oh, my God—no, Jeremy, no." She grabbed his wrists to punctuate her point. "The truth is I came because when I was a girl my uncle brought me here and took me to one of the upper levels where the old books were kept."

"Your uncle? You've never mentioned any uncle. Was he an academic?" Nichols laughed out of relief that she seemed not at all suspicious of anything *he* was doing.

"No, my uncle was...well, he had heard about what happened to one of the professors here at the Hendley."

Nichols was jolted by her admission. "Wait. How old were you when he took you here?"

"I was in middle school. Jeremy, are you all right? Did someone tell you about the professor who killed himself?"

"Killed himself?"

"Yes, back then. They found him up here—on one of the levels."

Finally, Nichols saw a way out of his confusion. "Tell me I'm not really hearing this. Elizabeth, the reason I came here was to...well, to see the place where another professor, Jackson Lawrence, was murdered this past February."

They remained in the stairwell as Nichols informed her who Lawrence was and spoke of the tour Beauchamp had given him five days earlier, adding that the professor emeritus was a close friend of Lawrence. Nichols assured her it was simply a matter of his curiosity having been peaked, and that he wished only to see the spot again. "I don't know, Elizabeth. It's like some kind of historical landmark. And since I'm going to be teaching here, I just wanted to...well..."

"But didn't Doug Finneran ever tell you about what happened here?"

"Doug. That reminds me...Anyway, yes, he had mentioned it, and besides that, I had heard about it when I went to a conference in the spring. But it's different now that I'm going to be teaching here the next three years."

"I understand. I don't know if I would ever have come myself if I hadn't met you." She paused. "Did you hear that? 'If I hadn't ever met you.' I can't imagine where I'd be if I hadn't."

Nichols smiled and touched her pretty face. There was more he could tell her, but he thought it prudent to wait before he spoke more specifically of his interest Lawrence's murder. Nor did he think it wise to mention the call he received from the woman with the British accent. There were enough complications in his life as it was. He didn't wish to share another with Elizabeth—at least not at present.

"Jeremy, I had long ago forgotten what floor my uncle had taken me to. I was walking around blindly on the sixth level and thought maybe it was the fifth when I ended up here."

"I was told about that suicide. It's on the seventh level. Come on, I'll show exactly where you were when you were in middle school." Since she had just turned thirty, he guessed she had come with her uncle to the Hendley in 2002 or 2003.

As they climbed back up the stairs, Nichols remained troubled by Elizabeth's account of having been brought to the very location of a suicide when she was so young. When they reached the seventh stack level, he asked how her uncle explained his bringing her to such a place.

"He never told me why he needed to come here—at least not that I can remember. My father had broken his leg while skiing with his buddies in Vermont, and my uncle was visiting my mother and me, checking up on us since he was in the area and knowing that his brother was away. When we got the call about the accident, my mother insisted we drive up and be with my father. We got a very late start—my mother told me later that my uncle kept delaying our leaving for some reason—and so he decided to stop here for the night since it was a university town and would have a nice hotel and restaurant. Again, I recall my mother telling me all this later."

"Then why did he bring you to the Hendley? Your mother wasn't with you, was she?"

"No. After we ate, she wanted to lie down. She was still pretty upset." She paused. "About my father, I assume. My uncle promised me ice cream, so we both went out to get it."

"Okay, but..."

"I don't know why, Jeremy. All I remember is that he said he had to stop quickly and look at something in the library. I remember being scared to death by the building and especially when he brought me up here. I know I was terrified because there was no one else on this floor the whole time we were here. My uncle was definitely upset about something. He grabbed my arm, and...well, ever since that time I always had the shudders whenever I thought of the Hendley. For a long time, this very place—right where we're standing now—was in a recurring dream of mine, a very scary dream. I guess I just wanted to come here as a thirty-year-old woman, look at the place where my uncle took me, and then I'd laugh and finally shake off an unpleasant childhood memory. I never thought I should tell you all this, so I decided that, since our hotel is so close, I'd come here while you were talking to the retired professor. I'd have a quick look and then get back before you returned. I'm so sorry, Jeremy. I must sound like a complete zany brain."

Nichols smiled broadly at her colorful phrase. "But, Elizabeth, you forget that I deceived you as well."

She took his hand. "So, the murder of Professor Lawrence was on this floor too. In which aisle?"

"This one. Ready to see the spot?" Elizabeth had stopped suddenly as Nichols pointed down the aisle. He could tell she was still frightened. The dim lighting on the seventh stack level only contributed to her anxiety.

"Yes, I'm ready."

"Okay, it's exactly here, Elizabeth. Here's where they found the body. Do you remember where your uncle said the other professor killed himself?" Nichols firmly held her hand, fully respectful of the significance of the spot to her memory and active imagination.

She looked down the aisle of books and pointed toward the far wall. "Somewhere over there, I think." She stared toward the spot for some fifteen seconds. Finally, she sighed and looked at him. "Thank you, Jeremy." He wasn't prepared for what happened next.

Elizabeth pulled his head down to her mouth and kissed him as passionately as she had ever done since they had fallen in love. He assumed that for her the kiss was as cathartic as it was reflective of her affections. He hoped he was helping to purge her disturbing childhood experience. But he also realized that tonight being in their hotel bed would be cathartic for him. His desire for her was as intense a feeling and frustration as he had ever known.

When she broke the kiss, she stared into his eyes for several moments. He could see she was still grateful for his understanding. As she playfully turned her head to regain her composure, she noticed the yellow legal pad resting on top of several books on one of the shelves. "Someone was actually here doing some research, it seems." She reached for the pad. "Just some shorthand names for books. Hardly impressive calligraphy."

Nichols wanted to smile at her unconscious slap at his penmanship, but he was too confused by the fact that the shelf from which Elizabeth took the legal pad wasn't the one on which he had left it earlier. He had placed it on books two shelves lower when he thumbed through the edition of Dickens's Christmas stories.

Elizabeth sighed and replaced the pad. "Well, we'll just leave it. Its owner will be back, I'm sure." Jeremy smiled easily now. She had no idea how right she was.

"Come on. It's time for dinner. Do you have any idea what restaurant your uncle took you to when you were in middle school?" She cast him the usual "Are you kidding me?" look. "Okay, the hotel restaurant will do nicely. Let's go."

As they reached the end of the aisle and turned right toward the stairwell, they were startled by the presence of someone else on the floor. They had heard no one approaching.

"Hello, Jeremy. And who is this lovely lady?"

Nichols was barely able to articulate a reply. "Elizabeth I'd like you to meet Professor Emeritus Fred Beauchamp."

CHAPTER 22

Helena opened her bureau drawer. She hesitated for a moment before touching the undergarments, closing her eyes and leaving her hand resting against the soft fabric. Just as she'd done this past winter, when she was deciding what to wear under her corduroy pants, flannel shirt, thick sweater, and ankle-high boots.

Outwardly, the choice of clothing wouldn't have surprised anyone who knew her. She deemed her chosen style as "ruggedly casual"—even more pronounced than the informal outfits she preferred in England before moving to the States. Her American contemporaries at the university had for some forty years refined the ruggedly casual style and made it a statement of character as well as comfort. Although she never considered herself a conformist, Helena took to this fashion style enthusiastically.

But on the evening of February 6, 2019, Helena debated whether she would wear the undergarments—bra, panties, and pantyhose—she had purchased earlier in the day. Each item was particularly feminine in the traditional sense—sheer, silky, and alluring—and reflective of what a resourceful young woman might choose to slip on if seduction was in her plans. And seduction was indeed on Helena's mind as she prepared to meet Jackson Lawrence at his place later that night. She imagined herself removing the sweater immediately upon entering. She would then cook dinner on his stove. After the meal, she would remove her boots and make herself comfortable on his sofa.

The meeting was his idea. The location and the dinner were hers. In fact, she had already refused to see him if he desired to meet at either the Hendley again or at some safe public haunt. Lawrence protested, but she felt his heart wasn't really behind the appeal for prudence. She reminded him that their student-teacher relationship ended with the *A* grade she received in the Dickens seminar the previous fall term. She didn't have to add that he would be denied further examination of the Dickens manuscript unless they met at his place for an innocent dinner and glass or two of wine.

Helena shook free of the memory and gently pulled some of the items from her drawer as she kept her eyes on the mirror above her bureau. She offered a weary smile at the recollection of the hours spent imagining what her face would look like in her mid- to late-forties. Not at all a beautiful young woman, she hoped her later years would be kinder and somehow permit her at least some freedom from the kinds of drastic change she saw too frequently in her family. Both in old family photographs and in person, she witnessed the physical appearance of the female members deteriorating by their mid-thirties—with their hair and clothing conceding to some unspoken rule about what a woman should look like by the time she reached forty.

But she assumed one thing would not change. Since puberty she compensated for her plainer facial features through her aggressive personality, which often included playing the active partner, and pursuer, in her relationships with boys and then men. She was sure her personality and sexual allure would remain her strong points as she grew older and that she would more than hold her own against those women who were deemed pretty in their teens and early twenties but had transformed into plain or even ugly women by their late thirties — a thought that often comforted and delighted her.

On the evening of February 6th, she arrived at Lawrence's residence with the rust-colored folder in her arms. The string that secured the flap was tightly wound. She would open it only after they enjoyed the dinner she had planned, made from the ingredients Lawrence agreed to purchase earlier in the day. At the time, she wasn't at all ashamed of what she was doing; nor did she care that any interest Lawrence might show in her was primarily stimulated by his need to possess the journal for a few days so he could read every page and revel in the manuscript's authenticity.

Jackson Lawrence's being over forty was of no consequence to her, even though she was not yet twenty-two. And why should it have been? She was physically attracted to him—to his handsomeness, yes, but more to his charm and his incredible voice. She wanted to imagine herself as the only young woman he had slept with since he left his thirties. If he found the opportunity to make love to a woman her age merely an opportunity to validate his virility, so be it.

The dinner was pedestrian. She made pasta and a simple salad. The wine was a modestly priced red. A cordial served them both as a dessert, and as they sat on the sofa, she followed her plan and removed her boots, smiling invitingly at him. She was unhappy that his smile wasn't warmer than it was.

"Helena, I appreciate so much your willingness to let me keep the journal for a day or two. As you can imagine, I am most anxious to read every word." She was furthermore disappointed that he sat as far away from her on the sofa as he could, almost wedging his torso into the corner of the arm rest. She considered lifting her legs and placing her feet in his lap, forcing him to touch if not massage them, but her pride demanded that he give at least some indication he was interested in being intimate. Their conversation over dinner was by and large a series of inquiries about her life in England. He offered nothing at all about himself. Too much the gentleman, she thought, as she sat back against the rear cushion, her corduroy covered legs now demurely crossed at the ankle.

"Helena, may I see the manuscript now?"

"I assume the pasta was all right?"

"Yes. Yes. Delicious. As was the salad. Thank you so much for preparing it."

She was quickly becoming frustrated by his reluctance to speak with any literary flair, as he always had in the classroom. Accordingly, she said in an almost dismissive tone, "You can open it now." Finishing her cordial, she held out the cordial glass for him to fill again. That he seemed put-off by the request, even though he granted it, made her indignant.

Lawrence unwound the string securing the folder and carefully removed the journal pages. The brief experience handling a few of them at the Hendley was nothing compared to holding the entire manuscript in his hands in the privacy of his own home. Helena was envious of the way he looked at and handled the journal, even softly sighing as he did so. Would that he had paid half as much attention to her, she reflected.

"Helena, how many times have you read these pages?"

"I don't think I have ever read more than two or three of the pages since I've had them." She exaggerated the level of her indifference because she wanted to anger and frustrate him.

"I find that hard to believe."

"You may believe it."

Lawrence didn't react to her increasingly unpleasant tone; he was too enamored of what he held before him. He skimmed several pages just to get a sense of the subject matter. "Again, assuming that all of these pages are genuine, Charles Dickens is speaking freely and privately here about Ellen Ternan, the young woman he loved—whom he deeply desired but could never really have."

"Are you sure about that?" she replied. "I mean you've only taken a brief glance at only some of the pages. Are you sure he never had her?" He wished to keep skimming through the document, but she moved across the sofa to him and put her hand down on the pages he hadn't yet seen. "And he was how old when he dearly loved this young woman?"

"In his forties. Forty-five when they first met."

"And she?"

"Eighteen."

"Twenty-seven years difference, then. Close to the difference between you and me. And he desired her, you say?"

Lawrence was distressed and embarrassed by her behavior and the implication and tone of her inquiry.

"Helena, I don't know if I've inadvertently said something to make you believe that I—"

Before he could finish, she jumped to her feet and began searching for her boots. When she finally found the second one, she sat on the dining room chair slipping it back over her nylon-clad foot. The doorbell startled them both. Lawrence walked to the door without once looking at her.

"Sandra? What are you doing here?"

"I wanted to talk to you. I have to talk to you. It's very important."

"Of course, of course. But..."

Helena called toward the door. "He has to assure one of his students that she's on the right track for her first important paper of the semester." Helena grabbed her heavy sweater and headed for the door. The resentful tone of her words made clear to Sandra that the young woman had come for more than advice about her critical prose.

"Hello, I'm Helena Allingham, one of Dr. Lawrence's..." She was about to stick out her hand when she saw the lovely features of Sandra Stark, the woman who so bedeviled her mind the past number of weeks. Her face flushed.

Sandra's did as well, as she too remembered the young woman who sat with Lawrence at the library that day. The two women stared at each other for several moments, each formulating painful conclusions, both of their expressions disturbingly the same. Helpless to make the moment less unsettling, Lawrence stepped away from the open front door, feeling the cold air rush in. Helena was the first to remove her eyes from her adversary's. She said nothing further, but slowly turned her head and looked at Lawrence. She dropped her eyes, nodded, and then walked through the door, shutting it firmly behind her.

Sandra lifted her delicate hand to her mouth. Lawrence could see she was trembling. "Jack, how could you be...? Why would you...?" She completed neither of these thoughts, but he knew what she had assumed. He tried to embrace her, but she put her hands out defensively and wouldn't let him approach her. She glanced at the dining-room table and observed the clear evidence that Lawrence had eaten dinner with the young woman. The two wine glasses still contained the residue of the wine they shared.

"Sandra, please. Let me tell you what her visit was all about."

"No. I can't listen to you now. I have to think. I have to think. And I really wanted to talk to you tonight about... and now I can't." Without another word, she left.

Lawrence poured himself a stiff bourbon. Not the ideal drink after pinot noir and a cordial, but still the necessary crutch for moments and events that bore down on him. In his desperation to get Sandra to understand, he knew he was in love with her in spite of the many reasons why he was a fool to feel that way. He was confused. What was she alluding to that she had to speak to him about? Did she wish to end their relationship? If so, she might have reacted less emotionally at what she assumed was going on between him and one of his former students.

And what of Helena? She wished to share something romantic with him—that was evident enough. But now that he had rejected and humiliated her, how might she react? With some exaggerated pronouncement about his intentions and behavior? Who the hell would believe his denial of anything untoward, given his history, or at least the assumptions made about him, true or not? But most important to him now was that Helena's anger, no matter where it might lead, would preclude his examining the Dickens journal.

The journal? Lawrence whipped his head around toward the sofa. There it was, still resting on one of the cushions.

• • •

Softly laying aside her memories, Helena Allingham placed enough clothing in her bag for several days' wear. She would leave in the morning. She smiled. She hadn't seen her beloved mentor Fred Beauchamp in quite a while.

CHAPTER 23

"It's a pleasure meeting you, Elizabeth. First time in the ancient and elevated catacombs of the Hendley Library?"

Nichols felt Elizabeth's hand reach for his forearm.

"No, Professor Beauchamp, I was here briefly many years ago."

"Please call me Fred. And don't be like Jeremy and take your sweet time about it, either." Beauchamp's face was luminous with delight. "You said 'briefly many years ago.' Then you weren't a student here?"

"Oh, no. I stood absolutely no chance of being accepted here when I applied to colleges."

"Did you apply anyway?"

"No. I didn't see the point."

"Then you cannot make so confident a judgment about your chances. But if the two of you are through looking around these antiquated stacks, might I buy you both a drink?"

Nichols felt her fingers dig into his arm. "Fred, thank you, but I still have to see the realtor about a house for my sister." In truth, Nichols had earlier called the realtor and made a 9:00 appointment for the following morning.

"Of course, of course. Real estate before real pleasure, they always say." Elizabeth smiled. She relaxed her grip on Nichols's forearm. The older man was beginning to charm her in spite of her nervousness. He continued, "Then I will say goodbye for now. Jeremy, might I give you call when you get back home? I need to dish the dirt on all your new senior colleagues, of course." Beauchamp winked at Elizabeth. "I've always been the biggest gossip in the English department." She again smiled at his teasing wit.

"Fred, I'll look forward to your call. I should be back by late tomorrow afternoon, so feel free to call any time after that."

"Good, Jeremy, good. Then let me say how much I have enjoyed meeting you, Elizabeth. I do hope to see you again—soon. Please enjoy your stay at the University Plaza Hotel. Goodbye." He took Elizabeth's hand and gently shook it. He stuck out his hand to Nichols. "Not goodbye, Jeremy, but until later, my young academic squire." Beauchamp kept his firm grip a little longer than necessary, as he looked straight into Nichols's eyes. After the emeritus professor entered the elevator, Elizabeth asked, "How did he know where we're staying tonight?"

Nichols had failed to see the implications of Beauchamp's allusion to the University Plaza Hotel. "I imagine he just assumed we were. It's the best place that's closest to campus and...nearest the Hendley."

"Did you talk to him about me when you were here earlier?"

Nichols hated having to answer her truthfully. "I didn't think it was the—"

"No, never mind. Please don't say it. I understand."

Nichols looked around the seventh stack level like an adolescent in the school hallway. Satisfied they were alone, he kissed her gently on the lips.

"Jeremy?"

"Yes?"

"What was he doing up here?"

"Probably, ...I guess he was looking for an old book in his specialty." Nichols knew that the older books on Poe and nineteenth-century American literature were down on stack level six. "Ready to go? I'm getting hungry."

She didn't answer but took his hand and pulled him toward the stairwell. She made clear by her movements that she didn't wish to take the elevator down.

• • •

Janis began to pull into her brother's driveway with her daughters and young niece. Belinda wanted two of her favorite dolls to keep her company until her father came back home tomorrow afternoon. Janis saw a dark-colored automobile parked a few feet from the garage door. She jerked the wheel quickly to the left, keeping the car on the road in front of the house.

"Why aren't you stopping, Aunt Janis?"

"Because, little Belinda, I'm hungry for ice cream. How about you?" Belinda and her cousins shouted gleefully. Janis took as many looks over her shoulder as she could before they progressed too far down the street. All she could detect was the car which didn't appear to have anyone in it. Then she remembered. Jeremy once told her that the city's water meter checker occasionally pulled up in his own vehicle. Janis began to relax, although she decided to come back and check the house for any sign of a break-in—just in case.

By the time Janis's vehicle turned onto the thoroughfare, the person in the dark sedan had finished examining the rear door and windows to the house. Within two minutes of Janis's passing by, the sedan backed out of the driveway and headed off in the opposite direction.

• • •

On the morning of December 19, 2018, Coy Mallory arrived twenty minutes late for the breakfast with Fred Beauchamp and Jack Lawrence in their favorite local coffee shop—not long after Mallory finished a voice-over project in New York.

"Late as always."

"Right, Fred. Some of us do have a night life with 11:00 p.m. being more a wake-up call than a 'lights-out.'" Now in his mid-thirties, Mallory felt comfortable jabbing at the more polished and conservative—and much older—Fred Beauchamp. "But Professor Lawrence knows what I mean, don't you, Jack?"

Beauchamp answered for his good friend and academic colleague. "No, I don't think he does, Coy. Jack's success with the ladies doesn't include the making of financial transactions with third-parties as part of the wake-up call. With Jack, the 9:00 p.m. 'light's out' phase is most often initiated by the lady's eagerness—without any third-party serving as romantic catalyst, right Jack?"

"Fred, there is such eloquence in your bullshit. There really is. Wouldn't you agree, Coy?" Lawrence was leery of offending the younger man's masculine pride. He had once witnessed Mallory drive the face of a tavern loud mouth down on the top of a bar counter, fracturing the man's nose and jaw. The victim had made the mistake of insulting Mallory's judgment and manhood.

Mallory liked Lawrence generally but resented the man's easy way with women much younger. Still, Mallory had no problem paying for sexual services. He claimed he had neither the time nor the desire for anything beyond the most ephemeral sexual relationship. After the three men ordered food, Mallory flipped through the small notebook. "Okay, as I noted some time ago, although I'm out of the spy business as a full-time, send-my-sorry-ass-to-any-shit-hole-in-the-world worker, I'll still keep my motor warm on a temporary basis when asked and adequately paid. But that does leave me more time for fun and games—such as your so-called project 'Roderick.' And why did you pick that name again?"

Beauchamp nodded. "Because Jack particularly likes Roderick's line from 'The Fall of the House of Usher.' Jack?"

Lawrence gave the line with his characteristic literary flair: "To an anomalous species of terror I found him a bounden slave."

Mallory cast a mildly hostile look at Beauchamp—recalling their disagreement over the name of the emeritus professor's dog—but found the "project" amusing, nevertheless. "And I suppose you want Dryden to know that you have evidence that can make his life miserable if revealed."

Lawrence nodded. "You have it perfectly, Coy. I possess some incriminating photos, but I want something more substantial. And that's where your knowledge of the professional ladies comes in."

"And you're in on this too, Fred?"

Beauchamp sipped his coffee. "Not so much *in on it* as in *full support of it*, Coy."

"And you don't want to arrange all this by yourselves?"

Lawrence played along. "We're too old for the game, Coy. We need a young handsome buck like you to handle it."

"And I get what again?"

"We can pay—I mean Jack can pay you—five thousand dollars, if you won't do it out of a sense of camaraderie."

Mallory laughed and lightly punched Beauchamp on the arm. "I have no sense of fucking camaraderie—especially with you two."

"But we're your mentors."

"You *were* my mentors—in another life. Besides, I don't stand on sentiment. I'll take the fucking five grand."

Lawrence and Beauchamp shared a look. Mallory's profane epithets and bar-room metaphors traversed far different ground than the one they kept their feet on. As Beauchamp once told Lawrence, "You know, Jack, you and I enjoy caressing the English language; Mallory just wants to bend it over and..." Beauchamp was always too much a gentleman to complete the analogy.

"What the hell are you doing?" Mallory had become annoyed at Lawrence's eating his omelet with one hand and doodling something on a paper napkin with the other.

"Anagrams, Coy. It relaxes me."

Beauchamp explained further. "Perhaps you don't know that my good friend here has one of those peculiar brains that must always deconstruct and rearrange. Why do you think he's been occasionally valuable to the agency over the years, Coy? He never shuts down—even though he has his academic duties, scholarly writings, and romantic liaisons to devour his time. Show our young gun Coy what you've got there, partner."

Smiling at Beauchamp's feigned cowboy accent, Lawrence held up the napkin in front of Mallory's face.

Mallory sighed with affected boredom "It says 'Morally.' So what's that supposed to mean, Jack?"

"It's an anagram of your last name, Coy."

Mallory was visibly embarrassed. "Of course. How could I have missed that?"

Lawrence wrote another. "Beach Puma."

"Well, Coy?"

Mallory studied it for a few seconds but quickly lost his patience. "Fuck it. I don't know."

Beauchamp coughed, in an exaggerated manner. "That's the nickname Jack gave me soon after we became friends."

Mallory laughed. "Somehow I don't see you, Fred, as a puma prowling on the beach for feminine prey. I think that's more a fitting description of our friend Jack here."

"True, Coy. I don't prowl. I just set traps. And rarely catch anything. My dear fellow, 'Beach Puma' is an anagram of 'Beauchamp.'"

Mallory swallowed the rest of his orange juice. "Just finish your fucking waffle, Fred."

CHAPTER 24

"Elizabeth, I want you to enjoy your food, so please don't feel you have to hurry." In truth, Nichols was anxious for her to finish the meal so they could be alone in their room.

"I'm sorry. Was I eating too fast? It's not like we have any place to go or anything to do, right?"

They both broke out laughing, causing other patrons in the hotel restaurant to look their way. The couple returned to their food and slowed their pace, but only slightly.

As soon as the hotel elevator door shut, they kissed ardently, and as soon as they reached their room, they were left only to remove their clothes and pull the covers back from the queen-sized bed. It was as if they had both rehearsed the moment many times, for there was no hesitation or clumsiness in their lovemaking. Their bodies moved together as intensely as they were able.

• • •

As Nichols slept, Elizabeth knew he would awaken later in the night and they would make love again, this time more casually. She struggled against the comparison of this unsanctioned moment with the last sexual experience she had with her lawful husband. In the past year, he had reached for her less and less frequently, and she understood that on those occasions Steve merely wanted sex, not her. Since she had fallen in love with Jeremy, she could barely endure those times when her husband touched and required more of her in bed. For several months, Steve had desired only one position for intercourse—his wife on her stomach, her face not even resting on a pillow. Elizabeth could see why women would find the position degrading, but she preferred having sex with her husband this way because she didn't have to look at him, and she knew he didn't want to look at her. She wouldn't be expected to say anything erotic because her face was pressed against the sheets and mattress. But most of all, it was a position that made it seem as if she were being violated—taken against her will. And she knew that in essence that's what it was.

Gently rubbing her lover's back—and now for the first time Jeremy was indeed her lover—she made up her mind to confront her husband about a divorce when he returned late Friday night or sometime on Saturday. If he wouldn't agree, she would see a lawyer on her own. She had to. She couldn't wait any longer for Steve to make it easy and painless for the both of them. The thought that the next several days and weeks would be dreadful ones chilled her palpably. She pulled the covers up to her neck and waited for Jeremy to awaken.

• • •

Beauchamp called the de facto leader of the English Department's junior faculty and suggested that the young woman send an invitation to Jeremy Nichols to join her and three or four others for dinner on Sunday night.

"Jessica, make clear to him that the reservation will be limited to just the five of you. Because I think it's best he come back up here alone and not with his new love interest. No, that's all right. You didn't know. Yes, it will. It would be his fourth trip here in the span of eight days." As Jack Lawrence used to say, it was one of the advantages of living in the northeastern United States. Everything being a train ride or a moderate drive away. A college or university on every block. "Good, good. Thanks so much, Jessica. Call me later and let me know if he'll be coming. Goodbye."

Beauchamp needed to get Nichols back on the seventh stack level, applying his knowledge of Charles Dickens to whatever clues Lawrence left behind six months earlier. Jack and his damned puzzles and anagrams. Beauchamp was certain Lawrence didn't expire among the stacks until he left some sign, something telling that would challenge the intellect to discover. Beauchamp wondered if at the autopsy the medical examiner found Lawrence's tongue wedged deeply into his cheek.

Checking the nearly imperceptible powder he had placed in the morning along the edges of the Dickens volume, pages 178-79, Beauchamp saw that the page had been opened and that Nichols had found the blood-stained section of the book. That much he'd seen, but he had the woman with him and couldn't have devoted much time to analyzing the peculiar check-mark streaks. Regardless, he wanted Nichols back as soon as possible. The young scholar would have dinner with his new junior faculty colleagues on Sunday night, and then Beauchamp would be sure Nichols spent the entire next day, at least, trying to make a connection between the Dickens story *The Chimes* and the fertile and infuriating mind of Jack Lawrence. There had to be a link.

Beauchamp was satisfied he had already taken steps to see that Elizabeth Ellertson remained near her home. He would have to depend on others doing their part, but he'd always been excellent at anticipating the behavior of others. And not only anticipating, but charmingly and subtly programming it as well. It was for good reason that Beauchamp had the agency nickname "B.F. Skinner"—the famous behaviorist of "Skinner Box" fame.

• • •

Dryden poured his second drink of the new day. It was one-thirty in the morning. As always, alcohol cracked the door to his memory. This time to a phone call he had received in early February past when he was away from Washington, recuperating from a balloon angioplasty with stent, spending the week at his old home, less than a mile from the Hendley Library.

"Stuart? Jack Lawrence here."

Dryden remembered the voice as being anxious and almost giddy. He could tell Lawrence had been drinking.

"I don't think I have anything I wish to say to you, Jack."

Lawrence ignored Dryden's dismissive tone. "I just read your journal review, Congressman. I do so appreciate your honesty about my place in the profession, you prick."

Dryden understood this day was coming. From the moment he agreed to take a look back at his academic life and remark on scholars writing on the Victorian period, he was well aware of what the consequences of his printed assessment would be. Still, he refused to lower himself any further by pleading with Lawrence to be discreet about the photograph he picked up from the floor of the Hendley. Besides, the men simply despised each other—in ways that defied any rational explanation—regardless of all the professional courtesies they had earlier extended to each other. Their debate about Stoker's *Dracula* revealed Lawrence's aggressive and nasty side. Since he'd heard nothing so far about the photograph since their chance meeting at the Hendley in November, Dryden assumed Lawrence hadn't told anyone of significance. Therefore, he would just inform anyone who asked that whatever Lawrence said about that day was a lie prompted by the severe though, Dryden believed, completely fair judgment in the article now published, which noted Lawrence's place in the profession as a teacher and scholar.

Dryden felt confident and assertive. "Jack, you've lost your eloquence and *savoir faire*. A 'prick' did you call me?"

Instead of fuming, Lawrence laughed. His voice sounded calm and brutal. "Stuart, I want you to look for something at your place and then I want to read you something I have in my possession. Are you sitting down?"

"I have better things to do than play one of your games, Jack."

"No, not a game, Congressman. No, no. Not a game at all. Are you ready?"

"Fine. I'll humor you. Go ahead."

"The folder in which you keep your ongoing research materials, including some interesting photographs of Victorian women—go get that."

"Fuck off, Jack."

"Oh, Stuart, come now. Afraid of what you'll find? Or rather, afraid of what you *won't* find?"

Lawrence heard the phone drop, and after a minute or so, Dryden returned. "You lousy son of a bitch!"

"I bet you'll never guess in a thousand years where the choicest of your photos are at this moment. You know, the ones that have your notations on the back of each. Let me read one or two." Lawrence was surprised Dryden didn't hang up. "Still there, Congressman? Okay, let's see. Oh, here's one I especially like. You wrote on the back, 'A mouth perfectly shaped for my cock. Such sweet swallowing of my offering.' And this one is good too. 'Slap and fuck her, pull out—slap and fuck her again.'"

"What do you want for those photos, Lawrence?"

"The ones with your inimitable handwriting on them, you mean?"

"How fucking much? I'll see to it that you get the sabbatical. We can start with that."

"You know, I remember your once telling me that your wife never bothers any of your books, papers, or notes. You said she knows that it's all off-limits and that you're not to look at or make snide comments about her romance novels. Must have made you feel safe about not locking up some of your more erotic research and commentary."

"God damn it, what do you want, you lousy son of a bitch?"

"If I were a lousy son of a bitch, I would insist that you give me something for the photos—which I haven't copied, by the way. I believe there is honor among extortionists, after all. What was I saying? Oh, yes. If I were the kind of low-life you think I am, I would get something nice for the photos and not tell you at all about the video recording."

Dryden quickly replied, "What video recording?"

"This is beautiful, Stuart. There's absolutely no dread in your voice—only understandable confusion. Let me put you out of your misery—or rather well into it. You recall the young and very attractive hard-working young female graduate student at Georgetown who served your table and told you about her thesis on Thackeray—your old scholarly interest? What was it? She wanted your opinion on old Thackery's moral vision and its effect on female readers of the day—isn't that right?"

"Jesus."

"There—there's that dread I was talking about. I guess you also recall inviting her to discuss her scholarly work over drinks at a place outside the capital—namely in Falls Church, Virginia? And I suppose you also remember going to her place near Arlington for further 'discussion.' And you no doubt will never forget what happened next. Well, to borrow the old cliché—let's cut to the chase. She wasn't really a graduate student at Georgetown—and even better, what the two of you did wasn't exactly a *private* moment between two consenting adults. Which brings us back to the video record I have in my possession. Well, I think I've given you enough to ponder for this evening, Stuart. Sweet dreams—bye."

Dryden remained seated in his reading chair for the next hour. When he finally rose, he headed to his bedroom and withdrew from the closet his overnight bag. When he finished packing, he zipped the bag and brought it to the front door. He would get up early in the morning and drive to the hotel down from the Hendley Library. As he lay in bed, he went over in his mind what he packed. When he assured himself he had everything he'd need, he closed his eyes and slept. He wasn't aware that he forgotten to pack his gloves.

CHAPTER 25

The following morning, two more pages were taken from the manuscript. There had been no attempt to read the Dickens journal pages sequentially. There was no plot to uncover, for the literary world knew the novelist and his love Ellen Ternan never married. Accordingly, anywhere in the manuscript one chose to extract a page or two would reveal a stunning insight into the mind and heart of the famous novelist. Again, the reader considered the extraordinary historical and financial significance of what now rested on the table.

Everything has exploded. The difficulties in getting Catherine to accept a separation agreement were of course to be expected.

Yet, I thought it done. She settled on a house of her own and six hundred pounds per annum. Living arrangements for our children were agreed to. But then her family once more ignited my rage. Her mother and sister began disseminating the supposed fact that Ellen was my mistress.

That they intend to blacken my name and so wreck my children's lives in the bargain would be enough to summon my contempt, but to forget so easily all I have done for the family over the years and to hurl invective and untruths without shame simply cannot be forgiven. And what they have done to poor Ellen, my darling girl.

I am told that Thackeray announced I was having a love affair with some 'actress.' I have written him expressing my disdain for his having made such a claim.

Yet how can I so love her and leave her exposed to such scandal? Indeed, how can she love me knowing what pain I am causing her? How much longer will it be until she refuses to see me completely?

So are my thoughts on this June evening in the year 1858.

• • •

After dropping off Elizabeth at Caitlin's apartment, Nichols felt more confident of their future together. They had consummated their relationship, and as far as he was concerned, there would be no turning back. She had promised to speak with her husband as soon as he returned home from his trip, perhaps as early as this evening.

The Hendley Library was for once out of his thoughts as he headed to his sister's house. He knew Janis wouldn't receive with much enthusiasm his assurances of a contented future with Elizabeth Ellertson, but he knew who would. He pulled to the curb and hit the programmed number on his cell-phone menu. The voice picking up on the other end was not the one he expected to hear.

Nichols hesitated before speaking. "Excuse me, who's this?"

The person on the other end also waited a moment before answering. "Can I ask you the same question?"

"I obviously have the wrong number. Sorry."

"No, no, wait. Are you trying to reach Douglas Finneran?"

Nichols hesitated. "Yes, I am. Who is this again?"

"My name is Ken Oliphant. Amherst Police."

"Oh, God. What happened?" Nichols heard no reply. "Please—what happened to Doug?"

"Sir, will you identify yourself?"

Nichols gave his name and explained that he and Finneran were very close friends.

"Mr. Nichols, I'm very sorry, but Mr. Finneran is dead."

"I don't understand. You're saying...?"

"Sir, we'd like to speak with you as soon as possible. I'm afraid that Mr. Finneran has been stabbed to death."

Nichols's head dropped on the steering wheel. "In a fight of some kind?"

"It was murder, Mr. Nichols. He was stabbed from behind while he was standing in the kitchen of his apartment."

"My God, I..." The thought flashed in his mind. Heather—his wife? Could their troubles have been that serious? Did they have a heated argument that got out of hand? Nichols assumed Doug had probably been seeing someone else, but he knew his friend loved his wife and would never willingly leave her permanently. In any event, he felt he had to find out if she had killed him. He asked Oliphant if Heather Finneran knew what happened to her husband.

"I'm very sorry, but she's also dead."

"Also a murder?"

"Yes. With the same knife we think. But they weren't together when each of them died. She was alone at her house."

Nichols was unable to formulate a response. After a few seconds, Oliphant broke the silence. "Mr. Nichols, we would of course like to speak to you about anyone you know who might have had a motive to do this. But most important is a sealed letter here at Mr. Finneran's apartment. It has your name on it. We'd like you to open it in our presence, if you don't mind."

Nichols couldn't believe he was still thinking rationally. "Of course. Do I need to come to Amherst?"

"I see no reason at this point. We'll come to you. Tell me where you'd like to meet." Nichols suggested his home and gave the address. "New York? For some reason I assumed you lived in Massachusetts. All right. Let's see, today's Friday. We have some more work to do today at the apartment and at Mrs. Finneran's residence and will probably need to continue tomorrow morning. So, we'll likely hop on over to I-90 sometime late tomorrow afternoon, although we might not get to your place until evening. Even so, I would appreciate your being home after four tomorrow afternoon, but I'll try to call you when we cross into New York. Is that okay?"

"Yes, of course."

"Again, I'm sorry to hit you with all this. But we need to see what's in this letter addressed to you. There's no postage and no address. It just has your name on the envelope in big letters—underscored three times."

As Nichols pulled back into traffic, a car sat in the driveway of a vacant house down and across the street from Nichols's residence. The driver had been waiting close to an hour for Nichols's arrival. Perhaps Nichols went somewhere else first. If so, the driver knew where.

• • •

"I am delighted to hear that, Rob. You deserve all the accolades you've received—as well as those you haven't gotten but should have. I've been telling you that for, what, some two or three months now? Anyway, excuse my delay in calling you back, but they've kept me busy all day at the Hendley. What? Go to law school? Me? No, no. I've told you I'm much too scattered for that. Besides, I love my job and the career I've chosen."

"Okay, but, as you know, there are some fine libraries in Manhattan."

Sandra frowned at the implication of Porterfield's assertion. He wanted her to move with him if he took the recent offer from the Manhattan law firm who had been actively courting him. They wouldn't need to marry—ever, if she didn't wish to. "I just want you with—or at least very near me," he said on more than one occasion.

"You know I'm committed to the Hendley, Rob. Look, I'm very happy for you, and if you take the offer, we can see each other more often than you think—either up here or down there."

Sandra was genuinely happy for him and viewed their relationship primarily in terms of a brother and sister, fully supportive of each other in all the other did. Therefore, she had a younger step-brother Will and an older boyfriend-brother Rob. She wondered how different all would have been if she had grown up with a biological brother—a big brother watching over his kid sister, ready to step in whenever she was headed for disaster.

Sandra considered herself fortunate in that for the most part and in spite of his assumption that matters would change between them, Porterfield allowed her to determine the parameters of their relationship. No woman could ask for more than that, she reasoned. Still the influence of the other man in her life remained profound. How could she not think of Jack Lawrence whenever she stepped inside the Hendley? Occasionally on weekends, she would come to the library for a short time until her loneliness abated. And everyone who knew her simply assumed it was a love of books that drew and invigorated her.

While talking to Porterfield and without realizing it, she jotted down Jeremy Nichols name on a post-it. It was clear to her why the young professor was on her mind frequently since she saw him yesterday. She had dismissed the possibility he would discover anything of significance in the Dickens volume Lawrence had in his hand at the time of his death, but now she wasn't so sure. Did he satisfy his curiosity about the area where the murder had taken place? Or would he return to the seventh stack level often when he joined the junior faculty? Sandra pondered what Nichols knew or what he *wanted* to know. And even more important, what Jack Lawrence wanted someone like Nichols to know. Might Nichols in fact make another trip to the Hendley before he began teaching his classes later in the month?

These thoughts brought to mind Lawrence's discussion of travel the first time they had dinner. At the time, Sandra found his series of inquiries somewhat trite but far more charmingly delivered than the usual "What music do you like?" and "What type of food do you usually prefer?" These kinds of questions she had heard innumerable times during a series of bland dates during her high-school and undergraduate years. When she told Lawrence she dreamed of spending a year in the Hawaiian Islands but assumed she wouldn't live long enough to have money enough to make it happen, he took a note card from his coat pocket and wrote down three words: "Obituary Luau Fee." She laughed and shook her head in mild confusion. He told her to read it again. She smiled and thanked him, not knowing what else to say. Yes, the three words somewhat encapsulated what she said about her wish to go to Hawaii and about not living long enough to save enough money for the trip. But she didn't think what he had written was at all clever or charming.

"Sandra, where would you like to go if you could never afford Hawaii—on a shorter visit, I mean?"

"I guess it would be New Orleans. I would love to walk down Bourbon Street at Mardi Gras time with twenty strands of beads around my neck."

Lawrence reached for another note card. On this one he wrote "A Bayou Future Lei." This time she saw something in the words that titillated. Was this handsome man hinting that he'd soon ask her to accompany him to New Orleans in early March? Followed by a trip to Hawaii?

When they rose from the table, Lawrence whispered, "You're wondering about what I jotted down on the note cards, aren't you?" She knew she had blushed, for she was still fantasizing about walking and dining on Bourbon Street with him.

"No, I understand what you wrote."

"No, you don't. Let me explain. They're both anagrams."

"Anagrams?" She looked at them again, but couldn't imagine how she could possible rearrange either of the multi-word phrases without online help. Like anyone else, she could do short one-word anagrams, such as "Eros" for "Rose," but not any of such complexity.

"Now I'm going to write on the back of each note card what I was really saying to you. To save my embarrassment—because you know I am by nature a very shy person..."

"Uh-huh."

"Don't read either of them until you get back to your place. Promise?"

Sandra waited until she was in bed before she read the note cards. She still anticipated that on the back of the second one he had written "Will you come with me to New Orleans?"—even if it couldn't be an anagram of the phrase he jotted down. She looked at the first, "Obituary Luau Fee," and turned the card over. "You are beautiful." She warmed with pleasure and kissed the card. She reached for the second, "A Bayou Future Lei," and turned it over. It also said "You are beautiful." She took this card and held it to her breast. She'd heard this exact compliment so often since she was fourteen, but no one had paid it as wonderfully and creatively as had Lawrence. She remembered how annoyed she was when Porterfield paid the same compliment when he asked how well she knew Jackson Lawrence when he saw her chatting with the professor at the Hendley. She quickly dismissed the implication of the question, to which Porterfield added, "You *are* beautiful, Sandra. I wouldn't be so blind to his interest in you."

From that time until his death three months later, she came to understand Lawrence's fascination with puzzles, riddles, anagrams, and code games of various kinds. It was a fascination they didn't share, for she preferred that which was more direct. She marveled at his patience to create and solve such word challenges, and she teased him about being perfect for government service as a code-breaker. He only laughed.

Getting up from her desk, Sandra balled up the post-it with Nichols's name. The young man surely couldn't break whatever code Jack Lawrence might have included in the antiquated Dickens volume. She left her office feeling more secure about the past remaining locked away forever.

• • •

"I didn't tell him where you went, but he made it impossible for me to sound convincing when I lied about who you were with. I'm so sorry."

"Oh, Caity, it's all right; it really is. I've decided to take the initiative and tell him that we need to begin divorce proceedings right away."

"But what if he...?"

"Then I'll tell him that I'm calling a lawyer, regardless of what he does or refuses to do."

"Oh, Elizabeth, I'm so glad. I've wanted you to make the first move for months now."

"I know. At first, I just wanted to be sure it was the best thing for the both of us. And then, I don't know, I guess I felt guilty because I was seeing Jeremy and falling in love with him. I wanted Steve to take the first step away from the marriage. But now I can't wait any longer. I love Jeremy and want to be with him. I no longer care if the divorce has to be difficult."

"Whatever I can do, just tell me."

"Thank you, Caity. So, how angry was Steve was after he guessed I was with Jeremy?"

"He demanded that I tell him, just remember that. He said not to give him "any more crap" about your being with friends in Saratoga. When I refused to admit he was right, he calmed down. He shook his head, but I couldn't tell if it was from hurt or from anger. He was silent for the longest time. I couldn't believe that he said 'Thank you, Caitlin, you've verified what I already knew' when he left. That's not like Steve. He's never been polite to me before."

"So, did he call my phone before he came over?"

"I assume so."

Elizabeth left her cell phone with her friend so she wouldn't have to talk to her husband when she was with Jeremy. Nor did she want Jeremy affected by any phone call he assumed was from Steve.

"Did he leave a message?"

"I don't think so, but here."

Caitlin handed the phone to Elizabeth, who checked her voice mail. Nothing. She looked at the number of the last caller. It was one she didn't recognize. The area code said 413. Massachusetts.

CHAPTER 26

"I'm sure you're weary of our university already, and you haven't even started teaching yet."

Nichols was grateful to hear a cheery voice on the phone in the wake of the news about Doug and Heather Finneran. "Not at all, Jessica. I'm most anxious to make the move up there."

"So can you come back and join us for dinner on Sunday? It's a tradition those of us in the untenured netherworld willingly embrace. On the second Sunday night of each month we get together and bemoan our second-class citizenship. So what do you say?"

Nichols already liked Jessica Tillman, although he had only spent ten minutes with her on his first trip to the university. She was half-way through her second three-year stint, but still with no chance of tenure. Nichols wondered whether he'd get an offer to stay another three and whether he'd take it. That would depend on how much Belinda, Janis, and his nieces liked the area. And he hoped to have input from Elizabeth as well. After all, by the end of three years, she would be his wife. All the same, it was going to be rough being separated from her as she went through the trials of her divorce from Steve.

"Jeremy, there's more we'd like to talk to you about—and to show you of course—so you'd have to promise to stay all day Monday as well. We'll take care of your accommodations. But I have to say...and this sounds crass, but we'd like you to come alone this time so that we can have you all to ourselves."

How did Jessica know Elizabeth was with him yesterday? Fred Beauchamp must have told her. "Look, Jessica, I would love to come up and join you, but I received word today that one of my dearest friends and his wife were killed."

"Oh, my God, Jeremy. I am so sorry."

"I really appreciate that. So let me get back to you tomorrow. I'm not yet sure what arrangements are being made and whether I'll have to go to Amherst and...Well, I'm just a little unsure of what the rest of my week is going to look like."

"Of course, of course. Just call me if you can break away. And again, I'm so very sorry for your loss. Let us know if we can do anything for you. Goodbye, Jeremy."

Sensing the dinner invitation a ruse of some kind, Nichols speculated on why Beauchamp would want him to return so quickly. Was he still going to recruit him for intelligence work? Would he again bring up details of Lawrence's murder as a kind of incentive or as some kind of warning that he should seriously consider the offer Beauchamp seems already to have made him?

Nichols's emotions sagged. Not only was he thinking in terms of a conspiracy against him, but Doug and Heather Finneran had been murdered. Stabbed to death, as was Jackson Lawrence. And it was Doug who told Nichols about Beauchamp's intelligence connections. Was there a connection between Beauchamp and Doug and Heather's deaths? It was all too bizarre for any of it to be true. In any event, he had to pull himself together. He needed a drink.

As he downed a double Jack Daniel's, the questions continued to bedevil him. Why hadn't Elizabeth called by now? She promised to contact him before he went out for pizza with his family. He hated the fact that he couldn't call her without risk. Had she already spoken on the phone with her husband and mentioned divorce, or was she going to wait, as she said, until Steve came back later that night? Nichols wanted to share the news about Doug and Heather, but he'd hold off until she talked with her husband. Her leaving Steve was the most important thing at the moment, and Nichols didn't want her affected in any way that might lessen her resolve.

• • •

"Usher! Come here boy!" Beauchamp held the rear door open until the dog scampered across the lawn and back into the house. This nightly ritual always satisfied the retired professor, if for no other reason than it suggested the kind of simplicity he longed for in his life but never truly achieved. Give a command and have it obeyed. Hear an order and obey it. A relatively uncomplicated existence. The life he believed he was choosing for himself in early twenties.

He'd been recruited by the agency while an undergraduate. Swayed by the government's case that his talents would be better employed outside the classroom, Beauchamp concluded that the best life life for him would be one of incident. And, if need be, a life of dangerous and violent incident.

A year after he received his B.A. in English, Beauchamp was in Nigeria in the immediate aftermath of the Nigerian-Biafrin civil war with orders to report on the activity of the Soviets in the area. But Beauchamp couldn't handle seeing first-hand the effects of the violence and devastating famine in the area. He asked to be sent home, and after his debriefing in Washington and hearing the personally insulting and gratuitous compliment, "You did your race proud," he realized he wanted the life of a scholar after all. He accepted the agency's good wishes, and he began graduate school in the fall. But it wasn't long before they contacted him about both keeping his ear to the ground on campus and recruiting those who might make excellent agents.

Admiring Usher's physical abilities as he romped across the backyard, making a full circle around the property before he returned to the rear door, Beauchamp thought of Jack Lawrence's circuitous nature—always taking others on a journey that could have ended where it began with a simple explanation or revelation. But Jack loved teasing too much—not only his colleagues and acquaintances but also the women who were infatuated with him and his closest male friends. He informed Beauchamp he possessed highly incriminating evidence on Stuart Dryden but made his older friend guess what it could be. Lawrence finally confessed to having Dryden's nineteenth-century pornographic images but made his colleague wait until two days before his death before he mentioned the video evidence of Dryden's sexual deviancy. But Lawrence wouldn't say where this evidence was or what exactly he planned to do with it. At the time, Beauchamp assumed Lawrence would reveal it to someone, either Dryden's wife or someone in Congress—or at least in the press—a scenario that made Beauchamp highly uncomfortable. It was conceivable such a revelation would also cast negative light on Lawrence himself and Lawrence's good chum—Fred Beauchamp. For those two days, Beauchamp allowed every worst-case scenario to shape itself in his mind. Did Jack have evidence relating to Beauchamp's lone extra-marital affair fourteen years earlier with a fellow scholar he had met in New York at conference? Did Jack record any of their conversations in which Beauchamp expressed his dislike of and occasional contempt for colleagues and members of the university administration? Could Jack be true to his promise not to reveal that Beauchamp had shared a number of details about his agency activities he had taken an oath to keep to himself? By the beginning of this past February, Beauchamp had become frightened of Lawrence's power to compromise or destroy the final years of his friend Fred Beauchamp's life.

Following Lawrence's murder, Beauchamp was relieved no one had discovered the evidence damning Dryden. It wasn't in his nature to play the game of personal destruction. But soon Beauchamp wondered if that evidence had been partnered with other material damaging to others—Beauchamp included. It was then that he began searching every place Lawrence could have hidden it. Failing to locate anything incriminatory, Beauchamp became cautiously confident such evidence would never be found, although he believed that Lawrence was trying to leave a clue on the seventh stack level of the Hendley. It was only more recently, however, that he wanted to find that evidence for something far nobler than personal reasons.

And now there might be a chance—just a chance—to find out what Lawrence had. That chance came in the person of Jeremy Nichols.

CHAPTER 27

I seem to have deserted my novel writing as I devote more time to my public readings. It has been over a year now since I completed **Little Dorrit***. What will be the next book? I have been thinking of a story set during the French Revolution, a historical book so much different from my usual fare. I can see my own misery assisting me in the shaping of the characters. But I cannot begin it now. My thoughts rest too much with my lovely Ellen.*

I have begun writing to her and sharing some of what I feel. I must do something to express what she means to me at this time of my life. Will I write more intimately as the weeks pass? Will I in fact speak my heart and passion to her face when the opportunity permits? I do not fear timidity. Rather, I fear vulnerability and subsequent pain should I see in her eyes that her feelings come nowhere near equaling mine. In any event, she has told me that no one will ever see my letters to her. She says she will burn every page.

The reader was interrupted by the sound of the phone. The manuscript page was replaced in the stack and the full manuscript returned to where it was safely kept. By the time that was done the phone had stopped ringing.

• • •

Nichols took a second look at Belinda's latest sketch. The stick-figured man—whom he now knew to be himself—was standing outside a tall building reaching his hand toward the handle of the front door. Including the two drawings of her father lying outstretched on the floor, Belinda was beginning to depict scenes of what she saw and in this case what she recently heard. Experiences—hers or her father's—rather than simple scenes from her imagination. But still the empty oval was in its usual place.

Satisfied she was asleep, Nichols's mind shifted back and forth from Doug and Heather's murder to his night with Elizabeth in the hotel room. She'd finally called to say she was definite about speaking to Steve when he returned home—although she hadn't yet heard from him about when he'd be back—and that she wasn't afraid. Still, Nichols wanted to think of something else to help facilitate his getting to sleep at a reasonable hour. He shouldn't have taken another look at Belinda's painting. That damned Hendley.

If not for the heightened suspicion over what Beauchamp had in mind for him, Nichols was certain he would be most eager to drive back and spend more time on the seventh stack level. He'd at least seen the volume and the pages on which Jackson Lawrence left his bloody mark. Had Lawrence purposely put his hand to his neck so that he would have some "ink" with which to identify his killer. Did he intend to write the assailant's initials, perhaps? Were there two thicker daubs on the page touching two letters of the text? Two letters that began a first or a last name or indeed the murderer's initials? Nichols might have thought to look for that evidence the previous day, but the library employee Sandra Stark had interrupted his examination of the superannuated Dickens volume.

If that wasn't Lawrence's intention, then what was the purpose of calling attention to those pages? *The Chimes*. Did this particular work have meaning? Did it provide a vital clue? Was the plot some kind of parallel to the identity of the killer—or perhaps reflective of something the assailant and Lawrence shared?

Nichols ran quickly through what he recalled of the short novel. The full title ran *The Chimes: A Goblin Story of Some Bells that Rang an Old Year Out and a New Year In*. Did the murderer compose ghost stories—being a fellow academic or writer friend of Lawrence's? Or was there some connection to the previous New Year's Eve? Someone Lawrence met some five and a half weeks before his death? Someone he celebrated that night with? Was the perpetrator someone who had a serious quarrel with Lawrence—over some kind of longstanding issue? An insult going back to Lawrence's days in graduate school or when he first began his scholarly career? Might the perpetrator have been the loyal and misguided student of a scholar Lawrence had deeply offended or embarrassed in print? Nichols couldn't help his next thought. Did Beauchamp have a son?

Nichols knew *The Chimes* was composed in 1844, while Dickens was in Italy. Staying in a villa near Genoa, the novelist had reacted to the sound of the city's bells, which provided him the title for the story he was then constructing. It suddenly hit Nichols that the novelist's friend John Forster had written something about Dickens's reaction to those bells. Nichols went to one of the boxes in his living room that held books taken from his office in preparation for his impending move. Having marked each box for its contents, Nichols knew exactly where to find Forster's biography of Dickens. He pulled out the pertinent volume of that work and turned to the section dealing with Dickens's stay in Genoa. Nichols read about the novelist's problems coming up with a title for his new book, but then "such a peal of chimes arose from the city as he found to be 'maddening.' All Genoa lay beneath him, and up from it, with some sudden set of the wind, came in one fell sound the clang and clash of all its steeples, pouring into his ears, again and again, in a tuneless, grating, discordant, jerking, hideous vibration that made his ideas 'spin round and round till they lost themselves in a whirl of vexation and giddiness, and dropped down dead.' He had never before so suffered, nor did he again; but this was his description to me next day, and his excuse for having failed in a promise to send me his title. Only two days later, however, came a letter in which not a syllable was written but 'We have heard THE CHIMES at midnight, Master Shallow!' and I knew he had discovered what he wanted."

The passage mesmerized Nichols. He recalled Dickens's familiarity with the line from the second part of Shakespeare's *Henry IV*, but he hadn't remembered the exact wording from Forster's account. The intense pressure Dickens felt from hearing the chimes—the "grating" and "hideous vibration," the "whirl of vexation and giddiness," and the "maddening" phrase "drop down dead" now seemed to Nichols so relevant to aspects of his own life and of course to the demise of Jackson Lawrence. But still any direct linkage to the crime continued to elude him.

He pondered further any possible motive for the murder. Was there a scholarly project relating to Dickens that Lawrence was co-authoring but failed to complete his part, causing resentment from the other scholar, perhaps a younger man—someone trying to make his mark in the profession? "Damn it, Jeremy—enough!" He had to stop these speculations now, but such games of intellect had intrigued him since his youth. He was probably the only English major at Penn who sought the refuge of mathematical problems from the demands of literary analysis and scholarly searches.

In any event, he would have to look at the text of *The Chimes* because he didn't know it as well as he should have. The short book was rarely taught in the classroom, and Nichols had only dipped into it for his previous research. His edition of Dickens was still in his office awaiting packaging and not here at his house. He could have examined it online, but he always preferred the book in his hands or spread out before him. Besides, he could form no proper conclusions about the text until he examined the volume Lawrence touched and marked the night of his murder. Therefore, Nichols was satisfied to leave the matter alone for now. Yet, one more thought intruded. What if Lawrence simply grabbed the book and for some reason jammed his finger between two pages? Not a clue in fact but a simple unintended action by a dying man? It might have had nothing at all to do with the murder. But Nichols refused to accept that explanation—because he didn't want to accept it.

As he grabbed a bottle of water from the frig, he thought he heard two knocks on the front door. He checked the time—9:50 p.m. Three knocks followed. He smiled, assuming it had to be Elizabeth. Perhaps Steve came home and they talked. Was it possible they'd already come to an agreement about the divorce? Nichols re-opened the refrigerator door. There was still one bottle of Prosecco left. He took the bottle and jogged to the door.

"Hey, baby, I wasn't expecting..." The punch caught him on the edge of his jaw but mainly on his right shoulder. The bottle of Prosecco dropped to the floor and rolled several feet across the carpet.

"You mother-fucking son of a bitch." Steve Ellertson's voice hardly reflected the violence of his act. He delivered his profanity in a breathless and subdued fashion. Seeing that his punch had only barely clipped Nichols's jaw, Ellertson tried to step up into the house so that he could use the full weight of his two hundred and thirty-five pounds against his lighter opponent.

Because he wasn't knocked off his feet by the glancing blow, Nichols was able to push Ellertson off the threshold, causing the larger man to lose his balance and fall back down the steps. By the time Ellertson regained his footing, Nichols was down the steps and on the walkway. Although outweighed by forty pounds, Nichols lifted his fists and prepared to defend himself. Ellertson could see by Nichols's stance that his adversary was no stranger to boxing.

In fact, Nichols had fought two years for the Pennsylvania Golden Gloves when he was in high school, and he had maintained his skills as well as one could who wasn't actively training, winning the only fist-fight he found himself in since that time.

Nichols saw that Ellertson was a "swisher"—throwing his punches more side to side and thus easier to defend against. He just couldn't let the larger, more muscular former football player grab him. True to expectation, Ellertson threw two roundhouse punches, a right followed by a left, from which Nichols easily backed away. Praised by his boxing coaches for his pin-point left jab, Nichols threw three quick darts into Ellertson's face before the larger man tried to grab his arms. Nichols moved to his left and hit the larger man twice more. Blood spurted from Ellertson's nose.

Completely out of breath, Ellertson stopped and pawed at his face with the back of his hand. Nichols thought he was trying to say something but articulated nothing more than a grunt. Ellertson could only point his finger at Nichols before turning and walking to his car, which was parked on the street a house away from Nichols's.

As Ellertson drove off, Nichols headed to the phone to call Elizabeth. He was fearful Ellertson would harm Elizabeth when he got home, if he hadn't done so already. Elizabeth had assured Jeremy that her husband never slapped or pushed her, but the situation was different now. Ellertson had his face punched five times by the man he believed had cuckolded him. Nichols thought it prudent to insist Elizabeth leave her house until she talked to her husband by phone. There had to be some way of keeping what had just happened from getting any worse.

"No, Jeremy, he hasn't come home yet." The anxiety was evident in her voice.

"Elizabeth, he was just here."

"Don't tell me that. Oh, God." She'd earlier made the decision not to tell Nichols that her husband had already guessed the truth. She assumed Steve would call her before he came home. She highly doubted he'd just barge in on her. And his going to Jeremy's house was the last thing she expected. She felt foolish and naïve.

"Elizabeth, he obviously knows about us. He took a couple of swings at me."

"Are you hurt?"

"No, he just grazed me with a punch, but I hit him several times in the face. I may have broken his nose." He heard nothing on the other end of the line. "Elizabeth. Elizabeth? Elizabeth, are you still there?"

"Yes." Her voice was barely audible.

"I don't know what he might do when he sees you. I think it's best you go to a hotel for the night. Just don't go to Caitlin's. He's likely to look first for you there. Do you understand? Elizabeth? Elizabeth?"

"Yes, Jeremy. I'm sorry. I'm just... All right, I'll go to a hotel. Will you come too?"

"I have Belinda. I can't."

"Of course. She didn't see you and Steve fighting, did she?"

"No, I don't think so."

"Okay, I'll pack some things and go."

"Leave as quickly as you can."

"I will, I promise."

• • •

After throwing some of her things in a tote bag, Elizabeth grabbed her keys and opened the front door. She quickly fell back into the house. She dropped the bag and grabbed at her forehead, feeling blood. She never heard the shot.

CHAPTER 28

Ellertson stood over his prone wife, his nose packed with blood-soaked tissue paper. Elizabeth's eyes were closed. Her left hand showed evidence of blood, while her right hand shook. When he called her name, her eyes cracked open.

"Steve, why did you do this to me? Why?"

Her husband quickly turned and stared at the open door. The area over his left cheek bone had swollen, further evidence of the punches he had taken from Jeremy Nichols. His wife hadn't seen the damage done to his face. She refused to look at him.

Ellertson dropped to his knees and pulled her hand away from her forehead. She tried to prevent him, but she lacked the necessary strength to do so. Ellertson saw four small blood-clotted areas above her left eye, near the hairline. Some of her hair was matted with blood.

"Please, don't hurt me anymore, Steve. Please don't. I'm sorry. I'm so sorry."

Seeing that she was terrified, he tried to assure her. "I won't. I won't. Talk to me; talk to me. Do you have any idea what—?"

"How could you? How could you?"

"No, I...no. Listen to me."

"I won't!"

"All right, all right. Come on, let's get you up." He helped her from the floor and assisted her to a chair. "Here, sit. I need to... Just wait right here." He ran to the downstairs bathroom.

Just moments before, she was standing at the front door when she felt the force of something hitting her above the left eye—then the sharp stinging sensations coming from the small wounds on her forehead. She still couldn't understand what exactly her husband had done to her. Had he shot her? Had he truly done that? Why had he waited so long to come in through the door? She heard him shout from inside the bathroom. "God damn it! God damn it!" She also heard his jerking open drawers in the bathroom vanity and clawing through the contents of each one. What was he looking for? What was he going to punish her with?

Finally, he came out. "Stay here, Elizabeth. Don't move. Do you hear me? Don't move!" He ran out the still open front door, and she could see him heading for his dark blue car parked halfway up the driveway. Seeing her overnight bag lying just inside the doorway, she thought to grab it and run out the back, but she couldn't rise from her chair. Whatever he was going to do to her now, she would be unable to prevent.

Her cell rang. Her first thought was of Jeremy. She reached for the phone on the table beside her and peered out the door. Her husband was bending over in the front seat of the car, seeming to retrieve something from the glove compartment. She assumed he kept a pistol there, but she had never seen it, never wanted to see it. Twice he had told her he was going to the local firing range to "work off a little steam." She hated that expression and told him so just a few days earlier. That was the only time he seemed angry enough to strike her. He always kept control of his temper, but she feared that if he ever gave in to it, he might do something violent to her. And now she knew he had good reason to do so. She answered the phone.

"Hello?"

• • •

Nichols was frustrated. He had failed to suggest a specific hotel where Elizabeth could spend the night, and he didn't think to ask for a call when she arrived. He had to trust that she would contact him.

Surely, she would have arrived at one of the local hotels by now. Yet, she might have driven out of town to be further away from her husband. That would make sense, especially if she was frightened, as he knew she was. Still, why not call?

Nichols concluded she was in no shape to think as precisely as she normally did. Much had happened in the last twenty-four hours. Perhaps she was hungry and was eating something in the hotel restaurant before calling. Or maybe she was so exhausted she fell asleep as soon as she lay down on the hotel bed.

In any event, Nichols wasn't anywhere close to sleep. His mind was open to thoughts about her, Beauchamp, Lawrence, the Hendley Tower, the fight with Ellertson, his daughter, and even his sister and how she might judge her brother's recent behavior. To make us of the time, he sat at his computer to work on the Dickens essay he had for too long put off finishing.

As he clicked open the file, his eye caught a shadow in the darkness outside the den window. "Jesus Christ. Ellertson." Nichols had no doubt the man had made a return visit. And why hadn't he expected it before now? Ellertson might well have gone home and retrieved a pistol. Elizabeth revealed that her husband enjoyed spending time at the firing range. Cursing himself for his stupidity, Nichols rose from his desk and walked to the other side of the house, in the direction the shadow was moving. He looked out the bathroom window but saw nothing. He did the same toward the front of the house. Again nothing. He stepped into the kitchen for something to drink. Listening for any sound, he hesitated before opening the frig door. Hearing nothing further, he took a beer.

He reasoned that had Ellertson kept a gun in his car, he would have retrieved it right after he had his nose broken. Still, the man had pointed at him in that familiar gesture that said "Just you wait." He most likely didn't keep the weapon in his automobile. Or was "Just you wait" a threat to do harm to Elizabeth? Why the hell hadn't she phoned?

On the other hand, the shadow outside might well have been sixteen-year-old Nick Jansen, the neighbor's eldest boy, who kept his parents on edge by frequently coming home later than his Friday-night curfew. Once before, he knocked on Nichols's back door and sought refuge—or more accurately an alibi for his tardiness. Perhaps this time the lad was walking behind the house in order to sneak in his back door. After all, the shadow was moving in the direction of the Jansen house. Satisfied with that plausible explanation, Nichols took a refreshing swallow of beer. When he finished, he heard the slight tapping on his kitchen door, which led to the small backyard patio. Nichols smiled and thought of Fred Beauchamp's love of Poe. Steve Ellertson, he knew, wouldn't be gently rapping on his kitchen door.

"Coming, Nick." Nichols flicked on the patio light just as he unbolted the door.

He saw the gleam of the patio light radiating off the edge of the large knife pointed at his throat. The knife looked familiar, but he had no time to consider why because he also noticed the small .22 caliber handgun in the intruder's other hand. He raised his eyes and stared into the trespasser's face. His chest and stomach collapsed when he did.

"Meredith."

He hadn't seen or heard from her in almost four years, not since she was in the hospital immediately after giving birth to Belinda. His initial thought was incongruous given her menacing presence. He was disappointed in the style of her hair. It hardly suited her. She looked slightly heavier and healthier, but not much else had altered.

"Sit down, Jeremy and be quiet." She motioned to one of the kitchen table chairs. "Wait. Turn the chair around with its back against the wall. Sit with your back to me. Then grab the back legs of the chair with both your hands."

He did as she instructed, bowing his back as he grabbed the chair legs, with his forehead pressed awkwardly against the back of the chair. His only thought was of Belinda. If Meredith made a move to the bedroom, he was going to let go, spin, and leap from his position to stop her. That is, if she didn't stab or shoot him first. His only chance was to reason with her.

"Meredith, what are you planning to do?"

"I'm going to talk to you, Jeremy. And I want you to listen."

"When did I ever *not* listen?" It pained him to recall how attentive he had been to hearing all her problems and attempting to sooth all her discomforts.

"Just listen to me now." Her volume was soft; her tone smoldering. "Do you know I had just recently decided to come back to you, Jeremy?" He closed his eyes. Clearly, she had become more emotionally disturbed since she left him and Belinda. He long feared as much, but he expected to get word of her suicide, not such a visit as this.

"Meredith, can I help you? Do you need anything? I want to help you. Can I talk to someone who might—"

"No!" Her voice rose with her anger. Then she hissed a long "Shhhhhh." Her almost histrionic extension of the expletive unnerved him.

"All right, Meredith. Just talk. What do you want from me?"

"As if you had to ask." Her tone turned sarcastically sweet.

He knew she would say "Belinda" and demand to take her daughter—and that she would kill him if he tried to stop her. She would shoot him with the .22. But why the large knife in the other hand? The knife? It hit him. The uniquely shaped handle. It was part of the culinary set he had given to Doug Finneran.

"Meredith, were you recently in Massachusetts?"

"So you know?" Her voice sounded childlike.

Did she kill *both* Doug and Heather Finneran? But why? Just to get back at the man who once adored her? After all this time? Even though he'd done nothing but love and care for her? Nichols began to dread that in her disturbed state of revenge, she would take her own daughter's life.

"You killed Doug?"

"Yes."

"And Heather too?"

"Yes."

"And now you want to kill me?"

"Yes."

He was becoming infuriated by the bland repetition of her reply. "But you didn't want me then, Meredith. Why are you doing this to me now?"

"You wouldn't understand. The truth is that you never understood me. That's why I left you."

Nichols realized she yet hadn't mentioned Belinda's name. Had she simply put her child so far out of her mind as to deny the fact of her birth? Now he dreaded the possibility of his daughter walking out from her bedroom. What would Meredith do then? Could he turn and get up from the chair in time to stop her from harming Belinda? He had to keep

Meredith engaged in conversation. He had to feign a deep caring, which he had lost over three years ago.

"Can I turn around? I mean so that I can look at you when while we talk."

"No."

"At least let me sit upright." His back had already stiffened in pain.

"No."

"Will you tell me why you're angry with me now, after all this time? Is it because I didn't understand you then?"

"I'm not really angry, Jeremy." Her voice was placid, as if they were having a respectful conversation about their relationship. "But I am really hurt. I was finally ready to come back to you and *immediately* I found that you betrayed everything we had together."

He was puzzled by her emphasis on "immediately." "Meredith, I want to understand you. Tell me exactly what you mean."

"I believe her name is Elizabeth."

"Meredith, please."

"You've made me hurt her too, Jeremy. It's all your fault."

Nichols couldn't disguise the rising panic in his voice. "What did you do to Elizabeth?"

"I shot her. Right as she was coming out the front door of her house. She had a little bag packed. Coming over here, I assume, so you could fuck her." Nichols sensed Meredith's approaching him. He felt the edge of the large knife touching the bottom of his bowed neck. "You hated making love to me, didn't you, Jeremy? You were always so quiet. I knew you were bored to death."

"No."

"Yes, you were. Don't lie. But maybe it was your own fault that I wasn't more passionate. Maybe you just didn't do it for me. Did you ever think of that? You were just such a nice guy that it made me sick. I can't be excited by nice. You see, I learned that after I left you."

"Meredith, you have to stop this." He was trying desperately to keep Elizabeth's fate out of his mind so that he could survive—so that his daughter could survive.

"Still, I thought that I could teach you to give me what I needed, so that we could enjoy each other the way we never did. But *immediately* I found that *she* was teaching you." Meredith sighed. "I hope she's dead now. That's what I hope."

Nichols resisted the temptation to ask what she meant. He would take her words as hope that she had only wounded Elizabeth. And yet was the woman he now loved lying unattended, losing blood? Would anyone find her in time?

Nichols was desperate. "Meredith, please have a drink. Okay? I remember how much you liked vodka and orange juice."

"Screwdrivers." He felt the knife lift from his neck as she stepped back from him.

"Yes, there's vodka in the cabinet behind you and orange juice in the refrigerator. I want you to have a drink." He was banking, of all things, on her continued preference for the cocktail. "I'll sit here facing the wall. Look, I'm still grabbing the chair legs. I won't move. I promise."

"Trying to get me drunk, Jeremy?"

"You know better than that." He found the pressure on his neck and torso making his words more difficult to articulate.

"I always wanted you to get me drunk and then take me to bed and do whatever you wanted to do, but you never would."

Nichols heard the cabinet door open and the sound of her knife being placed on the counter. Then the clanking of bottles, followed by the vodka dribbling into the glass. He continued to stare at the kitchen wall, praying that Belinda remained asleep. Meredith opened the refrigerator door, found the orange juice, and poured it into the glass. To Nichols all these sounds were amplified, even the spoon softly hitting the inside of the glass as she stirred the cocktail. She would take it without ice. Now all he heard was the sound of her swallowing.

Nichols remembered that he put his beer down on the edge of the kitchen table. If he only could reach the bottle. But she still held the .22, aimed at his back. He wasn't aware of how much time passed in this relative silence, but it seemed considerable. Finally, he heard the empty glass hit the counter top.

"Jeremy, do you remember the time that you tried to get me interested in that Tennessee Williams play?"

He was grateful she was talking again. The long silence had taken its toll on his nerves. "Yes, *Cat on a Hot Tin Roof*."

"Right, that was it. I couldn't stand any of the characters except for Maggie. Do you remember that line of hers I liked so much?"

He felt the perspiration on his forehead as he recalled the line. "Yes."

"What was it? Tell it to me. Every word."

He knew the danger of telling her, but he had no choice. "If I thought you'd never, never make love to me again...why I'd find me the longest, sharpest knife I could and I'd stick it straight into my heart."

"Yes, that's it. Thank you very much." Nichols heard the knife being briefly slid across the counter before she picked it up. His heart raced; the pain in his body intensified. Was she going to kill herself with that knife? Was that how it was going to end?

"Meredith?"

"I'm sorry, Jeremy. But you were not there for me when I needed you. You betrayed me. You didn't wait for me to come back. You lied. You told me you loved me and that you always would."

He couldn't deny it. He had once told her so. "Please Meredith, think about what—"

"I've done so much thinking, Jeremy. I can't let you do this to me. I'm sorry."

His back in agony, he expelled a deep breath. She wasn't going to kill herself. She was going to kill him. He sensed that she was only a foot behind him. His upper back and neck were completely exposed.

"Goodbye, Jeremy."

"Meredith, no!" He shouted the words as loudly as he could, as if the increased volume would cause her to drop the knife.

He let go of the chair legs and instinctively began to twist his torso as he heard the sound of the knife hitting the kitchen floor. The sound seemed louder to him than the gunshot that preceded it.

He winced in pain as he lifted his body from the chair. He caught sight of the pistol—just fired and still aimed at the spot where Meredith had stood. Then the horrified expression on the shooter's face.

"Janis!"

CHAPTER 29

After firing the shot, Janis flung the pistol on the sofa and ran to Belinda's bedroom to prevent her from coming out. Still in pain, Nichols made his way to Meredith's body. The bullet had entered just below the right ear lobe. There was movement, a quivering of her head, but Nichols knew she wouldn't survive. With the blood pooling on the kitchen floor, he stepped back to the entrance of the kitchen. Behind him he saw Janis whisk his daughter out the front door. Belinda's head was covered with a blanket so she wouldn't see the horrendous scene behind her. As he heard her muffled crying, he called out to say that he was all right.

Nichols made a slow path to the door, still attempting to manipulate his torso to counter the stiffness and pain. A car he recognized was parked in front of the house. It belonged to Janis's best friend, who was driving. Both Belinda's cousins were in the car. As soon as his daughter was buckled in, the car drove off. Janis hurried back into the house, slamming the door behind her.

"She's dead—or very close to it, Janis."

His sister seemed much in control—almost regal, like a lioness. "Jeremy, call an ambulance. The police should be here any moment. I called them on my cell right before I arrived. I don't know why I didn't call immediately after I talked to Belinda on the phone. I guess I was panicking." Nichols thought her decisions and actions suggested anything but panic.

Janis revealed that Belinda had called her from her bedroom and said that a "lady was walking behind the house and that she had a big knife."

"I told her always to call you or 9-1-1 and never run toward danger. I guess she followed my..." Nichols trailed off, his emotions now having their full effect.

"You were very smart to keep a cell phone in Belinda's room and program my number into it. I told her to be very quiet, lock her bedroom door, and hide under the blankets stacked on the floor of her closet. You have a very brave girl there, Jeremy."

"Not to mention a sister." Nichols was utterly flabbergasted.

Suddenly, her demeanor changed."Oh Christ, why the hell did I have to give up cigarettes?" Her hands were shaking and her right leg was bouncing up and down as she sat on the edge of the living room sofa.

"Janis, did you have any idea that it might be Meredith?"

"Oh, yes. Damn it, yes. I knew she'd come back one day and want to take Belinda. Over my dead body was what I said then. And I meant it." Janis looked past her brother, aware of the irony of what she just articulated. There was Meredith's body lying lifeless on the kitchen floor.

"Thank God she didn't try to kill you any sooner than she did." Nichols was grateful he thought of the vodka and orange juice. "But I almost forgot to take the gun with me when I left the house. Oh, Jeremy, I almost forgot." His incredibly brave sister was now coming apart.

She continued, "I saw the strange car parked between your house and the neighbors, so I moved as quickly and quietly as I could to your front door and unlocked it with my key. I thought you would have heard the turning of the deadbolt."

Nichols offered a weary smile as he opened the front door and located Meredith's car. It was the same dark green sedan he had recently seen parked in the driveway across the street. "Janis, I'm so glad you agreed to take lessons on using that pistol."

"Are you kidding? I was terrible. I barely hit any of the targets. I thought the best I would ever do was to scare off an intruder."

"But you were only shooting at paper targets, not at someone who was going to kill your brother."

"Yeah, I guess so." They both expelled considerable tension with a mutual laugh. "Jeremy, what did she say about Belinda?"

"She never mentioned her at all."

They heard the sirens. Nichols put his arm around his sister and kissed her on the cheek. "I love you, Janis. How can I ever thank you enough?"

She laughed as she was sniffling. "That's what big sisters are for."

The mention of "love" brought Elizabeth Ellertson's fate back to mind. He reached for the phone. "Janis, Meredith took a shot at Elizabeth. I don't know if she's alive or dead." He let the phone ring until he heard Steve Ellertson's voice on the answering machine. He dialed Elizabeth's cell number just as they heard the EMTs pounding on the front door. He aborted the call and opened the door.

After being informed that Meredith was indeed dead, Nichols walked with the body as it was taken out to the ambulance. The police had arrived along with the EMTs and were already questioning Janis. The neighbors standing on their lawns made clear that tomorrow he would have to explain to them what had happened—at least in part. After he thanked one of the EMTs, he took a chance and asked, "Do you happen to know if anyone named Elizabeth Ellertson was taken to a hospital tonight?"

"Hell, yeah. We took her earlier. Do you know her?"

Nichols closed his eyes. "Yes. Is she...?"

"She'll be okay. Someone took a shot at her. They think the bullet hit the edge of the brick work framing her front door and some pieces of brick probably cut her forehead. Hell, we were just talking about that on the way over here. Seems her best friend called her, and when she found out that Mrs. Ellertson was hurt, the friend called us and the police. Ask the cops in your house; they might know more about what happened."

Nichols stepped inside and gave the police his account of Meredith's visit and the basics of their earlier relationship. He moreover informed them that she had admitted to killing Doug and Heather Finneran in Massachusetts and that a Detective Oliphant was coming down from Amherst to show Nichols a sealed letter to him from his old friend. Nichols added that Meredith claimed to have taken a shot at Elizabeth Ellertson.

One of the cops shook his head. "Really? Jesus, we have the husband in for questioning right now. Mrs. Ellertson believes he's responsible for her injuries. From what we've just been told, he claims it was you who shot at her. Someone else will be getting in touch about that tomorrow. Strange. From what we heard, Mrs. Ellertson's friend contacted us after talking with her on the phone, and when the officers arrived at Ellertson's house, he was nursing his wife's wounds, complaining that the first-aid kit in his car was half depleted and he had to make do with a couple of band aids and some toilet paper. Oh, yeah—something else." The officer laughed. "They said Ellertson's face looked like he'd gone ten rounds. So, tell me, Mr. Nichols. How do you know Mrs. Ellertson?"

• • •

After he finished answering the initial round of questions, Nichols and his sister locked up the house—now a crime scene in any event—and drove to Janis's friend's home to pick up the girls. Belinda remained peacefully asleep as she was carried into one of her cousin's rooms, where she always slept when she spent the night. Nichols accepted the advice of his sister to speak tomorrow with a professional who specialized in child trauma.

It was past two in the morning by the time he closed his eyes in Janis's guest room. Tomorrow he'd call Elizabeth again. He would even risk running into Ellertson to see her if she was still in the hospital. But if the wounds weren't serious, she might have already been released. He lifted his head and reached for his cell, his back and neck still aching from his ordeal in the kitchen.

"Caitlin, please forgive me for calling this late."

"Oh, Jeremy. I'm so glad you called. We tried your house but got no answer. I wanted to call your cell, but Elizabeth didn't want to wake you. Now understand that she's all right, but something happened tonight that—"

"I know, Caitlin. I know what happened."

"You do? Okay, here she is."

His conversation with his exhausted lover was brief. He understood there was more he needed to share about this night and about his previous relationship with Meredith Jamison. He'd merely told Elizabeth that Belinda's mother left them at the hospital and was never heard from again.

"Meredith came back, Elizabeth. She was horribly disturbed. She took the shot at you. Steve had nothing to do with it." He didn't reveal all that happened in the kitchen, but he informed her that Meredith was dead.

"I don't understand, Jeremy."

"I know. I promise to tell you more later."

"The police called a half hour ago. They're sure Steve didn't have anything to do with shooting at me. They checked the pistol in his car. It wasn't fired. I feel badly that I immediately blamed him."

"It's understandable. Try to put it out of your mind for now. Get some sleep."

Steve Ellertson's state of mind was unknowable at this point, although Elizabeth said he promised to leave her alone for a few days. Nevertheless, a police car drove by Caitlin's every half hour.

• • •

By 4:00 a.m., Ellertson had finished all but one can of the six-pack he started consuming when he finally returned home. He reflected on his miserable day. He had learned for sure of his wife's infidelity, had his face busted up by the man who had cuckolded him, and endured the pain of having his nose set after a long wait in a crowded emergency room. But perhaps most distressing was the fact that his wife believed he had taken a shot at her. His accusing Nichols to the police was only a release of his anger and hurt, and he was at least relieved when they told him they had a strong suspect who'd just been killed. However, they couldn't tell him why his wife was targeted. As he reached for the sixth beer, he felt he had no choice but to blame Nichols for all of it. Every bit of it—even the shot taken at Elizabeth. Ellertson pressed the remaining cold beer firmly against his swollen cheekbone.

CHAPTER 30

"I'm sorry, Helena, but it seems Professor Nichols won't be making it up here on Sunday as we hoped. From what Jessica told me, his close friend and his wife were killed this week. Therefore, Nichols doesn't know if he'll have a funeral to attend or not."

"I understand, Fred. And I'm sorry to have called you so early this morning, but it seems that lately I can't suppress my impatience to have this opportunity pursued."

"You're preaching to the choir, Helena. I'm of the same mind."

Beauchamp thought better of informing her that apparently his effort to encourage Nichols to return sooner than later had incredibly taken on a life of its own. A call earlier this Saturday morning informed him of the shootings involving both Nichols and Elizabeth Ellertson. Beauchamp learned that Nichols was unharmed and Elizabeth only slightly worse for wear, but as of yet, there wasn't any solid information on who did the shooting or why. Beauchamp immediately assumed it was the woman's husband, and he now regretted having the anonymous note delivered to Ellertson's Music Department mailbox. Informed that the Ellertson marriage was likely headed toward divorce, Beauchamp wished to manufacture a reason the woman would have to remain home and not travel to the university. That she had accompanied Nichols on his Thursday visit had been totally unexpected.

Helena interrupted his thoughts. "Fred, you know I care for you more than anyone in the world, so please tell me why it's still so important for you to locate the Dickens journal. I have a hard time believing you only want to find it for my sake. Please tell me the truth."

"My dear, there is nothing I wouldn't do for your sake. But, since you press me to be truthful, I will tell you that there is indeed another reason."

"And that would be?"

"The most obvious one. And I'm surprised you don't see it."

"Hmm. I hope you haven't gone daft since you retired."

He laughed. "My dearest Helena, I'd like Jeremy Nichols to find something on the seventh stack level of the Hendley Tower that might tell us who killed our special friend Jack Lawrence. Isn't that a worthy motive to tag onto your own?" Beauchamp trusted she would accept this as his only desire.

"Sorry. The forest for the trees."

"Please. No clichés—not before I've had my breakfast."

Now it was her turn to laugh. "Didn't you just say 'preaching to the choir'? So, we're even. All right, I'll end our conversation by wishing you a most delightful and digestible morning repast."

"That's better."

"My dear Professor Beauchamp, I do believe I'll give Professor Nichols another call."

"I do believe that is a splendid idea, Ms. Allingham."

"Might you have his cell phone number in case I can't reach him at home."

"Of course."

After she hung up, Helena replayed one phrase Beauchamp used during their conversation: "our special friend Jack Lawrence." She had never spoken disparagingly of Lawrence to her mentor Fred Beauchamp. Indeed, she only agreed with the emeritus professor's warm assessment of his old colleague and never contradicted his belief that she had simply lent the Dickens journal to Lawrence for one evening and expected to retrieve it the following day. Nor had she ever mentioned the dinner she invited herself to and her expectation of something amorous with the handsome professor, even though Beauchamp would later ask if they had indeed been intimate.

When she left Lawrence's the night of February 6, she was as upset as she had ever been in her life. Her thoughts were centered on her "rival"—the beautiful young woman who worked at the library, whom she painfully knew had occupied the darkest part of her mind since December, when she first concluded that Lawrence was sexually interested in Sandra Stark. Among other vengeful ruminations, Helena entertained several violent scenarios relating to what she might do to the woman if given the chance. But she quickly turned her antagonism toward Lawrence, believing he had invited the beauty to his place knowing she would assist in the rejection and humiliation of his plain, star-struck, and, surely to his mind, annoying student. It was after several hours of such bitter ruminations that she finally remembered the Dickens journal.

On the morning of the 7th of February, she made the first of five calls to Lawrence's residence. None were answered. She affected a cheerful voice as she left messages after the first three calls, leaving none for the final two. Right before noon, she drove to his place, but found his car gone. As each hour passed, she became more agitated, even though she'd always resented the responsibility with which she had been burdened—the legacy of all the women in her family who treasured the pages in Dickens's hand and saw themselves as caretakers of something far more significant than a valuable manuscript. But now that the journal was in the possession of another, Helena's sensibilities underwent a profound change. Whereas she had always dreamed about flight and escape, now she saw herself wandering alone searching for what had escaped her possession. For the first time, she imagined dire consequences in the afterlife.

At 2:00 p.m. that day, she made the decision to search for Lawrence in Myers Hall. He wasn't in his office. She asked other faculty members where he might be. One suggested the Hendley, since Lawrence expressed to him a need to spend an hour or two that afternoon or evening doing research.

Knowing Lawrence had a study carrel on the third floor, she decided to look there first. Then she would search for him in the stacks on that same floor, where the more recent books on Victorian literature were housed. If need be, she'd even go up to the seventh stack level, in case he was looking through one of the dated volumes on Dickens.

But as she entered the library, she saw that a young man was behind the circulation desk. The beautiful young woman was not there. Helena was surprised she hadn't even thought of encountering Sandra Stark when she came into the Hendley, nor what she would say when she saw her. But now, noticing her absence, her mind leaped to an inevitable conclusion. Jackson Lawrence was at that moment in her rival's company.

Helena walked to the circulation desk and asked the young man where Sandra Stark lived. She claimed they were acquaintances and that she had something she needed to drop off before the day was out. Trusting her word, the young man provided the address. If she didn't find Lawrence there, Helena would come back to the Hendley at a later time and wait for him. She was relying on the other professor's assertion that Lawrence had research to do at the Hendley later in the day. If she failed to see him there, she would go to his house in the middle of the night. If he left town, she would consider breaking in. She tried to suppress her growing anger and thoughts about another course of action she could take.

• • •

"We got a much earlier start as a result of your misfortune, I'm afraid." Police investigator Ken Oliphant and his partner sat outside on Janis's small deck. "They'll check the knife with the M.E.'s report about the wounds to both Mr. and Mrs. Finneran. I'm sure it's the murder weapon, and it seems from what Ms. Jamison told you in your kitchen that she committed both crimes. But still there's the why." Oliphant dropped a sugar pellet into his coffee. "So Jeremy, if I may call you that, why do you think she killed your friends?"

"Just for that reason. Because they were my friends. She wanted to get back at me any way she could. That's why she also..." He stopped, not wishing to say anything about Elizabeth.

Oliphant's eyebrows lifted. "Then why didn't she go after your sister and your nieces? Your sister told us she was certain she earlier saw Meredith's car drive slowly by the house at least twice before your former wife paid you that night call."

"We were never married."

"Sorry."

"Look, I'm just going by what Meredith told me last night."

"All right. Well, as I said on the phone, we'd like you to open this letter Mr. Finneran addressed to you. It's likely nothing, but it does seem odd that he would leave it, with your name in big letters, underlined like this. If he wanted to communicate he could have called or emailed, right?"

"Right." Jeremy took the letter and hesitated. Oliphant had a point. Why would Doug have tried to communicate with him in this fashion? "Wait. Do you know what the funeral arrangements are for Doug and Heather? I haven't had the chance to call their families."

"It's been planned. It was in each of their wills. Cremation. Immediate family only. No services. Sorry."

"No, it's all right. Thanks."

"Okay, would you open and read it out loud?

"Yes, yes. Of course." The flap of the letter was pressed tightly against the seal. Nichols carefully ripped off one of the ends and slid out four folded sheets. The letter was dated a week earlier. Nichols cleared his throat and read.

Jeremy,

If you're reading this, it means that I didn't have the guts to say all this to your face or over the phone. Email seemed too impersonal, so this is the best I could come up with.

First, you know I love you and Belinda. No matter what you may think of me after you read this, I do love you guys. And I'm happy to say that I now know deep down that I truly love my wife. It just took me a while. I've been a fool. No, more than that, I've been a lousy son of a bitch. Of the worst kind.

I know you've been thinking that I was fooling around with someone and that led to Heather and me separating. You were right, as you always seem to be. The other woman was Meredith.

Nichols hesitated before he went on and took a quick glance at Oliphant. Doug once said he'd always been attracted to Meredith and that he would have asked her out if she and Jeremy hadn't gotten together. Nichols continued reading.

I made some asinine comment to her—half in jest, really—to the effect that, if the two of you split up, she might call me and we could have a drink and talk about it. Then she got pregnant with Belinda, so I really felt like shit about what I'd said to her. You have to believe that.

Finneran repeated some of what Nichols already knew—that he then began his "three-year academic gig at the holy of all holies," moved up there, and met Heather." It was in January, he went on, that Meredith called him and said she was in town and wanted that drink he'd promised her. Finneran admitted he was intrigued and eagerly set up a meeting.

I knew how affected you were about her just leaving you and Belinda, so I guess I wanted to feel her out—to see what she was thinking and why she did what she did. We chatted for about two hours. She seemed lost, so I told her to email me whenever she wanted to chat. She was quite put off by my suggestion, which surprised the hell out of me, and I thought I'd seen the last of her. Forgive me, but I just didn't think it was worth telling you about it. I didn't want to upset you.

Finneran added that at the time of his marriage he had only seen Meredith that one time, but then in the fall she came by his office to pay a visit. Finneran confessed he was delighted to see her, but he did inform her he had recently gotten married.

> *Jeremy, she just sat there, her face showing no expression, so as a peace offering, I took her for some coffee across the street from the Hendley Library. We talked for about thirty or forty minutes and then parted. I didn't hear from her again until I received a Christmas card in my box at the department. She included two pictures of herself. You can imagine what she was wearing. And she made clear what she was inviting me to do with her.*

Nichols read further that Finneran's next eight or nine months were marked by Meredith's periodic calls, cards, and visits—one a month, Finneran estimated, until he first saw her at night. They shared a kiss; that was all. But by the end of the fall, they began sleeping together. Finneran knew he was trapped by his fascination for her.

> *Jeremy, I don't know why—but maybe you can understand, if anyone can, why I got so caught up in her. I was risking everything, but I knew it was going to end. Even Meredith assured me it would, so I guess I just kept seeing her while waiting for her to walk out of my life as she did yours. You must know how petrified I was that she'd allow herself to get pregnant.*

Finneran continued by noting that some ten months ago he told Meredith they had to stop seeing each other. He had moved out of the house by then and into his own apartment. Still, he was visiting Heather every day at least for a few minutes. He was certain his wife wanted him to clean up his act and make another go of the marriage. That was why she didn't file for divorce.

Finneran added that when he took the job at UMass, his wife moved to Amherst with him and got a house, although she insisted he rent his own apartment until he was ready to commit just to her.

> *Jeremy, Heather still didn't trust me completely, even though I assured her it was over with the other woman, and that it had been for quite a while. The last time I had sex with Meredith was some two months before Heather and I moved to Massachusetts. I swear I thought Meredith had accepted that we were finished when I said goodbye to her right before we moved. But I made the big mistake of telling her where I was going. So this past Thanksgiving I got the first of her emails. Then the same pattern. À visit in early December. The*

Christmas card. The photographs. Then in January, she came to my office to tell me she'd moved to Amherst. I was panicking by this time. And I couldn't call you and ask your advice. I had a long talk with Heather about Meredith and she insisted I call the police and take out a peace bond of some kind. I didn't because I still felt that I could convince Meredith to go away for good. I refused to have coffee or talk on the phone, even though she frequently came to my apartment and wanted to spend the night. Thank God, Heather was living in the house and not with me.

Nichols turned to the last page of the letter.

I made the mistake of letting Meredith spend the night on my sofa. She came during a March snow storm and was trembling like a scared child. I made her tea and talked with her for several hours. I left her asleep and went to bed. Sometime later, I could feel her hand rubbing me under the covers. She then whispered in my ear, "bong...bong...bong. It's three o'clock and time for you to please me, Doug." That's when I lost it. I pushed her away and told her to get out of the bedroom—and from now on to leave me alone. She slapped me as hard as she could and left the apartment. I thought it was finally over. No word from her the next four months. Never saw her. I assumed she left Amherst. And then just this week, she arrives at my place as if nothing had happened. As soon as she saw the boxes I was packing up, she screamed. And then kept screaming until I had no choice but to place my hand over her mouth. I struggled with her until she stopped. Then the tears. "You're going home to your wife, aren't you?" she said. I told her I was. She stopped crying and pulled my hand away from her face. "I'm sorry I slapped you so hard." She said that as calmly as I had ever heard her say anything. Then she left. Jeremy I really think she's finally accepted the truth. I feel sorry for her, I really do. But she needs to get help. Serious help. Anyway, after she left, I knew I had to tell you everything. I've never been more ashamed of myself in all my life. I want a new start. I've got one with Heather. I can only pray that I'll have one with you. I'm so deeply sorry.

Doug

Nichols's head sagged. "Here." Jeremy handed the letter to Oliphant. "I think this answers the 'Why?'"

CHAPTER 31

Once more the journal was removed from its place of concealment and two more of its pages pulled for perusal.

I know my separation from Kate won't end my unhappiness. I cannot have my Ellen. Never was a man so seized and rendered so helpless. I have decided to remove myself entirely from Tavistock House. Indeed, the city has become more unappealing with every passing day. I will spend most of my time now in the country, although coming to London will be necessary if I am to see Ellen in any respectable way. My heart has been devoted to the girl for three years now—beyond what anyone would call a normal courtship period.

I feel it most peculiar, but something is happening to my view of the past. I suddenly want nothing to do with any of it. Since I have fallen in love with Ellen, I have wished that I had no memory of anything before her. I love my children but cannot bear remembering what I did to conceive them.

I am committed to effacing my personal history. I shall begin the process of burning all the letters and miscellaneous papers I have kept for over a period of twenty years. I will also destroy all correspondence I receive from this point forward. Only my novels and this journal will carry my memory, my pain, and the true feelings of my heart.

• • •

Sandra Stark barely slept during the night of February 6-7, 2019. The visit to Lawrence's house that evening had left her shaken and depressed. She had gone to tell him something that wouldn't please him. Something she had to share that frightened her. She needed his comfort and assurances, if not his advice. As she arrived, her mind spun with intense thoughts of love, loyalty, sacrifice, and pain. And then she saw that young woman.

Sandra had little room in her thoughts to accommodate jealousy along with her other emotions. But it pushed its way into her sensibilities nonetheless, roughly expelling for a few moments everything else she'd been feeling that evening. The weight of possibility fell heavily upon her. Was she nothing more than just the last young woman Lawrence had seduced—that plainer English girl now being the most recent?

On the table were the nearly empty glasses of red wine. Sandra fought her initial anger. She couldn't give in to it, for she had to process the questions flashing through her mind. Had the man she had fallen in love with quoted verses to this young woman too? The very same verses that won her heart? Had Lawrence and the English girl made love in his bed, on the very spot where she had lain with him only two nights before? In the same room where hung the Waterhouse print of the Lady and her knight? And yes, the meal. Lawrence never cooked for her or asked her to cook for him. And yet with this other young woman he apparently had.

Sandra warned herself the first night she saw Lawrence socially that he would quickly tire of her. She knew nothing much of his academic specialty. In high school she read only two of Dickens's shorter works, *A Christmas Carol* and *A Tale of Two Cities*—and in the Nineteenth-Century Novel class she took from him, they covered but one Dickens novel—*Bleak House*. What could she say about her work at the Hendley that would interest him? It would take time before she'd know the library as well as he did. She of course understood that he was taken by her appearance, but throughout her youth she was told that good looks were a trap not only for the man but for the woman who possessed them. And events in her past had made her regret her beauty and shape of her body, even blaming herself for something that occurred when she was in her later teens. What she had never spoken of in the years since.

But Lawrence didn't pay her the same compliments she had become used to receiving. Each time they were together, he charmed her with something creative and new. He took interest in what she read—even though he was ignorant of some of the titles. He found it delightful that she had a taste for Wagner's majestic and intimidating *Ring* cycle, especially her fascination with its second part, *Die Walküre.* He teased her by calling her his "warrior goddess" and humming the famous opening to *The Ride of the Valkyries* when she walked into a room. Sandra became convinced that no other woman had heard exactly what he said to her. And now she assumed everything he told her was a lie. A well-rehearsed lie at that. And that English girl looked far more like a warrior goddess than she did.

In addition to Sandra's deep humiliation was the galling awareness of her ignorance and naiveté. She was used to handling superbly everything she did. Her love for Lawrence was in large part predicated on his feeding her desire to be unique. But now she felt foolish and used. Her intensifying bitterness convinced her to speak to him no more.

She wasn't scheduled to work on February 7th. From his office, Lawrence first called at 9:00 a.m. He was being polite, trying to show her he had indeed paid attention to her assertion that she liked to sleep until 8:30 when she didn't have to be at the Hendley. The phone rang again at 9:15, 9:45, 10:30, and 11:00. She refused to answer any of the calls and left her apartment at 11:15. She expected Lawrence to drop by and ask her to lunch, and she was determined to avoid seeing him. She ate by herself and took in an early afternoon matinee. She then did some marketing and returned home at 4:30. When she arrived, he was sitting on her front door stoop. Although bundled up in his winter coat, he was evidently freezing.

"Sandra, you will give me a chance to explain?"

"Excuse me." She opened the door and closed it softly between them.

Lawrence knocked. "Sandra, will you let me in? It's really cold out here. Please. Sandra, what you saw last night was very, very misleading. I can explain." She didn't respond. "Sandra? Sandra?"

Lawrence tore a blank page from the 3 x 5 notebook he had in the pocket of his coat. He jotted down a brief message, folded the paper once, and placed it in the crack of the door. He returned to his car, but before driving off, he checked the envelope containing the materials and thumb drive proving Stuart Dryden's perverse behavior. Everything was there, ready to be released at the right time.

Pulling aside the edge of the front curtain, Sandra watched Lawrence pull away. She couldn't believe she had shown him such indifference. She hadn't frowned or replied to him in an indignant tone because she refused to act so predictably. Nor did she soften and invite him in, to listen with hope and gullibility written on her face. She wouldn't trust him again. He'd just lie to her about last night. After all, he was a superb actor, as she now assumed most mature seducers of younger women were. Moving to her kitchen and pouring a glass of sherry, she felt momentarily proud of herself for demonstrating integrity and strength. She understood she couldn't prevent him from trying to call or see her. Nor could she prevent the tears that began to run from her eyes. Only once before had she gone through anything like this, and she vowed then not to let it happen again—but it had.

Almost three hours later the phone rang for the first time since Lawrence's five morning attempts to reach her. After her first glass of sherry, she had drunk two more. She let the phone ring without answering. Stepping outside to retrieve the mail, she saw drop the folded piece of paper Lawrence stuck in the door. She opened it against her better judgment. "Darling Sandra, you are the only one—the ONLY one." A few seconds later the phone rang again. This time she answered.

When she hung up, she knew she had to see Jack Lawrence as soon as she could.

CHAPTER 32

Nichols awoke Sunday morning feeling optimistic that he could begin putting behind him the last two excruciating days. Perhaps nothing eventful would occur today. Perhaps too he would have a relatively relaxing week ahead. He had spoken twice the previous night to Elizabeth, who revealed that Steve called but had promised to honor her request for privacy. But by Tuesday they would have to talk, he said, although she wasn't sure by the sound of his voice whether he wanted to begin the dissolution of their marriage or commence the healing between them. Regardless, as she told Jeremy, "As soon as I see him I will say that we need to end it."

Nichols was relieved. After all that had happened to the both of them the previous two days, he feared she would no longer find their relationship worth the toll it had taken. "And how are your wounds, Elizabeth?"

"The physical or emotional ones?" She immediately regretted her reply. "I'm sorry. I guess I've just been feeling sorry for myself this morning."

"You have every right. I meant the ones on your forehead."

"One of them is definitely going to leave a visible scar, about an inch above my eyebrow. The others are a little higher up and weren't as deep." She offered a raspy laugh. "So how would you like me in bangs?"

"I'd be your biggest fan."

"Are you taking Belinda in for counseling today?"

"Yes, Janis got her an appointment at 1:00. The counselor's coming in to the office just to see Belinda. She didn't want us to wait until Monday. So far my daughter seems fine, thank God. She just keeps asking me if I was hurt and whether I should go to the hospital to get the doctor to look at me. But I will tell you I'm very nervous about seeing her next painting."

• • •

Wishing further to divert his mind from all that went wrong the past two days, Nichols sat at his computer and returned to the same Dickens piece he was examining when Meredith's shadow moved past his window. Again, a knock—the front door this time. He hesitated but opened it after stepping to his right where his body might be protected by the door frame.

"Yes? What can I do for you?" Nichols expected a request for a donation of some kind.

"Are you Professor Nichols?"

"Yes. Wait, are you...?" The voice was unmistakable. The British accent. "Were you the person who called me last week about—"

"About the Dickens journal. Yes, I am. My name is Helena Allingham."

"Please come in."

After inviting her to sit, Nichols offered tea and some of the pastry he had earlier picked up for Belinda.

"Thank you. Tea, yes—but sweet treats, no. I'm currently in a state of confectionary denial." Helena surveyed the house which showed clear evidence of the impending move. "You have a young daughter, is that right?"

"Yes. She's almost four. I'd love to introduce you, but she's with her aunt and cousins." Nichols noted the time. 10:40 a.m. Janis was going to pick him up in less than two hours for the trip to the counselor's office.

Helena noticed the framed eight-by-ten of Nichols's daughter. "She's a most beautiful child."

"Thank you. You've no doubt come to talk to me about the journal and whether I've begun looking into the Dickens volumes."

"Yes. I was merely going to call you, but I decided we should meet. Therefore, I took the chance you'd be home this morning."

Nichols indulged his burgeoning curiosity about this woman. "And from where have you come to see me?"

"It's not important." She smiled and lifted her head toward the kitchen.

"Ah, yes. The tea. Excuse me." He continued to speak from the kitchen. "Ms. Allingham, I really haven't had time to make an adequate examination of the vintage Dickens editions. It's been...an eventful couple of days."

"Please know how sorry I am about the deaths of your friend and his wife."

"Excuse me, but how did you know about that?" He returned with the tea,

"I suppose it would be all right to tell you. Professor Beauchamp informed me."

"I see." The emeritus professor obviously learned about Doug and Heather's deaths from Jessica Tillman, but did he know they were murdered as well?

"I can see you don't quite understand. Professor Beauchamp and I have been the dearest of friends for the past two years. He was my favorite professor." She smiled warily as she took the first sip of her tea.

Nichols debated whether he should tell her about having examined the volume containing the Christmas books. Surely, she must know about the volume marred by Jackson Lawrence's blood. As a former student at the university, she might well have located the volume and opened it herself.

"Professor Nichols,..."

"Please call me Jeremy."

"Very well, Jeremy, I hope you can see your way to come back soon to the Hendley Library and continue your search."

"I probably need to stay here for the next several days or so. But I'll bring my family up soon enough to see where we'll be living for the next three years."

"You daughter, you mean?"

"And my sister Janis and her girls. They'll be moving up with us."

"Of course. You're fortunate to have such a close and loving family. I envy you."

"Thank you. I *am* fortunate. I most certainly am."

"Will anyone else come with you?"

Nichols stared at the smiling young woman, who was wearing a blue long-sleeve silk blouse, a tan skirt to the middle of her knee, light brown tights, and flats. Appropriate and attractive, though conservative, he thought. Her comforting appearance belied the discomfort he felt at everything she seemed to know about him.

"Well, what I can do this weekend is retrieve an edition of *The Chimes* from one of the boxes here and see if I can find anything that might give a clue as to the location of the Dickens journal you say Jackson Lawrence possessed."

She was insistent but still pleasant. "No, no. You will have to come back to the Hendley and spend a full day there at least. You must examine the *actual* volume Professor Lawrence handled. That book will offer information no other edition could possibly give you."

Nichols had already come to a similar conclusion. "I wonder if there's a way for me to have the volume here? An interlibrary loan? Perhaps you or Professor Beauchamp could talk to someone at the library."

Helena's demeanor altered dramatically. Her smile evaporated, and she stood up, turning her back to Nichols. "No, that won't do. The book had Professor Lawrence's blood in it. It cannot be taken from the Hendley. It must be examined *in* the Hendley, *on* the seventh stack level of the Hendley Tower. What you must find is *there*. It is not just that one book, Professor Nichols."

Her return to a formal address made clear that she was upset and losing patience with him. He understood he had every right to ask her to leave if she wasn't content with how he wished to proceed in the matter. But he was mesmerized by her manner and even further intrigued by what it was she was looking for other than the supposed journal manuscript.

"Forgive me, Ms. Allingham. You're of course right. It's just that I've had a very difficult time here recently."

When she turned around, the smile had been restored. She carefully sat, folding the back of the skirt with her hand as she did so. He studied her face again. She wasn't traditionally pretty, let alone beautiful, but she was appealing in another way, which her self-assuredness and general bearing enhanced. As she returned to her tea, Nichols decided he had to know more about the purported Dickens journal before agreeing to return to the Hendley. If Jackson Lawrence was murdered because of this manuscript, it was all the more important to know everything he could about.

"Ms. Allingham, forgive my repeating anything I asked during our phone conversation, but what led you to believe that this journal was authentic? I mean that it's a document in Charles Dickens's own hand?"

She turned her face away. "Jackson Lawrence examined it and he was convinced." He knew she was holding back. It had to be something to do with its ownership. Nichols was of course aware of several famous examples of literary discovery—with manuscripts, letters, and journals uncovered a century or more after their composition. Bound and separated pages had been stumbled upon in attics, basements, cabinets, storage sheds, and toy boxes. That there would be a Dickens journal unknown until the present day was completely plausible. Did Helena Allingham find it at the bottom of a clothing chest in a farmhouse where she grew up in England? Had someone else found it—a grandparent or a sibling —and given it to her because she was the one in the family who knew something about English literature?

He continued, "So it disappeared right before Lawrence died, and you think he left some kind of clue as to where it might be?"

"Yes. But you already know that."

"But what I don't know is how the journal came into your possession and why now, after all this time, it is so important to get it back."

"It has *always* been 'so important to get it back,' Professor Nichols."

"Sorry."

"Very well, then, I'll tell you." She took out a compact and checked her lipstick after finishing her tea. "The journal had been passed down through my family, and it came to me as a responsibility. No one had ever considered selling it or donating it to the Hendley or to any other library. I've learned that one can no longer ignore responsibility handed down through several generations of one's family."

"But had you attempted to find it before now?"

She tensed. Nichols could see that she was unsure whether to answer him truthfully. "What matters at present is that I want to find it if it still exists. I can say that months ago I did not believe it existed any longer. I thought it had been destroyed." She paused. "However—"

He interrupted. "Why did you feel that way?"

"However, I have come to believe that it now does exist—in its entirety."

He was amazed at himself for not having asked before. "Ms. Allingham, have you read the entire journal? Can you tell me what it includes?"

"I believe I never read much beyond the first page or two." He was stunned by her admission. "I was unappreciative of its importance when I received possession of the journal. It was, as I suggested, a responsibility I didn't at the time want."

Nichols understood she was refusing to tell him everything. Or was she only teasing him—forcing him to show further interest? "But on those first pages, what did you see?"

"A man deeply in love with a woman he couldn't truly have. I felt at the time that I understood what that was like. There was no need to read any further."

"Was the first page dated?"

"Yes."

"Can you tell me when it began?"

"In 1857."

Nichols easily concluded that the woman Helena Allingham alluded to was Ellen Ternan. "So, if you read only the first page or two, you don't know if Dickens shifted the subject at any point or if the journal included something in addition to his remarks about this woman."

She sighed. "The journal belongs to me, to my family. You have the chance to help me get it back. Once I see it—finally read it through—I will allow you to study it and publish a long essay or book that will make your career." She was aware that doing so would violate the agreement all the women in her family had made, the very charge given them all by Mary Bertram almost a century and a half earlier. Nichols had dropped his eyes and didn't notice her lips shaping into a sly smile.

Had he done so, he might have distrusted her promise to give him the journal for scholarly use.

"Excuse me, but I have to ask you this, Ms. Allingham. Another Dickensian could be asked—a senior scholar at another institution."

"*You* are the one I have asked."

"Yes, but..."

"I'm someone who has always believed in such quaint notions as kismet. Others come into our lives at the very time they do for a reason. I strongly feel we make our own tragedies when we run from the inevitable. The ancient Greeks knew that. Therefore, to offer excuses or rationalizations to the effect that we are not yet ready or that we are too young and under-qualified only masks our cowardice. But it's a gossamer mask everyone else sees easily through."

Nichols was taken by the manner in which made her point. She insulted him, but he took no umbrage. Rather, she fascinated him the moment she entered his house. She seemed far older and wiser than her years. He could easily imagine that Dickens himself had handed the journal to her before his death. "Forgive me, Ms. Allingham. I'm just—"

"Too modest. Let it go at that. Promise me you'll come to the Hendley as soon as you can, within the week."

"If I do, will you be there?"

"At this moment I can't say." She stood up and extended her hand. It was not in the usual position in order to shake his. Nor was it palm down in a manner of a by-gone era. It was at a slight angle, giving him no indication whether she wanted to shake his hand or have him take hers and place it to his lips. He gently took her hand and held it for several seconds before she said goodbye.

• • •

Returning to the rental car, Helena thought of Nichols implied suggestion that a more noted Dickensian should do the search in Hendley Tower. She wondered if Nichols would ever understand that he was chosen in part because he was relatively anonymous. Less likely to be noted—less likely to be missed.

CHAPTER 33

"Are you sure you don't want me to come? All right, but I'll be calling you later tonight. Just remember what I said. It means a lot that you confided all this to me. No, no, I understand. I do. Bye."

"Jesus Christ." Coy Mallory returned his phone to his front pocket. The caller had given him much to consider. Much to be apprehensive over and much to anticipate. He just had to be careful to avoid any mistakes this time. There was too much to lose—in the only two areas of his life that still meant anything to him. Still, there was enough he didn't know to leave him feeling unsure and vulnerable. Giving in to caution was one thing; being limited because of doubt was quite another.

For so long, he'd felt the debilitating presence of personal disgust. How much more ironic could it be? Confronting Jack Lawrence then was supposed to put an end to those feelings. And what had been the result? Being a slave to the same emotion—and every decision he made only exacerbating his self-contempt. Lies, deception, and betrayal marked his life, but wasn't that how he'd been trained when he worked for the agency? Had they noted something in his character that gave them confidence he'd use those qualities and talents to serve their ends—to serve, as they told him, his country's needs?

Mallory recalled the post-Christmas dinner at Fred Beauchamp's on the December 28, 2018. Following the meal, the men settled in Beauchamp's comfortable den. While Beauchamp constructed a fire, Mallory sipped brandy and noted he had gathered damning evidence on Stuart Dryden and had picked a young woman to seduce and encourage the congressman to act out an incriminating fantasy.

"Fred, I thought I would enjoy this assignment more than I have."

"So you're having second thoughts?"

"No. But it's quite different than the work I've done in the past."

"Not really, Coy. You've worked to destroy a few reputations at home and abroad, remember. And what you're doing now involves no violence."

"I still feel like the gods are frowning at me."

"Very melodramatic, Coy. I think Jack would like the touch."

"Yeah, I'm sure he would. And where is he by the way? You invited him to dinner, didn't you?"

"He had other plans. And they involved a young lady. The 'Aphrodite of the Circulation Desk,' as Jack put it."

"Well, I thought I'd ask if you'd hold on to what I have so far on Dryden." He pulled several folded sheets of paper from his jacket pocket. "But I don't want you to read any of it—at least not yet."

"Do you really believe I won't?"

"Yes. If you promise me you won't. You're the rarest of all creatures, Fred. A man of impeccable integrity."

"Come on, Coy. You make me sound like Don Quixote."

• • •

Moments after Mallory drove off, Beauchamp unfolded the sheets containing evidence of Dryden's interest in prostitutes and pornography—of any century. He hesitated and debated with himself. Finally, Beauchamp refolded the papers and wrapped a thin rubber band around them before placing the evidence in the back of a desk drawer. "No, I'm more like Quixote's Sancho Panza."

• • •

"Steve, you promised Elizabeth you wouldn't see her until Tuesday. Now go home and leave us alone."

A voice called from the back of the apartment. "Caitlin, who is it?"

"No one, Elizabeth. I'll be right there." Caitlin saw the menacing cloud on Ellertson's bruised and bandaged face.

"Let me talk to her. I just want to see her for one minute—that's all. Please don't fucking interfere, Caitlin."

She blocked his entrance through the front door of her apartment. "Don't use that language with me, Steve. Now go home." She recoiled from the stale liquor on his breath. He remained on the doorstep. "Go on, Steve. If you really care about her, just leave her alone."

"Care for her? And did she care for me when she *slept* with Jeremy Nichols? See? I said *slept*. Proper-enough language for you, Caitlin?"

"Caitlin, who is it?" Elizabeth approached the front door.

Ellertson pushed Caitlin forcefully out of the way, knocking her into the door jamb and causing her to sink to the floor in pain. Ellertson closed the front door behind him and stood facing his wife, who was barefoot and wearing one of Caitlin's terrycloth robes.

"I want to know why you did this to me. You're my *wife*."

Elizabeth was emotionally beyond fear; she felt only exhilaration at the opportunity to say now what she was going to say on Tuesday when they were scheduled to talk. She didn't hear Caitlin moan as she tried to rise from the floor. "Steve, our marriage is finished. We've both known that for a long time. It was over even before I met Jeremy last fall. You know that's true." Part of her still wanted to comfort him, for she saw he was in physical pain. He ran his hands through his thick hair and touched the bandage on his nose.

"I don't give a damn if it's over or not. You had no right to do what you did with him before we split. You had no right."

She was sensitive to his argument. "I know, but I—"

"You know. You're God-damned right you know."

"Steve, don't."

He felt Caitlin touch his arm from behind. He whirled around and shoved her violently into the front door. She slammed into it and fell to her knees, struggling to catch the breath that had been knocked out of her.

"Steve, stop it!" Elizabeth rushed forward. "Damn you. Stop it!" She pushed past him and knelt down to help her friend. Seeing his wife's bare breasts protruding from the borrowed robe, Ellertson lost all control and reached for a long-stemmed lamp sitting on a small side table. In a violent motion, he ripped off the delicate shade and pulled the cord from the socket. Elizabeth had no chance to protect herself and the bulb shattered against the side of her head. Ellertson threw the lamp across the room and headed for the back door.

A moment after Ellertson left the house, Caitlin made her way to the kitchen sink and soaked a dishrag. Still woozy, she returned and pressed it against the left side of Elizabeth's head and wiped the blood that was trickling down from above her ear. "We have to call the police."

More stunned than physically hurt, Elizabeth grabbed her friend's arm. "Wait. I need to make another call first. Bring me the phone."

• • •

"Jeremy Nichols, how nice to hear your voice. No, no. I'm not to bed yet. I've just let my dog out. I'm standing hear looking out at my back yard and listening to the breeze blowing through my *viburnum trilobum*."

"Sorry, Fred, I'm not as up on my bushes and trees as I should be."

"That's an American Cranberry. Edible fruit in late summer and orange-reddish leaves in the fall. Long been a favorite of mine."

"All right, Fred. I'm coming back up and I'll spend some time in the Hendley."

"Helena Allingham is quite a woman, isn't she, Jeremy?"

"I won't offer a counter argument. But I'd like you to tell me before I come up what—"

"Jeremy, just come and all your questions will be answered."

"No, really, you've got to tell me why I should drive up."

"Just come and ye shall be satisfied."

"Come on, Fred. Don't play with me. I'm told there's an authentic Dickens journal that I might be able to find if I decipher some code Jackson Lawrence might have left in that volume of Dickens Christmas stories."

"Yes."

"And that's why you've been wanting me to come back so soon? Why Jessica called? And..."

"Jeremy, you're telling me what the both of us already know. So I'll say goodnight for now. I'm looking forward to seeing you...when?"

"Tomorrow. I'll come up tomorrow."

"Good. Alone?"

Nichols hesitated. "Yes."

"Wonderful. Goodnight, Jeremy."

• • •

Nichols took another peek at his daughter as she lay sleeping. The time spent with the counselor earlier in the day was beneficial, although Nichols felt it helped him as much as it did Belinda. The counselor was impressed by his daughter's handling of what she saw and heard but cautioned that she might at any time run into a difficult stretch as she re-processed the dreadful events of that night. The counselor reminded Nichols that now was not the time to explain that Meredith was Belinda's mother, and she insisted that, when they moved to their new home, Nichols continue to solicit further professional advice for both his daughter and himself.

As he kissed his fingers and touched Belinda's shoulder, as he always did when she was asleep, Nichols saw a new painting on her nightstand. He took it to the living room and examined it carefully. The counselor had moreover advised that he study these sketches very carefully for anything suggesting that Belinda was beginning to have difficulties with her impressions of that night.

The scene was again a meadow. Belinda had painted herself and her father riding a horse. She sat in the front and Nichols behind her. There were no reins in either of their hands. Instead, her father's arms were wrapped around her. They were riding downhill toward the ever-present oval situated in the bottom right-hand corner of the paper. Nichols slightly gasped. The oval had hair on it and a crooked mouth, suggesting a frown.

• • •

At 3:20 a.m. a car drove by Nichols's dark and empty house. The automobile didn't quite stop but slowly drifted until it reached the mailbox down by the street. The driver checked the address on the mailbox and drove off.

Fifteen minutes later the car followed the same pattern as it approached the Ellertson home. But the garage door was open and a still-running car was half in and half out of it. Within seconds, it backed down the driveway.

Steve Ellertson had rushed into the house to pick up some cash, clothing, and a few toilet articles. As he came through the garage, he remembered a box of cartridges he had left near his workbench. He grabbed the box and threw everything into his front seat. He had driven by his house twice to be sure no one was in the home or waiting for him outside. The police had to be looking for him, he reasoned. Therefore, he wanted to get back on the road as soon as he could. In hiding since he left Caitlin's apartment, Ellertson made up his mind to stay away from the house for at least a few days. Now he would head northwest to Vermont and then perhaps to Maine until he figured out what to do. A good friend resided on a small farm near Bangor. Perhaps something could be worked out there.

As Ellertson didn't look behind him as he backed out of his driveway and swung to his left, he failed to notice the car parked along the street to his right. He wasn't a hundred yards down the residential road when the driver of the other car turned on the ignition.

• • •

Ellertson was growing concerned. The car behind him had been following at the same speed for over four miles. With the exception of one pickup truck coming the other way, the road was deserted. Ellertson expected the car behind him to turn on its blue lights, but he couldn't make out a light rack attached to the roof. Because the road narrowed to two lanes for the next fifteen miles, he slowed to allow the car to pass him. He had to get those damned headlights out of his rearview mirror. But the other car slowed as well and kept the same distance between them.

"The hell with this." Ellertson's head was throbbing from the pain from his cheek and nose. "Keep up with me if you can, mother fucker."

He turned up the volume on the classical music selection he was listening to and brought his car up to seventy. He knew the road well enough to anticipate where he would need to slow down to negotiate the turns. But the following car sped up enough to come precariously close to the rear of Ellertson's dark blue sedan. He began to panic and lost concentration on the road ahead, because he was keeping his eyes glued to the rear-view mirror. For a brief instant he felt no traction on his front wheels. Then none on the rear ones. He dropped his eyes from the rear-view mirror in time to see the large tree right before his car slammed into it. His sedan had left the road and been briefly airborne before the collision.

The car behind Ellertson's stopped, backed up, and stopped again. The driver emerged directly parallel to where Ellertson's car was wrapped around the oak. Lifting a pistol, the driver fired two shots toward the fuel tank, and within seconds the car was engulfed in flames. The driver wondered if Ellertson was already dead before the flames consumed the car. But then, it really didn't matter.

CHAPTER 34

Mallory headed to the university, intending to pay a visit to the Hendley Library, "for old time's sake," he jocularly muttered. Things had now been awakened. He'd prepared himself for such an eventuality, although the exact nature of his related actions was never clear to him.

The weather was most pleasant for this Monday morning in early August. A far cry from when he stood outside in the bitter cold of Washington D.C. this past winter and called Jack Lawrence from one of the dying-out open pay phones. He lamented the extinction of the old full-length phone booths. At least with those, he would have been protected from the wind on that early February day.

Lawrence hadn't answered his phone, either at home or in his office when Mallory tried him earlier. But the walk from the Capitol to his car was long enough to prompt another attempt. This time Mallory found his man.

"Jack, this is Coy. God damn it, are you going to pay me for the stuff I've given you on Dryden?"

"Ease up, Coy. I'm just deciding what I'm going to use. Then I'll pay you."

"You better fucking hurry. I'm leaving for London in two weeks. My agent has set me up with a gig for the BBC."

"Really? That's great. Your career is now going international. Look, Coy, will you do me a really big favor? Can you go to the British Museum and check on something for me?"

"I don't do scholarly errands, Jack. Look, I'll come up there and get the money from you. And I don't want to hear about this 'how much I'll use' crap. We agreed on the amount before I started."

"Fine. It would be great to see you before you go. Just give me a few days to look it all over."

"You're not hearing me. I said we agreed on an amount. Are you deaf?"

"Look, Coy. You forget what I do for a living. The first batch of papers has come in this week for the new semester. So I'm neck deep in grading. I'm also trying to finish up a paper on Dickens I'm scheduled to give at a conference in a few days."

"It would take but two fucking seconds out of your precious day to hand me what you owe me."

"Look. Today's the fifth. Just give me to the 12th—when I get back from the conference, okay?"

"What the hell are you up to, Jack?"

"Jesus, Coy. I'm not up to anything."

Mallory was exasperated. "I'll be up there in a couple of days. I'll expect the money or else."

"Or else what?"

"Don't fuck with me. I would imagine Dryden would give more for me to burn all the evidence."

"He doesn't have the evidence. Nor do you anymore. I do."

"You fucking bastard."

"Listen to me, Coy. You seemingly fail to realize that I could simply release the information and blame you for doing so. I can get in touch with the woman you used in the video tape and convince her to pin it all on you. You personally set it up with her, remember? You're in no position to demand any amount. You'll take what I think is fair—when *I get back* from the conference. Oh, and one more thing, Coy. If this gets out with your name attached to it, you're budding celebrity career is dead. Dead, do you hear me? I'll send the money before you leave for London—so be happy with that. Sorry to play hardball, my friend, but you leave me no choice."

• • •

Nichols started out at 10:00 a.m. Monday morning. He called Caitlin's the previous evening, but she and Elizabeth had apparently gone to dinner or a movie. Considering the psychological effect of the shot Meredith took at Elizabeth and the anxiety over her forthcoming talk with her husband, Nichols decided not to call back, in case she fell immediately asleep upon her and Caitlin's return. He also thought it best that she refrain from calling him. Given her emotional state, he didn't wish to put her in the position of having to make conversation. He left a voice message telling her that he was heading back to the Hendley in the morning—"I'll explain why later"—and that he would give her a call Monday night when he was in his hotel room.

Janis had initially fought with him about his decision to leave Belinda yet again, but he argued that, because he would be so busy seeing his new colleagues and the realtor, Belinda wouldn't be at all happy she accompanied him. His sister seemed to be handling well enough the fact that she had shot Meredith in order to save her brother's life, but Nichols was also concerned she might come undone once she was satisfied her young niece was going to be all right. At least she promised to see someone if she experienced undo anxiety over the event.

While on the road for the two-and-a-half-hour drive, Nichols turned off the radio and began to think further of what Dickens's *The Chimes* might have to do with Jackson Lawrence's life and ultimate fate. Nichols had agreed with Helena Allingham that he needed to examine the tale in the very volume Lawrence touched when he died, but Nichols found it impossible to ignore the matter until he arrived at the Hendley. He had re-familiarized himself with the basic plot line of *The Chimes* and now attempted to draw from it whatever might be relevant to Lawrence. The action began on New Year's Eve, not at Christmas. Dickens quickly established a depressing mood of immorality and crime. The tale dealt further with the love of man and woman, the inherent nature of evil men, and nostalgia for the past. Dickens, as usual, featured debt, poverty, and the issue of social displacement. He employed the supernatural element of spirits, goblins, disturbing visions, and the ringing of the chimes to comment further on man's concession to the worst in life. A character was said to have fallen to his death from the bell tower; other characters succumbed to financial ruination, alcoholism, and prostitution—and one character died, leaving his young wife with a child. The mother then considered her end and that of the child's through drowning.

But Dickens used the chimes as an audible reflection of conscience, and the central character learned his lesson and prevented the mother from the murder-suicide. Like Scrooge in the more famous Christmas book, the central character awakened as from a dream. The bells now signaled the New Year, to be filled with hope and promise.

Nichols couldn't make any distinct connection to Jackson Lawrence from the basic plot, other than a vague notion of the man's possible psychological state at the time of his murder. No, Nichols would have to look at the blood-stained section of the Hendley edition to see if there was anything hinted at on those pages. If he could recall the exact section of *The Chimes* that Lawrence kept open with his finger, Nichols could read the text for further clues, but he hadn't the time earlier to make proper notations, owing to Sandra Stark's interruption.

• • •

When the phone rang, Lawrence was about to head out for a late meal after a more than hectic day of playing hide-and-seek.

"Sandra, I'm so happy you called. Can I now have that opportunity to explain what you saw here last night?"

"I have to see you, Jack. Can I come over now?"

Lawrence checked the wall clock. 8:40 p.m. It was also February 7th—Dickens's birthday.

Lawrence had just returned home after seeing Helena Allingham. Why had all this happened to him at once, he wondered? He had used the same stalling tactic on her as he used on Coy Mallory. Although she was adamant about having the journal back immediately, he promised to return it just as soon as he read it through. Today, he'd been studying it at one of the smaller college libraries fifteen miles from the Hendley, where no one would think to look for him. His plan was to get what he needed for a long article, submit it, and then charm Helena into compliance for the "sake of literary history." And then, if she were considerably charmed, he could talk her into letting him edit the journal pages. Hell, he'd be more than willing to have her name with his on the title page. He just needed to be left unmolested by both Helena and Mallory, especially if the latter decided to drive up and confront him about his payment for the evidence on Stuart Dryden.

But what to do with that evidence? He wasn't about to give it back now. Hell, it was too late to give it back. He'd been in contact with a woman in the university president's office and with a reporter from the *Washington Post* as well as someone from one of the less-honorable publications who was most interested in seeing what Lawrence had, even though he refused to reveal what exactly he possessed or knew about. Lawrence wanted a wider audience for Dryden's tawdry behavior than the higher-ups at the university, who would likely do all they could to keep the story quiet, even if they cut ties with the congressman. Lawrence enjoyed imagining Dryden's sexual predilections being dragged out in front of readers of the *Post, The New York Times, Boston Globe, Newsweek,* and *Time* and viewers of the political programs on MSNBC, CNN, and FOX. And how sweet it would be if he received healthy payment for the materials—remaining anonymous to the university and the general public of course.

Lawrence intended to spend his nights out of town, at a colleague's empty cottage, until he knew Mallory was on his way to London and after he had finished his initial work on the Dickens journal. But thinking of financial gain offered another scenario to ponder—one that might temper briefly his visceral dislike for Dryden and his desire to see his political career destroyed. Surely, Dryden was desperate to protect his reputation and career but he might also dread this revelation of rot in the august and puritanical Dryden-Delacroix family tree. After he listened to Dryden whine and plead with him to give over all the damning evidence, especially the video recording, he might be willing to spin the dials of his family's vault and offer a sum Lawrence might not be able to turn down. Yes, Dryden might offer him a lofty amount, but money wouldn't satisfy what it was that fueled his desire for the congressman's destruction.

"Jack?"

"I'm sorry, Sandra, I was just thinking of how deeply, deeply sorry I am that I gave you the wrong impression last night." Lawrence nervously looked out the window. Helena was agitated over his refusal to bring her the journal, and he was concerned she might drive over and cause a scene—especially since she had been so humiliated the night before. He had two minutes earlier seen a car drive slowly by, almost coming to a complete stop before it regained its modest speed. And there it was again, slowing down and then re-accelerating. Lawrence clicked off the lamp near the phone.

"Sandra, can you meet me later?"

"I have to see you now. It's very important."

"It's getting near nine. Look, I have a couple of things to do. But I'll go over to the Hendley at 11:45 tonight. Meet me on the seventh stack level. I'll have something to show you—as a peace offering. We'll leave right at midnight, I promise." He expected her to soften at the understanding that there was no change in his feelings—and particularly that he hadn't betrayed her with Helena Allingham. But her voice still reflected suspicion and lingering anger.

"Okay. But it has to be tonight. It can't wait until tomorrow. It simply can't."

"It won't, my darling. Tonight at 11:45."

She hung up without speaking further.

Unwilling to leave his valuable documents at home for fear of robbery, Lawrence grabbed the Dickens journal and the packet of evidence against Dryden and left through the back door.

Chapter 35

On early Monday evening, another several pages were taken from near the end of Dickens's journal. The section was composed a little over two years before the great novelist's death.

Today is the seventh of February 1868 and I am celebrating my fifty-sixth birthday in Washington town. I have been in America since the nineteenth of November—25 years after I first came here in 1842. My earlier criticisms of my host country are now forgiven if not forgotten. The Americans have treated me as they have no other literary personality previously—or so I am told. I have been splendidly wined and dined, and my hand has been shaken to a jelly by hundreds of well-wishers.

I had so hoped to have Ellen with me during these five months I will spend here. I think of how our relationship has grown more public over the past nine years. So much we have shared—from such innocent pleasures as visiting her London home at Houghton Place, where we would play cards and sing duets to piano accompaniment, to the more daring—traveling together from time to time, even to Paris. I still shudder remembering how we almost lost our lives in an improbable train accident, when we came upon a bridge with a stretch of track removed. We found ourselves dangling like a broken necklace over the water below. I helped rescue dearest Ellen and several others. I felt like a knight of old. Had she fallen to her death, my life too would have ended at that very moment.

My spending more time with Ellen at her home and at my residence at Gad's Hill Place in Kent have lessened the need to record my thoughts in this journal, but occasionally my passion for her and bouts of despair over our limited relationship and dim prospects for a permanent union leave me little choice but to release my feelings in a paragraph or more. I have found, though, that at times I can write merely a brief sentence or a phrase—expressing everything honestly and without any concern for decorum.

I informed Ellen I would send her a telegram to let her know if she should join me in America. I am embarrassed now over my supposed cleverness. If the message said "All well," then she should come. If it was "Safe and well," she shouldn't. Sensitive to the difficulties of her coming and the inevitable public reaction if she did, I sent the latter message. How saddened I have been over having done so.

And to add to my general state of dejection, I have been giving thought to my own mortality. I have found it more difficult to sleep through the night, and my public readings often exact their toll on my weakening frame. On one occasion I resorted to oysters and champagne to restore my flagging energy during an intermission. My left eye often throbbed with pain, as did my stomach and chest. I cannot get things right internally. I once thought that my love for Ellen would have added years to my life and my strength even in my advancing age. And yet I feel as though the intensity of my love has shortened my days and weakened my constitution. Even so, I cannot imagine my life had I not fallen in love with her.

• • •

Nichols was relieved no one was on the seventh stack level when he entered the area at 7:35 p.m. He earlier checked into the hotel and eaten a leisurely dinner, not contacting Fred Beauchamp for fear that the emeritus professor would come to the Hendley and oversee the likely futile attempt to discover any clues in *The Chimes*. Then again, Beauchamp was a most intelligent man. He might well have realized his presence would be inhibiting and therefore counterproductive. But Nichols had the uncomfortable feeling that at this very minute, Beauchamp knew exactly where he was—in the Hendley Tower.

Since it was the second Monday of August and since the summer session ended on Friday, only a few students and faculty were scattered throughout the library. In the silence of the seventh stack level Nichols expected to hear a voice calling his name. And then he imagined hearing Sandra Stark asking why he had come back. Helena Allingham demanding that he employ sophisticated thinking to find the whereabouts of the Dickens journal. His daughter questioning why he was always coming up to this *ly-berry*. Steve Ellertson threatening him if he didn't stop seeing Elizabeth. And of course, there was Elizabeth herself pleading with him to be patient while she convinced her husband to agree to a separation and divorce.

But Nichols also heard the voice of his friend Doug Finneran. Perhaps when he taught at the university, Finneran had been up here chatting with someone about the Sox or Patriots, violating what seemed to be the cloister-like silence these stacks demanded. Finally, Nichols thought he could hear Jackson Lawrence as he spoke his final words, perhaps directly to the person who would kill him. Had Lawrence known the murderer? What might he have said in the seconds before he was slain? Did he plead for his life or hasten his death with an insult? Having been in that position with Meredith several nights earlier, Nichols wished he could know. But perhaps Lawrence had no time to articulate anything at all.

• • •

Lawrence waved at a current student who was standing at the circulation desk checking out a few books. Other than his student, he had seen no one else he recognized as he entered the Hendley at 11:30 p.m.—fifteen minutes before closing time. He smiled and whispered softly, "What a hell of a way to spend your birthday, Mr. Dickens." Lawrence walked to the current periodicals section and affected an interest in a recent number of the *Dickens Quarterly,* which he had just agreed to edit for two years beginning in July. He'd already talked to Sandra Stark about helping him with the increased correspondence his editorial duties would demand. After a few minutes, he headed to the west side stairwell of the Hendley Tower and began his climb to the seventh stack level.

In his hand he carried a folder containing the Dickens journal belonging to Helena Allingham. In the folder were also the incriminating photographs of Stuart Dryden examining his pornographic stash and of Dryden alone with the woman Coy Mallory had hired to seduce the scholar. In his pocket was the video thumb drive which left no doubt as to Dryden's betrayal of his wife and family and his unusual sexual preferences. Lawrence refused to leave any of the evidence at home. It would stay with him until he handed everything over to those who could do Dryden the worst damage. Evidence for which Dryden would give all he owned to have in his possession so he could destroy it. There was a warm flush of power in that realization. When he began ascending the stairs, Lawrence felt the heat of his body also rising. He stopped and removed his heavy coat, wrapping it around the folder.

Arriving at the seventh stack level, he traversed the entire area, checking for the presence of anyone else. He knew Sandra wouldn't be there, because she was always punctual to the minute and wouldn't step out of the elevator until exactly 11:45 p.m. However, there was someone else he feared might be present, and for reassurance he felt for the .32 caliber pistol in the lower pocket of his sports coat. God forbid he would have to use it here, of all places. But the entire stack level was vacant as usual, except for the hundreds of venerable books standing like rigid ancient monoliths very few had ever beheld.

The first deeply passionate kiss he had shared with Sandra Stark was up here—in the aisle where the superannuated Dickens editions and other volumes devoted to Victorian literature were interred. Weeks later, he asked her to accompany him again to the seventh level to see a very unusual early twentieth-century facsimile of Dickens's *Oliver Twist*, which had one of the chapters—number 47—bound completely upside down. He told her, "Since you are destined for a sterling career in the Hendley, you ought to know about this volume."

When they arrived at the seventh stack level, Lawrence ceremoniously pulled out the volume, and Sandra was delighted to look upon this bibliographical anomaly. The chapter from *Twist* was titled "Fatal Consequences" and included the murder of Nancy by the villain Bill Sikes. Again with flair, Lawrence flipped the volume upside down so that Sandra could see the section of the tale that someone had circled and marked with the words "This is my favorite chapter in all of Dickens!" The inscription didn't include a name, but added to it was the date of November 14, 1932. Lawrence skimmed several pages until he came to the dramatic finale of the chapter. He began to read the denouement in a menacing whisper.

"Sikes sat regarding her, for a few seconds, with dilated nostrils and heaving breast; and then, grasping her by the head and throat, dragged her into the middle of the room, and looking once towards the door, placed his heavy hand upon her mouth." Lawrence lightly placed his hand across Sandra's lips. "You know, you she-devil! You were watched tonight; every word you said was heard."

Lawrence removed his hand and with a seamless and complete change of character requested that she read one brief section of Nancy's plea for her own life. "Do it as though you were about to die, my dear Ms. Stark."

Little experienced in the dramatic arts, Sandra nevertheless felt some of Nancy's alarm at the moment before her murder. Sandra's body began to shake as Lawrence again assumed the character of Sikes. Her voice quivered naturally as she read.

"Bill, Bill, for dear God's sake, for your own, for mine, stop before you spill my blood! I have been true to you, upon my guilty soul I have!"

Lawrence took the volume and finished the chapter.

"The housebreaker freed one arm and grasped his pistol. He beat it twice with all the force he could summon, upon the upturned face that almost touched his own. She staggered and fell: nearly blinded with the blood that rained down from a deep gash in her forehead. It was a ghastly figure to look upon. The murderer staggering backward to the wall seized a heavy club and struck her down."

Lawrence closed the volume and returned it to the stacks. Sandra's expression remained as it had been throughout the impromptu reading. Apprehension, amazement, and desire fought vigorously over the terrain of her face.

Finally, Lawrence dropped his frightening persona and smiled benevolently. "Sandra, I want you to know that I understand the meaning behind the books and stories you are drawn to—as well as the

Wagner. Your own take on the damsels and *squires*. You remember I said my deepest feeling lies in the phrase "Lean Airy Outlaw"?

Her passions intensified, she could barely get the words out. "Yes, another of your anagrams, isn't it?"

"It is. Here let me translate it." After he whispered the restructured phrase to her, "You are all I need," he lifted her head and kissed her passionately.

CHAPTER 36

The yellow legal pad still rested where Nichols had last seen it on Thursday. He pulled down the "Christmas Stories" volume and found the opening pages of *The Chimes*. Taking the volume and the legal pad, he searched for a table at which to work. It occurred to him that he hadn't noticed any furniture on his previous visits to the seventh stack level. He made his way down to the very end of the aisle to the wall farthest from the elevator. There was a single short table flush against the wall and a lone chair pushed under the table. Nichols imagined these two pieces were holdovers from at least the 1940s if not earlier. The original light brown color of the table was now pocked and streaked with the darkened signs of age, use, and neglect. Nichols looked for graffiti and what else might reveal the table's history, but there wasn't a single marking written or carved into the wood. He imagined he was only one of a handful who had ever used this table since it was first placed there.

He pulled out the chair and sat, looking over his shoulder down the aisle he had just traversed. Reopening the volume and removing a pen from his pocket as he flipped the top sheet of the legal pad, Nichols was ready to record whatever hints he came across in the text. The illumination on the table was slightly better than it was anywhere else on the seventh stack level, owing to the natural light from the setting sun coming through the window directly above where he was sitting. But the window was narrow and placed very high on the wall. It was almost as if the architect didn't want any users peering out at the campus when they ought to be focusing on the academic task at hand. Or was it that the architect didn't want anyone peering in? Nichols looked straight ahead into a faded gray wall also scarred by age. Behind him were the stacks of neglected books. He believed it impossible that he could have felt any more claustrophobic—or vulnerable.

Nichols turned to the two blood-stained pages for any clue regarding the identity of his killer or, far less likely, the location of the Dickens journal. On first glance there seemed to be no evidence of Lawrence's marking a particular word or phrase with his finger. And how could there be any, Nichols thought? The man was bleeding to death. It was a miracle he was able to open the volume to the page he did—if he really intended to locate this particular section—and make the odd check mark across the two pages. A miracle? Might Lawrence's actions have simply been a reaction to the trauma of the moment, a response devoid of any intentions? Or might Lawrence have intended to leave a clue but was unable to open the book to where the clue lay. These two blood-streaked pages, then, might have merely been the place where he opened the book and dragged his finger. It might have been nothing more than that.

But Nichols had to continue on the assumption that the two pages did hold a clue of some kind—again, likely identifying the assailant who might have killed Lawrence merely to obtain the Dickens journal. If the assailant had another motive for killing him, then he probably took the manuscript after dispatching the professor. Resigned to his task, Nichols began jotting down words and phrases that might give him something to go on.

The Chimes was divided into four sections Dickens named "quarters," to suggest the quarter chimes of a clock. The bloody two pages were in the "Second Quarter." Near the top of the left-hand page, Nichols read, "'Bless him for a noble gentleman!' thought Trotty." A "noble gentleman"? Might the killer have been titled? Perhaps an academic colleague from Britain? But then Nichols came upon the passage, "My friend the Poor Man, has no business with anything of that sort, and nothing of that sort has any business with him. My friend the Poor Man, in my district, is my business. No man or body of men has any right to interfere between my friend and me." Was the assailant poor or downtrodden—or an untenured colleague? Nichols surprised himself by thinking first of his own murdered friend Doug Finneran. He refused to ponder further that connection and turned to the last sentence which suggested anger at anyone who would come between the narrator and this friend. Was there a disagreement between Lawrence and someone in the university hierarchy about a younger untenured colleague? Nichols frowned. Or could it have been about a student? A female student?

Nichols now allowed his imagination free rein. Had Lawrence and someone outranking him in the university been rivals for a young woman—a colleague or student? Given what he'd learned about Lawrence, such a scenario seemed more than possible. Nichols read on: "'Nice children, indeed, Sir Joseph!' said the lady, with a shudder. 'Rheumatisms, and fevers, and crooked legs, and asthmas, and all kinds of horrors!'"

Could this passage also be a clue to the identity of the killer? A man with physical and respiratory difficulties? Nichols shook his head. He knew he was trying too hard to make each of these passages serve as a clue not only to the identity of the killer but also to the narrative of Lawrence's social activities right before his death.

To relieve tension, Nichols massaged his neck muscles as he read the passage at the bottom of the page. "I do my duty as the Poor Man's Friend and Father; and I endeavour to educate his mind, by inculcating on all occasions the one great moral lesson which that class requires." The passage reminded him that the object of the narrator's concern was masculine and not feminine. Nichols's energies sagged. He was hoping a young woman was involved and that a rival had killed Lawrence and likely took the Dickens journal as an afterthought. Yes, it was possible Lawrence still meant a young woman, even though Dickens writes a "Poor Man," but only possible and not at all probable.

Ignoring the inner voice chiding him for this futile exercise, Nichols forced himself to read further: "If wicked and designing persons tell them otherwise, and they become impatient and discontented, and are guilty of insubordinate conduct and black-hearted ingratitude; which is undoubtedly the case." Although the passage might be relevant to the identity of the assailant, it didn't say much more than the killer was "wicked and designing" and guilty of "black-hearted ingratitude."

The right-hand page seemed to have nothing more substantial, except for one sentence: "Alderman observes (very properly) that he is determined to put this sort of thing down; and that if it will be agreeable to me to have Will Fern put down, he will be happy to begin with him." Nichols jotted down the names "Alderman" and "Fern." He would look in the campus directory for anyone with those last names and determine who served on local councils at the time of Lawrence's death. The rest of the second page included a four-line verse about loving "our occupations" and knowing "our proper stations."

Nichols dropped his pen on the legal pad. It was almost laughable—the whole thing. It would take time and much research to follow this trail, even if it were one. Would Lawrence have been that esoteric? Finding an authentic clue seemed more and more impossible.

But Nichols's stubbornness pushed him to come at the two pages in *The Chimes* from a different angle. Beauchamp had mentioned Lawrence's fascination with acronyms and anagrams. Nichols looked once more at the four verse lines.

O let us love our occupations,
Bless the squire and his relations,
Live upon our daily rations,
And always know our proper stations.

What of the beginning letters of each line serving as an acronym? O-B-L-A.

Four letters in a last name—possibly a first? The sound of Nichols's laughter echoed through the stacks. Popping into his head was the Beatles' song "Obla-di, Obla-da" from the White Album. Lawrence would likely have known of the album and the song, even though the tune was first heard in 1968, seven or more years before Lawrence was born. After all, if Nichols knew it... He ran through the lyrics of the song for names. There were two. Desmond and Molly Jones. Nichols wrote both names on his legal pad. For a moment he satisfied himself with the thought that he'd find a colleague or university administrator named Desmond and some proof that Lawrence taught a student named Molly at the time of or soon before his murder. If either had the last name of

Jones all the better. He also jotted down the entire four lines so he could run them by an online anagram arranger for anything else that might be relevant. Still, he couldn't resist attempting to rearrange at least one of the words. He took "stations," the last word in the four-line stanza and spaced the letters on the legal pad. He wasn't all that good at it, but he enjoyed anagrams if the word was short enough. But he cursed at what he came up with: *stain sot*, *oats snit*, and *ass it not*. Flushed with frustration, Nichols knocked the yellow legal pad off the table. "What the hell am I doing?"

Nichols stood and jerked the chair away from the table. He was about to close the book, return it to the shelf, and leave the library. He had already spent too much damned fruitless time in Hendley Tower.

But after standing, the slightly increased distance gave him a different perspective on the odd check mark Lawrence made in blood. Nichols placed his own finger on where the bloody mark began and then where it changed direction—and finally where it ended. Had he been wrongly looking for evidence of a slight rise on the line under one or two of the words. Nichols eyes magnified. "Oh, Jesus Christ."

CHAPTER 37

Dryden tossed the cell phone on the front seat of his car. He was going to enter the Hendley with the same feelings of purpose and dread he experienced the previous winter. It was much earlier in the evening than it was on the seventh of February. Earlier, he learned that Nichols was inside the library. Dryden assumed the young scholar was on the seventh stack level searching for the clues Lawrence likely left behind regarding the location of a treasured manuscript. The caller had implied as much. But it was what Nichols might also discover that had Dryden so anxious. Was it possible the incriminating evidence of his peculiar sexual appetites remained hidden somewhere *within* the Hendley? At the very least, he was certain the library contained either the direct information or a clue regarding where that could be found or to whom it was given six months earlier.

Wearing a ball cap pulled low on his head and a pair of non-prescription glasses, he stepped from his car and slid the cowhide sheath on his belt further rearward, so that it rested three or four inches past the point of his right hip. He checked to see that his sports coat didn't catch and bunch up on the sheath. The blade measured five inches long. It wasn't exactly what he brought with him on that February night, but it would do. Checking the traffic, Dryden made his way across the street and toward the entrance of the Hendley.

• • •

Elizabeth tried Nichol's cell phone a second time. It went immediately to his voice mail.

"Jeremy, it's me. 7:20 p.m. Please call me right away. It's important. I love you. Bye."

She pressed her fingers to her temple attempting to relieve the pressure of her splitting headache. Something wasn't right. She thought she might have been too blindly trusting this time. Soon after she shared the information, she wondered why it was so important that she give it. She didn't like the intensity of the caller's request. What was going on? She needed to talk to someone but didn't feel she could speak with Caitlin about her confusion or her fears. Yes, her fears. Why did she have to tell the caller everything? But she knew. She told him everything because she always had.

• • •

The night of February 7th, Jackson Lawrence checked his pocket watch for the time and felt once more for the .32. He wasn't trained to use firearms. Nor was he ever expected to be. He was merely to share information about visiting or permanent faculty of foreign birth who might be of interest to his government. How he got that information was his own business. Without doubt, he was good at it, whether he charmed someone to speak more candidly than prudently or whether he employed others—usually unknowingly—to gather information for him. He had even asked his young lover Sandra Stark to unlock the study carrel of an Iranian graduate student and take an inventory of what was lying on the small desk inside. He didn't require her to read anything or to open any notebooks, but merely to tell him what she saw. He explained that a colleague in the History department was concerned the young man was plagiarizing parts of his dissertation and that he wanted to satisfy himself that such suspicions were unwarranted. Sandra accepted the explanation and gave a cursory report of what she saw.

No, Lawrence had never fired a pistol. Fred Beauchamp had, but not that often. Coy Mallory, on the other hand, would wax poetically—at least for him—about the assorted weapons he carried when he worked for the government. Based on Mallory's colorful and graphic tales, Jackson understood that his younger friend and former student had shot three men and stabbed another to death. And now Lawrence saw the possibility that within minutes he would have to use the unfamiliar weapon in his pocket to save his own life, even though he at best hoped to use the weapon to deter and at worse only to wound.

Lawrence opened his pocket watch. 11:37 p.m. Sandra would meet him in less than ten minutes. He finally conceded to the idea he had formulated while climbing the west stairwell of the Hendley. He pulled down the volume of Dickens' Christmas books. The previous week, while waiting for Sandra to join him, he searched for a quotation in *The Chimes* he wished to use for his next article on Dickens. He wasn't sure where it was exactly, so he flipped through several pages until he came to the section in which the character Trotty speaks of being "the Poor Man's Friend and Father." Lawrence grinned at Trotty's line, "I endeavor to educate his mind." He had shared it with his young lover during a playful moment—before, that is, she discovered him alone with Helena Allingham.

As Lawrence looked over to the next page, his eye settled on two words having relevance to his situation with Sandra and then on a phrase at the end of the four-line poem—"And always know our proper stations"—which gave him further pause. He determined that, should something happen to him tonight, he had to leave a clue so that Sandra could locate Coy Mallory's potentially explosive evidence about Stuart Dryden's sexual antics and preferences. Lawrence placed a pen between the two pages and closed the volume around it. He placed the volume back on the shelf, and walked a short distance down the aisle with the Dickens journal still wrapped in his winter coat, and arbitrarily stopped in front of another section of books.

Lawrence knew prudence was only one reason for deciding to leave clues. His love of puzzles and games and anything cryptic also encouraged his actions. When he returned to the section where the superannuated Christmas Books volume was sitting, he thought about leaving another two clues as to the identity of the person who just might try to kill him. He'd already spotted the clues on the two pages of *The Chimes* he examined—although no one else but Sandra Stark would understand them. He simply had to figure out how best to mark the clues so she would find them.

• • •

Helena Allingham sat in the hotel lounge nursing her cocktail. From her table, she could plainly see the lights of the Hendley Tower now that the sun had set. Six months had passed, but the memory of what she felt that February night was impossible to suppress. As a teenager she occasionally entertained thoughts of violence against several boys who played with her sexually and then ridiculed her to others. And there were the dark imaginings of her father's death, occasionally by her own hand. But nothing before or since compared to the hatred she felt for Jackson Lawrence on the evening of February 6 and the entire next day and night.

Following Lawrence's death, she tempered the intensity of these violent thoughts against those who used her cruelly. Yet, in aftermath of the loss of the Dickens journal, she periodically contemplated suicide. Fred Beauchamp had saved her, she believed. It was Beauchamp who finally encouraged her to stop actively hating the young woman she believed was her rival, Sandra Stark, and Beauchamp brought them together in late May for lunch and some honest conversation about past feelings and their respective impressions of what happened on the night of February 6. Helena remembered the disappointment on Beauchamp's face when neither woman wished to talk about that time or their feelings for each other. But at least he was pleased by the cautious cordiality the women extended to each other.

Helena never wavered from the belief that Beauchamp had been the most important man in her life. In spite of their chronological and racial differences, she was certain she would have married him if he had asked. But he served the role of loving and forgiving father to her, which she long ago acknowledged was what she needed most.

Now inside the tower of the Hendley Library was a young Dickensian scholar searching for whatever clue Jackson Lawrence might have left behind relating to the location of the journal. She had several times been to the seventh stack level to search for herself—but to no avail. Months earlier she tried to accept that the journal would never again be in her possession and that she needed to stop longing for its return. But all her attempts to divorce her mind from the manuscript only made her want more desperately to have it again in her hands. Should she find it now, the deceased women in her family, even Mary Bertram, would understand what had happened. Surely, they would forgive her. She dreaded to think what would happen if they didn't.

• • •

Nichols continued to stare at the peculiar check mark Lawrence traced with his own blood. It started on the second word of one of the lines on the left-hand page, "Every quarter-day he will be put in communication with Mr. Fish." The trail of Lawrence's finger then went diagonally downward to the bottom of the page and across several more lines of text, ending at the beginning of the words "I am their Friend and Father still. It is so Ordained. It is in the nature of things." The line going down to this place was jagged, as if Lawrence was having difficulty making the mark. That was the first elongated diagonal line of the odd check-mark configuration.

The longer line angling up and to the right cut across to a place a little down from the top of the second page, resting on the phrase "at the house of our mutual friend, Deedles." Nichols rapidly nodded his head up and down at his epiphany. The odd check mark made by Lawrence's index finger with his own blood began on the word "quarter" and ended on the phrase "our mutual friend." Nichols concluded that Lawrence was identifying the fourth volume of Dickens's 1865 novel *Our Mutual Friend*.

Nichols left the Dickens volume on the single study table and walked rapidly back into the stacks, locating the section housing the moldy editions of the 1865 novel. It was in the next section past the one that contained the Christmas books. There were several antiquated editions of Dickens's last completed work, two of which Nichols handled in other research libraries. He pulled down the fourth volume of the first set he came to and began sifting through the pages for anything that hinted at being a clue to the murder's identity or to the location of the Dickens journal. The first three examinations offered nothing. Could it be that the clue was in a character name in *Our Mutual*

Friend? Or a location? Or a plot device? Once again, Nichols felt overwhelmed by the task before him.

He reached for the fourth volume of the next edition on the shelves. This one was published in Leipzig in 1864-65. Nichols could see that this edition—in English—was published with copyright for Continental circulation. Volume four of this edition was in particularly bad shape. The binding was torn, the edges of the pages discolored and clotted with the remnant of some liquid. It seemed to Nichols as though the edition had been dropped into a pond, retrieved, and left to dry by its own devices. As he opened the volume, the odor was unmistakable. The dank smell of age and disuse. Nichols noticed that past midpoint of the volume, a series of pages had melded together at the bottom edges. This edition had obviously been ignored for a very long time. Nichols had occasionally come across two pages similarly stuck together by moisture and the subsequent drying process and he'd always carefully run his finger between the pages and broken the unintended seal. But the series of pages in this volume had formed a bulging pocket. Nichols opened to the section and saw that he could place four of his fingers down into the pocket from the top of the book. His quirky habit of straightening all folded corners and pages in the volumes he consulted prompted him to do so now. As he placed his fingers into the pocket, he felt loose paper.

Nichols brought the unsightly edition back to his table and pulled out several loose pages—all of them small, three by five inches in size, made even smaller by having been folded in half. He reached into the pocket again and retrieved several photographs and a computer thumb drive. He had already unfolded each and spread the loose sheets on the table when he heard a metallic click behind him.

"Don't move a muscle, Professor Nichols. Now shut your eyes tight and lower your head toward the table." After doing as he was told, Nichols felt the barrel of a pistol pressing forcefully into the back of his head.

CHAPTER 38

This time the intention wasn't to pull pages indiscriminately; rather it was to read the final pages of the unknown journal in Dickens hand. It was impossible to ignore how much this literary treasure might bring at auction. The reader knew that a single sheet December 1863 letter from Dickens had sold for close to fourteen thousand dollars at Christie's and another letter went for over nine thousand. How much, then, might this incredible journal command? But the reader knew the journal would never be offered to the public.

I write again after neglecting this journal for so long. It is the 7th of February 1870, and today I turn fifty-eight years of age.

In spite of my ailments and fatigue, I have remained insistent on projecting dramatic intensity into my public readings. I have added a violent scene from Oliver Twist, in which the villain Sikes brutally murders Nancy. Friends and family have begged me not to read it again for fear of the toll it might take on my health, but I remain insistent on including it. I have even joked about the need to release my murderous instincts. But more depressing to family and friends are the signs of paralysis on my left side. I wonder if the forthcoming fall lecture tour might not in fact finish me.

At Christmas I made arrangements with dear Mary Bertram to keep my journal when I felt I could write no more in it. Since my return from America two years ago, my relationship with Ellen has undergone an alteration. I have, for months, questioned whether my deep feelings for her have not been misplaced. After today, I will say no more about her in this journal. I simply cannot bear the thought of recording anything that speaks of the end of my love for her or hers for me.

London, Edinburgh, Belfast, and Dublin have all delighted in my readings, and in each I taxed my strength to the utmost, especially with the murder scene from ***Twist****. I cannot help wondering if I have been attempting to kill myself through exhaustion these past two years. I wonder if I was also trying to kill my love for Ellen by putting such effort into depicting for an audience the death of Nancy.*

Last summer I entered into an agreement for a new book. In October I read to one of my friends the opening chapters of ***The Mystery of Edwin Drood****. What a tale to choose for what may be my last book—an exquisitely lovely heroine and a madly jealous and potentially murderous villain, who has an inordinate desire for opium.*

I have written my will and have left Ellen Ternan a thousand pounds "free of legacy." I am well aware that a public airing of the bequest will raise public ire after my death—but I hardly care. Of my other bequests, I have arranged to have my dear friend Forster receive the manuscripts of all my novels. And to Mary Bertram I have left several books she has long admired, and I have added "What I have given her she may keep under the terms previously agreed to." She now possesses a letter expressing what I want her to do with this journal, which I will now place in a box and never open again.

Secured to the last page of Dickens's journal were two additional sheets in a woman's hand—that belonging to Mary Bertram, as the prefatory notation revealed.

Dr. Beard came to every one of Mr. Dickens's final readings to check his pulse rate, which elevated dangerously the more dramatic the scene was that he performed. On one occasion, it took Mr. Dickens a full ten minutes of lying prone on a sofa at intermission before he could speak an intelligible sentence. On March 15, 1870 he looked at his public audience, among whom I sat, for the last time, tears well visible in his eyes. He said to all of us, "I now vanish forevermore, with a heartfelt, grateful, respectful, affectionate farewell."

During the final months of his life, Mr. Dickens remained active. He saw the Queen, socialized with friends, gave receptions, and presided over dinners. He continued working on his Drood book, publishing several installments by late spring. He moreover took charge of an amateur theatrical at the home of friends, rehearsing his eager cast, and I feared then that the experience opened the door to the memory of his initial meeting with Ellen.

On Wednesday June 8th he wrote on his novel all day—he did not take his usual walk—and he composed several letters, one of which quoted Friar Lawrence from **Romeo and Juliet**: *"These violent delights have violent ends." Before long, his devoted sister-in-law Georgina noticed a look of pain on his face. He stood up and said he had to go to London at once. But he began to collapse and would have fallen had she not gotten to him in time. Dr. Beard and Dickens's daughters Mary and Katey arrived to find their father lying unconscious on the sofa. The paralytic stroke predicted for months had finally paid its unwelcomed call. Georgina wondered why her father wanted to go to London. Who was it he wanted to see, she asked?*

In the afternoon, Ellen Ternan looked down at the man whom she had loved and comforted for over ten years. I know, for I accompanied her to the Gad's Hill house. It was apparent she did not feel the same as she had when she first wished to be in his company and desired to give him all that he could not receive from his wife. Now thirty-one, she knew that in a matter of hours she would finally be free to marry and to bear her own children. She turned and looked at me. We had been friends, but we had never shared anything intimate. She knew that Mr. Dickens had destroyed all correspondence he had received from her, and Ellen was certain that she would soon burn whatever she still possessed. Everyone would guess but no one would ever fully know the depths of his love for her.

Several hours later, the great novelist Charles Dickens expelled a soft sigh and died. It was a little past six o'clock in the evening on June 9, 1870.

• • •

Lawrence glanced at the elevator. The doors were closed. It was 11:52 p.m. He stepped back to the Dickens section and took another look at the superannuated Christmas Books volume resting on the shelf just above his head. The Dickens journal lay on the rolling step unit, still wrapped in his winter coat. "Come on, my beautiful Sandra. Please don't tell me you've changed your mind." He looked down and across the aisle and found it amazing that after over twenty-five consecutive years in a university setting—as both student and professor—he still had a visceral reaction whenever he felt surrounded by books, especially those of more ancient vintage. They made him feel both secure and unsettled—the "womb and tomb" dynamic he often mentioned to his students.

At that very moment, Sandra sat in her car, which was parked across the street from the Hendley. Shaking from the February cold, she gently touched the tears trespassing on her beautiful face. Her deep hurt over Lawrence's betrayal with the English student Helena Allingham had drained almost all her strength until finally at 11:55 p.m. she managed to shut off the engine and open the driver-side door. As she headed across the street to the Hendley, she looked up at the tower. It had never appeared so menacing.

CHAPTER 39

I assume you've examined the photographs and noted the thumb drive, right Professor Nichols?"

"No, I just put them on the table. I didn't have a chance to look at anything."

"Keep your hands spread on the table. Spread them wider. Wider!" Nichols winced from the pressure of the gun barrel driving into the back of his head. He stretched his arms further across the table. Again, his body was painfully contorted by someone apparently about the kill him. The increasing tightness of his neck muscles made articulation difficult.

"What the hell do you want? If it's the thumb drive and the photos, then take them. I haven't seen your face or even looked at the photos."

The man laughed. "I'm not as poorly educated as you might think I am. Please don't insult my intelligence."

"All right, I know they're of a sexual nature, but I didn't recognize either the man or the woman."

The pressure from the gun barrel lessened. Then it no longer touched his head, but Nichols knew it was only an inch or two away. He lifted his head slightly with the release of the gun barrel's pressure.

"Look, I promise you I haven't identified anyone in the photos or read the notes. Just take what you want and go. I'll stay right where I am for the next hour if you want."

"Oh, I'm sure you will."

"I'll keep my eyes closed until you've gone. How the hell could I identify you? Jesus, man. Think about it."

"Don't tell me you don't know who I am."

"I *don't* know. How could I know?" Nichols felt the gun barrel lightly brush against the nape of his neck.

"Elizabeth hasn't told you, is that what you're trying to say? You've been seeing her on the sly for months and you recently brought here from New York just to sleep with her, correct? Oh, and I'm sure she hasn't told you about her loving family—right?"

"Family? Jesus Christ, what are you talking about?" Nichols had immediately ruled out Steve Ellertson as the man standing behind him. The two voices were nothing alike. Was this Ellertson's brother, then? A close friend? Someone Ellertson hired who wished to indulge a twisted wit?

"I'm sure she's mentioned me to you."

"Are you Steve's brother?"

"Don't fucking insult me, Nichols. Anyway, were you not such a super academic sleuth, you'd be thanking me right now for removing that little impediment from your life."

Nichols felt his fingers curling into fists. He immediately straightened them again. He couldn't risk being shot. Not like this. Thinking of his precarious situation several nights earlier, he wondered if this man wasn't somehow connected to Meredith Jamison.

"What do you mean removing an impediment? What impediment?"

"Let's just say that poor Steve went a little too far and tried to run away without being punished. Let's also just say he had an unfortunate traffic accident. Oh, with a little assistance from yours truly. But what does it matter now? I'm afraid you now won't have the chance to marry my beautiful niece, the former Elizabeth Mallory."

"You're her uncle?"

The man laughed. "Very good deduction, Nichols. Your PhD has finally come in handy."

"You brought her here when she was a teenager."

"And I hurt her arm. I've whipped myself often for that, I can assure you. I made a vow that no one would ever harm her without a visit from me."

Nichols recalled what Elizabeth told him earlier. "Your brother broke his leg skiing, and you visited Elizabeth and her mother. A trip here to the Hendley and then ice-cream."

"So she did tell you about me. But not all about me, it seems. Well, that's understandable. For one thing, she doesn't know exactly what I used to do for a living—when she was in high school. I had a daredevil of a much older brother, true. But I also had a sister-in-law I was sexually attracted to, even though she was thirteen years my senior. The forbidden fruit of my life, which I tasted on three occasions before she convinced me we needed to stop. As for my niece, I've been crazy about her since I first laid eyes on her, and although I haven't always been physically present in her life, she knew I was always there for her and that there was nothing I wouldn't do for her. And that includes avenging any wrong done *to* her."

"You think I've harmed her in some way?"

"You're not paying attention, Nichols. I meant her husband, the husky music professor. Frankly, I was happy she was in love with another man. That being you. She's been giving me progress reports on your relationship for several months now."

"How did you know I was here? Have you been following me?"

"Elizabeth told me where you were."

"Elizabeth?"

"Now don't worry, Nichols. She didn't betray you. She doesn't know anything about these little old photos lying spread out on the table—or about the reason I want them and the thumb drive that goes along with them. She just told me that Steve roughed her up. She didn't want you to know. I simply asked where you were, and she told me. She wondered whether your visits here and my visit with her seventeen years ago were related in some way. Related." Mallory again laughed. "That's what she said. Related. Anyway, she doesn't yet know that her husband's no longer a worry in her life. But it's a god-damn shame that it can't all work out. I'd give anything not to have to do this, Nichols, but a very important person can't afford to have these photos and video get out. And I can't afford not to get the amount he's giving me to get them back."

"I keep telling you I don't recognize who the man and woman are. I don't know what they're about. Just take them. Then they won't get out."

"Now, now. You have to say that to stay alive—right? Oh, and please don't resort to cliché and tell me that you won't tell anyone that you didn't read the back of at least one of the photos and see the name of the man and the date of the "event" depicted in each shot.

Nichols knew the man was starting to lose his composure. The tone of his voice was providing considerable evidence of impatience and anxiety.

"Look, for Elizabeth's sake, don't do this. Think. Think what this might do to her."

"She'll survive. She'll see that moving away and starting a new life is the best course. She's a beautiful woman. Only thirty. She'll find love again before too long. You see, I'm giving her complete freedom from her past. Something I've never quite had. Now stand up. But keep your arms extended and move them slowly toward the center of the table and then clench your hands together."

Nichols guessed the man had stepped back toward the last stack of books. Nichols began slowly to bring his hands together until he finally intertwined his fingers.

"I just can't believe the irony—or is it coincidence—that you'll be the second person I've killed up here on the seventh stack level of the dear, old, venerable Hendley Library."

Nichols throat constricted in shock. Elizabeth's uncle was the man who murdered Jack Lawrence. But why? How did the men know each other?

"Now get up and back away from the table and keep your arms extended. Slowly. Slowly. Don't turn around."

Nichols began to push the chair rearward with the back of his legs. He realized that now might be his only chance.

In a sudden motion he moved the chair a bit further with his legs and immediately brought the bottom of his foot up to the chair's edge and shoved it behind him as forcefully as he could. Mallory cried out in pain as the chair caught him in the shin and knee. Tightly wired, he fired his weapon, but he had lost his aiming point. The bullet bore into the wall above the study table.

Nichols had already begun running down a long aisle of books toward the stairwell and elevator. He could hear the man running with difficulty toward him, cursing from the pain. Nichols knew he'd never make it to the elevator or stairwell without taking a round in the back. He jumped to his right and down one of the adjacent aisles of books. He thought he heard books dropping behind him and then the sound of the elevator doors.

He couldn't believe it. The man was leaving the seventh stack level.

Perhaps Elizabeth's uncle was only trying to frighten him. Or perhaps he'd lost his nerve. Nichols barely got a glimpse of the man when he shoved the chair behind him and turned to run, but Nichols could see he was only slightly past his prime physically, yet a time when caution and prudence had more veto power over an impulsive act. Nichols stopped before reaching the end of the aisle. He caught sight of some of the titles of the books on the shelves to his right and left. He had run right past the Dickens collection where he had found the edition of *Our Mutual Friend* and the volume including *The Chimes.* Peculiarly, he gave a moment's thought to going back and collecting the photos and thumb drive from the table, but he assumed the man had scooped them up and taken them with him into the elevator. Nichols decided to descend by way of the stairwell, but very slowly, making sure that the man had time enough to leave the Hendley ahead of him.

Nichols turned. Mallory was standing no more than ten feet away, the pistol aimed at the bridge of Nichols's nose. Nichols looked down at Mallory's lower leg and saw the blood seeping through the khaki pants.

"Close your eyes, Nichols."

Jeremy knew he'd have no chance to defend himself now. He felt more fatigue than ever in his life. He hated that he was conceding, but he couldn't fight it. His eyes closed involuntarily. He wondered whether he too would, like Jack Lawrence, grab at a volume when he was falling mortally wounded.

The shot was true. Nichols opened his eyes and saw the man lurching toward him. Mallory's face appeared gentle, his expression resigned. He fell to the floor, directly in the center of the narrow aisle. None of the books on either shelf unit were disturbed. Nichols looked up toward the end of the aisle and saw the detached expression on the face of Fred Beauchamp.

CHAPTER 40

Two hours later, Beauchamp and Nichols were seated in the hotel lounge across from the Hendley. It was just past ten, but the activity in front of the library was considerable. Students and locals had been milling around the front door, as if they expected at any moment for the police to stand aside and allow them access so they could run up the stairs and see where another killing had taken place on the seventh stack level of the mysterious and haunted structure.

Nichols kept his eyes on Hendley Tower, which was streaked with lights in odd configurations, from the few narrow windows in the tower itself to the lights shining from below. Automobile headlights and blue lights from police vehicles were supplemented by flashlights in the hands of the curious throng waiting outside the library. The sound of sirens cutting on and off added further grimness to the moment. But the Hendley seemed implacable and serene, even comfortable in the intense and austere glow of the lights and the attention it was presently receiving.

"Jeremy, I'm going to think awhile on what to do with the photos and thumb drive I *purloined* from the table." Nichols smiled at Beauchamp's choice of the 'Poean' verb. "I assumed that if I ever found them—or rather if *you* located them, I'd hand them over to a reputable publication. I always felt it was my responsibility to do so. That's why I said you could do your country a service by locating the Dickens' manuscript. But I did mislead you, my boy, and I feel awful for having done so. And to think that I've just killed a man I used to call a friend—a man Jack Lawrence and I used to call a friend. But Coy was someone who at heart had more self-interest than integrity. He never spent much time pondering right and wrong. I hoped that when he left the agency, he'd monitor his decisions and actions more cautiously—but that just wouldn't have been him."

"Fred, I'm not sure I understand the exact nature of Mallory's work for the agency, his connection to Jackson Lawrence, and why he felt he really had to kill me."

"I'll try to make more sense of it for you in the days ahead. God willing, we'll be together often enough the next three years."

"So, what are you really going to do with the photos and thumb drive?"

"The easiest thing would be to let the police have them. They have to consider a motive why he wanted to kill you, right? But on the other hand, I still feel it's my responsibility to prevent a despicable person from climbing any higher in government than he has. I fear the police would bury the evidence to protect him. I'd like a little more time to think about the matter, so I have to ask for your cooperation."

"Fred, I can't lie to the police. I can't."

"Not asking you to. Just hold back on telling all of it, that's all. From what you said a few minutes ago, Coy knew about your relationship with his niece and promised you would never have her. Besides, he's already committed murder on the seventh stack level of the Hendley—evidence of which will now come out from multiple, even if anonymous, sources. So..."

"I'm sorry to have to say this, Fred. But I can't depend on what you say about any of this."

"Why may I ask?" Beauchamp seemed not at all insulted.

"You made such a convincing case that you didn't know who killed Jackson Lawrence in February and from what you just said, you've known all along it was Coy Mallory."

Beauchamp's features constricted. "Come again?"

"You heard me, Fred. Mallory killed Lawrence. He admitted it to me—and you knew all along." Nichols reached for his wallet to pay for his drink. It was evident he was about to leave.

"Hold it, young man. Did Coy say he killed Jack Lawrence? Did he say that exactly?"

Nichols remained standing. "He said he'd already murdered someone on the seventh stack level. Who else could he have meant? Jesus, Fred. Now I've got to tell the police what you've known for six months but wouldn't reveal." Nichols voice and face reflected his deep disappointment in Beauchamp. A man he had come to like—a man who had just saved his life.

"Coy killed Professor of Comparative Literature Karl Bermann, not Professor of English Jackson Lawrence."

"What? Who?"

"I don't blame you for being confused. Sit back down and I'll explain."

Nichols reluctantly did as Beauchamp asked.

"Bermann was a colleague of ours who unfortunately did a little side work for the Russians. Seems members of his family were in the old East German *Stasi,* their official state security service. When Germany unified, these fine folks switched over to the Russians. Long story short, it seemed Bermann was carrying on the family trade as well as writing brilliantly on Schiller and Goethe. Jack and I were asked to keep an eye on him, but we made the mistake of talking about our suspicions with a young Coy Mallory—our prize student—and it he apparently wished to demonstrate he had the chops to do agency work and took it upon himself to kill Bermann in Hendley Tower, making it look like Bermann himself blew his brains out. The acceptable stories were disseminated and that was that—a tragic suicide by a gifted scholar. The university's loss and all such nonsense."

Nichols struggled for words as Beauchamp ordered another round. "But couldn't...couldn't Mallory have also killed Lawrence?"

"He was in Manhattan that evening being interviewed live about the latest Smithsonian Channel's historical program, which he narrated. He called me to insist I watch, which I did, once he told me how to live stream the New York channel. No way he could be back here leaving Manhattan at 11:30 p.m. or so. Perfect alibi, I'm afraid. Anyway, I'm asking for your discretion, while I come to a decision about what to do with the photos and thumb drive. I'm asking that you trust my judgment."

"As I told Mallory, I never saw who was in the photos."

"Oh, but Jeremy, I believe I let slip that the person is in government."

Nichols, tried unsuccessfully to suppress a smile. "So you did, Fred, but I certainly don't know what's on the thumb drive."

Beauchamp chuckled. "Good answer. You do have a future outside the classroom, if you want it. Remember. You *can* have both. I'm living proof of that."

"Right. And Jackson Lawrence is deceased proof of that."

Beauchamp now frowned. "Look at my hands. They're still shaking. I may have to ask you to hold the glass up to my lips. Firing a weapon for the first time in many years and the interview with the police about finished me. I'm just too damned old for any of this. To quote one of my favorite moments in Shakespeare, that old rascal Falstaff says to his companion, 'We have heard the chimes of midnight, Master Shallow,' to which Shallow replies, 'That we have, that we have, that we have....Jesu, the days that we have seen.'"

Nichols appreciated this particular literary allusion. "But you had no choice, Fred. He was going to kill me."

"I know. Thank you for reminding me."

"Wait. It just dawned on me. How did you know Mallory was looking for me and that you ought to come to the seventh stack level with a loaded gun?"

"I'll tell you in just a bit. Let me have a sip of this bourbon and then I can both shake at and revel in the fact that I made it up there at exactly the right moment. As they say, the essence of comedy is... timing. And so, it turns out, is life-saving."

"Fred, what can I say? You saved my life. I owe you. I owe you big time."

"Just keep thinking those happy thoughts, my boy."

Nichols finished his drink. "But we didn't find the Dickens journal." Nichols took a furtive look at Beauchamp's eyes to see if he could detect any telling sign that Beauchamp had it or knew who did, but the emeritus professor gave him nothing. "So, Fred, we don't know who killed Lawrence. Will we ever?"

Beauchamp lifted his head and looked toward the entrance, and a broad smile now appeared on his weary face. "Hello, Helena. Jeremy, I called Helena when I took a break from the police interrogation."

She gestured for the men to remain seated, but she made no motion to sit with them. "I just want to thank you for trying, Professor Nichols. I am so deeply sorry you had to go through all that."

"Fortunately, Professor Beauchamp remembered how to use..." Nichols cut himself off. He didn't want to make light of what Beauchamp had been forced to do to a man who was once a student and close friend.

"Helena and I were sitting here when I saw Coy heading toward the Hendley. It was Helena who suggested that I take the gun from her car. Oddly enough, I gave it to her earlier this year for her protection against the burgeoning criminal enterprise down in Washington. I told the police I retrieved it when I thought you might be in danger. You see, Coy called me and wanted to know if you were going back to the Hendley. I could tell by his manner that he was upset, so I wanted to keep an eye on the library's entrance to see if he showed up. It's a good vantage point here, and I thought, since Helena was in town, she might like to join me."

Nichols smiled. "I see. But I feel badly I could find no clue as to the whereabouts of the journal."

She wasn't looking at him. Her hand had taken Beauchamp's, and she was gazing at the retired professor with unqualified devotion and affection. Finally, she responded. "The journal was, no doubt, taken by the murderer last February. It surely would have been sold or offered for sale by now, but not on any open market—or we would have known. The sale price would have been astronomical. Individual letters have brought as much as five figures for a single sheet, so the entire journal would have..." She raised her head and stared intently into Nichols's eyes. "No. There's a better chance it was discarded or destroyed. I cannot spend the rest of my life dwelling on the possibility that it might be resting at the bottom of a clothing box in someone's attic or basement. And yet I will never be able to rest my conscience because it was my responsibility not to lose it." Beauchamp stood and embraced her.

Nichols parted and headed to the sidewalk outside the hotel, as a member of the police approached him. He knew he'd have to explain to Janis how she almost lost her brother for a second time. How many years would pass before he told Belinda about this night in the Hendley

Tower? And what of Elizabeth? Had she learned of her husband's death by now? And how could she understand what happened to her uncle? Who would explain to her the kind of life Mallory led beyond what she knew? Whom would she ultimately blame? Could the both of them get through all this and be with each other for the rest of their lives? Nichols only knew he would do whatever it took to make that happen. His cell phone chimed. It was Elizabeth. Although highly emotional, she informed him she'd been told about the fates of her husband and her uncle. She had just gotten off the phone with her local police and immediately afterward with Fred Beauchamp.

"It's noisy and hectic here, Elizabeth, but just know that I'm all right and that I'll call you again when I get to my hotel room. Look, the next few days are going to be rough, but we'll get through this. I love you, just know that. I'll call you back as soon as I can."

Nichols signaled to the detective that he was now ready to begin the interview. He pointed to the small coffee and sandwich shop across the street and suggested they talk there. Everyone had come out of the establishment as soon as the chaos began in front of the Hendley. The place would be quiet enough for the initial round of questions. Nichols was grateful the detective didn't insist on his going to police headquarters.

As they made their way across the street, Nichols thought again of what Elizabeth Ellertson would have to process in the days and weeks to come. She would have the deaths of her husband and her uncle to deal with, as well as what prompted Coy Mallory to visit the seventh stack level with her seventeen years earlier. She would have further interviews with the police and at least one of the government's agencies. Beyond that, she would have the trauma of her own escape from death at the hand of Meredith Jamison. As Nichols looked to the future, he realized that she would of course require some kind of counseling. He fought off the encroaching thought that she might never get far enough past everything to marry him. She was intelligent, determined, and, he believed, committed to him in her heart. He now prayed she would also be resilient. He made up his mind to follow the most commonplace advice—and take each day one at a time.

After he finished speaking with the detective, he came out on the sidewalk and took one further look at the Hendley. As he stared at the forbidding tower where two men recently died and he'd almost lost his life, he reached a decision. Regardless of all the difficulties it might cause for his career, he would try to break his agreement to teach here beginning in two weeks. If that was impossible, he would move on after this academic year.

CHAPTER 41

Among the dozens of students milling about in front of the Hendley stood Stuart Dryden. He had made it up the stairwell of the Hendley Tower, his face disguised by a thick wool scarf, and was poised to enter the seventh stack level when he heard a gunshot and then the rapid footsteps of someone running toward the stairwell, followed by the sound of profanity and a more labored movement by a second person. Dryden tried unsuccessfully to re-button the sheath that held his five-inch knife—the weapon he would have pulled on Jeremy Nichols to gain control of the incriminating evidence Lawrence had collected—should Nichols have discovered it in his search. Over the past few months, Dryden had grown deeply concerned that Lawrence left clues about the location of the damning evidence that only a Dickensian like Jeremy Nichols could unravel.

Dryden felt no different tonight than he did on that February evening six months earlier. Other than the disgrace and career damage he'd suffer as a result of this evidence getting out, the thought of sullying the name of one of the most honored families to come from this country's puritan stock was impossible for him to endure. He would have brought dishonor to his father and to the long line of Drydens who contributed so much to this part of the country and to this university and its famous library.

He moved back down the Hendley's antiquated steps as quickly as he could, reaching behind him on every landing to be sure the knife was still in the sheath. At his age, it had taken much out of him to climb the stairwell, but rapidly going down was even more exhausting. Between levels four and five, he heard the sound of a second gunshot. Beginning to panic, he bent over to draw in as much breath as he could and then continued descending. When he reached the bottom floor, he noticed only a few patrons, all of them in a complete state of confusion over what they heard from above. No one paid any attention to the man in his early sixties barely able to catch his breath, even if his face was partially covered by a heavy wool scarf. After a moment's rest, Dryden walked outside the Hendley and took up a position on one of the benches so he could see all persons leaving and what they might have in their possession. He had no idea whether Jeremy Nichols was alive or dead.

By the time the police and ambulance arrived, Dryden had seen no one exiting with anything resembling an envelope or loose photographs in their hands. He knew the photos, with his name likely written on the back of each by Jackson Lawrence, as well as the thumb drive, could be resting inside a jacket or pants pocket, but he had no choice but to keep looking for more overt evidence that someone had possession of them. While he was straining his eyes to evaluate those walking out of the Hendley, a policeman tapped him on the shoulder and pulled him to the side. Dryden's anxiety at having his attention diverted from the entrance to the Hendley made the officer suspicious, resulting in more questions than were absolutely necessary. What would he say had the officer discovered the sheathed knife in his possession? So far, the cop hadn't recognized him or ordered him to pull the scarf from the bottom of his face. But after another several seconds, the officer seemed satisfied and suggested that Dryden move along.

Fifteen minutes later, Dryden looked across the street and saw Jeremy Nichols on the sidewalk seeming to look right at him, as the younger man talked with someone on his cell phone. Dryden now became more anxious that he might be identified and so left the area without determining if the compromising material had been discovered. He reasoned he'd know soon enough.

• • •

Beauchamp arrived home and was greeted by Usher. After vigorously petting the dog, Beauchamp poured himself a stiff drink and sat in his favorite chair. His hands began to shake as he pondered what he had done tonight—especially at his advanced age. He knew he ought to call Nichols and warn him that someone else might want him dead, but how could he name Dryden—a sitting U.S. Congressman as the potential enemy. With his money, Dryden was in the position of hiring someone to do his dirty business, after all. Beauchamp could barely bring the bourbon to his lips thinking about the past twenty years, and especially the last six months. His grandfather clock struck eleven, and with each chime, he changed his mind as to whether he should inform Nichols of his fears regarding Stuart Dryden.

• • •

"Thanks for calling, Chandra. Yes, me too. I can't believe that it happened again in the same place. Yes, at least they know who this time. Well, I have to run. I'll see you tomorrow. Bye."

Sandra was barely able to maintain her composure during the conversation with her library colleague. As soon as she heard there was another killing on the seventh stack level, her mind reeled from the agonizing memory of her lover's murder in February. Surely, she would have been otherwise stunned to learn that Professor Emeritus Fred Beauchamp had pulled the trigger to save the life of the young scholar she met at the Hendley a few days earlier.

She recalled that a week after Jackson Lawrence's death, a sitting U.S. Congressman had come to the circulation desk at the Hendley with several questions. He informed her he was a former faculty member and dean, before entering politics, and was a good friend of Lawrence's. He was concerned about some scholarly materials and drafts he knew the professor was working on and asked if anyone in the library had seen or retrieved them. Maintaining her composure, she shook her head no and attempted to leave her station, but he quickly inquired if Lawrence had a study carrel, and if so, did anyone open it. If not, would she get the key and look inside for him? "I want to be sure my friend's scholarship is passed on to someone who will get it eventually published. I owe Jack that much." He seemed forlorn when she informed him that nothing had been found anywhere in the Hendley.

She had come to assume since then that Congressman Dryden knew about the Dickens manuscript and wanted to get his hands on it. Lawrence mentioned to her on several occasions that he loathed the man and wouldn't trust him to "sweep out the Hendley," let alone serve the state well as a member of Congress, especially in the Senate.

With Rob Porterfield in New York, she spent the evening alone at her place, sitting outside, sipping wine, and reading. Would she have done the same on the night of February 7th? Because she'd been careful that night to manipulate the blots of blood Lawrence left on the two open pages of Dickens's *The Chimes,* she felt the odds were long that Jeremy Nichols would find anything to identify the killer.

As the wind picked up, increasing the volume of the wind chimes, Sandra decided to finish her reading in bed. As she stepped into the living room, she passed the mirror hanging to the left of the framed Waterhouse print of the medieval knight and his lady she had taken from Lawrence's residence the night after his death. Sandra examined her hair and make-up, as if she were joining her deceased lover in bed—a peculiar act she had occasionally performed since February 7th.

Satisfied with her appearance, she placed her book and wine glass on the side table and approached a handsome bookcase which held all of Jackson Lawrence's academic books, and drew out his edition of Dickens's Christmas stories. As she pulled the green volume toward her with her left hand, her right hand reached to the bottom of the shelf unit directly behind where the book had rested. She manipulated a lever and stepped back. The section of the shelving swung open revealing a 24" x 24" fireproof wall safe she had installed some six months earlier. She pressed in the code as she had done so many times before—and every night for the past several days. She opened the door of the safe and pulled out the Dickens journal she took from the seventh stack level of the Hendley moments after the death of her lover. She had just finished reading the end of the journal; therefore, she didn't wish to pull out any more pages. Now she just wanted to touch it by rubbing her fingers lightly over Dickens's make-shift title page. Here they were—the most intimate words Charles Dickens had ever penned regarding his relationship with Ellen Ternan. Sandra knew them by heart, of course. How could she not, when she read them so often since early February?

But she never read them thinking primarily of Dickens or of his Ellen. To her mind, she was reading the impassioned confession of Jackson Lawrence regarding her. These readings of selected pages kept her relationship with Lawrence alive. At this time in her life, she was sorely dependent on doing so.

She was convinced her lover wanted her to read them and hear his voice speaking to and about her. Yes, that was why he brought the journal with him to the Hendley that night. Surely, he wanted to present her with the journal so she could keep it for the rest of her life. The journal's having once been in the possession of Helena Allingham was unimportant to Sandra now, even though that fact caused considerable anxiety in the immediate aftermath of Lawrence's death.

Sandra returned the journal to the safe and finished her wine. Finally, she swung the bookcase back into place, latching the unit with her finger. She took the green edition of Dickens's Christmas stories, kissed it once, and set it back on the shelf.

Smiling wearily, she examined the framed family portrait displayed on the living-room wall, taken when she was fourteen. Her mother and step-father sat on the sofa with Sandra and her step-siblings standing behind them. Aubrey, the summer-loving swimmer now at Dartmouth. And dear Will, a winter-adoring outdoorsman, now living in Ontario, where Sandra had visited him most recently at the beginning of July. Will was presently trying to please her and the rest of the family by finishing his education at one of Ontario's Applied Arts and Technology colleges, even though he said he felt very confined in a classroom. Sandra smiled at the thought that Aubrey and Will represented these two seasons to her. After they made love the first time, Jack Lawrence had jokingly called himself her "Autumn" and her his "Spring." Her whole life embodied in these three persons so important to her. All four seasons so happily identified.

On their most recent phone call, Will reported to his step-sister how many wolves he had seen. Wolves. Sandra once more smiled, thinking how responsible she had been for his fascination with the animal. She was the one who introduced Will to Bram Stoker's *Dracula* after she listened to Jack Lawrence wax so eloquently about the book, passages of which he read to her with his irrepressible dramatic flair, even once making love to her after reading one of the book's most enthralling chapters.

Jack Lawrence never met Will, although he knew all about him from Sandra's frequent discussions references to her family. He even gave the young man a nickname which pleased Sandra. Lawrence listened patiently to her concerns about Will's general insecurities, which she attributed to his mother's death when he was so young. Sandra's heart went out to Will as soon as he joined the family, because of the boy's loss and the personality that shaped itself from that point on. Whereas his biological sister Aubrey was outgoing, adventurous, and self-confident, Will strove to earn the compliments and displays of affection from everyone in his new family. He did so much without being asked—occasionally to the point of frustration on the part of the family, especially his father and step-sister Sandra. As he reached his teens, he seemed more interested in socializing with her rather than with girls his age. He had one adolescent "romance" that left him crushed, when the girl called it quits after two months. At the time, Sandra sensed he needed her approval and affection more than ever. Otherwise, he continued to demonstrate a pleasant and nonconfrontational personality and maintained the friendships he developed in middle school, in spite of the family's recommendation that he "branch out" and meet new people. Inherent in that suggestion was that he ask girls out from time to time, but he resisted. Sandra understood his reluctance. He didn't wish to risk another broken heart.

Sandra undressed and slipped on her favorite nightshirt, which included on the front the quotation "The Best Beauty Tip is to Love Yourself"—a Christmas gift from Jack Lawrence. She glanced at the framed pictures on her chest of drawers and focused on her high-school graduation family photo. Two months later, when she was eighteen and about to leave for the university, she learned that the sweet and loving relationship she shared with her step-brother wasn't enough for him. She discovered that summer, when stripping his sheets for washing that an article of her intimate clothing had been removed from her drawer and placed between his pillow and pillow case. Although upset, she remade the bed and kept what she found from everyone in the family. She wouldn't embarrass Will, even if others might advise she speak to him about such an inappropriate act. She behaved as always for the rest of the summer and only broke down when she arrived on campus. She knew she hadn't ever suggested anything sexual in their relationship, but subsequent research told her she didn't have to. She also found solace and understanding in books that featured the love relationship between siblings and half-siblings. Certain novels by the likes of Nabokov, Tolkien, Irving, and Durell made her realize that Will's feelings for her had at least literary precedent. She scoured the classics for brother-sister sexual liaisons and figurative thoughts of such.

Nevertheless, over the next seven years she continued advising but never criticizing Will—whenever she came home and through email and phone conversations. She always tried to reinforce the notion that he should rely on his own judgment and make decisions on his own. Finally, right after Christmas, Will became interested in a woman he said was slightly older than he. Unfortunately, he decided to engage in the relationship on social media without the complement of person-to-person meetings, although they had spoken on the phone. How they found each other, she didn't know. Will simply said, "We just did," when she asked. Perhaps, Sandra thought then, he might push it further once he gained courage and more self-esteem. After all, as he said, his "new girlfriend" made him feel "important and smart."

Sandra's eyes blinked rapidly and she put down her book and turned out the reading light. But as it did so often since February 7th, her mind insisted on replaying the events of that horrible night. After the devastating visit to Lawrence's home and seeing Helena Allingham and the two wine glasses, Sandra was determined to leave her job at the library and go to the west coast—far away from memories of Jackson Lawrence—to find some respite from her turbulent emotions. But first, Lawrence wanted that meeting on the seventh stack level of the Hendley at 11:45 p.m. She knew she couldn't go across the country without informing him face-to-face that she would no longer see him or accepts his calls or even his written correspondence.

No one saw her step into the elevator which moved almost reluctantly to the seventh stack level. When the doors opened, she stepped out and immediately heard Lawrence's voice. She hurried to the aisle that housed the older Victorian volumes. When she turned to her left, she saw him reaching up and grabbing one of the volumes near the top of the stacks. Then he fell and seemed to be manipulating the pages. The pen inside the book slid several feet on the slick floor. She witnessed Lawrence deliberately press down with his bloody finger on two spots on the open pages. It was only then she noticed the wound on his neck. She looked at her step-brother briefly as she made her way to Lawrence. The young man's mouth had dropped open; his eyes were clotted with tears.

"Jack, oh, Jack."

She could barely hear Lawrence as he spoke. "The Squire. The Squire." Lawrence's last words were the nickname he had given Will. Sandra wasn't sure Lawrence even realized she was there.

Mesmerized by the widening pool of blood on the floor, she finally cleared her head and saw Will standing near the end of the aisle, his body and features frozen in horror. She knew she had to maintain her composure for him. Carefully, to avoid stepping into the pooling blood, she bent down and picked up the pen that had fallen to the floor near the Dickens edition. Seeing the outline of the pistol in Lawrence's jacket, she removed it and backed up toward her motionless brother, refusing to concede to the tragedy before her. She turned to Will and extended her arm to make clear that she wouldn't desert him. It was then she saw the blade in his hand. Gently taking the weapon from him, she dropped it, the pen, and the gun into the deep pockets of her winter coat. She pushed Will toward the west stairwell, knowing the exact route they would use to return to the ground floor and exit the Hendley.

As she took a final glance at her lover, she saw again his finger in the partially opened volume of Dickens's Christmas stories. The two daubs of blood were underneath two words of text—as if Lawrence wanted someone to concentrate on those two words. Her breath halted as she saw the words "Squire" and "Will." She drew a handkerchief from her pocket and blotted then smeared those two blood marks so that there was no clear indication of any clue. As she stood to leave, Sandra caught sight of Lawrence's winter coat further down the aisle, lying folded on the rolling stair unit. She gestured for Will to stay where he was. She walked down the next aisle of books, turned, and came back toward Lawrence's coat from the other side. There was something wrapped up inside it. Unfolding the coat, she discovered the vintage manuscript pages.

Moving Will along with soft commands, they progressed down the stairwell to the fourth stack level. They crossed through it to the east-side stairwell and then to the second level, which had a little-used passage way leading to the rear of the library. With neither of them speaking, she drove them to her apartment, where Will spent the night on the sofa. When she closed the door to her bedroom, she began to sob violently.

The next morning, the 8th of February, she drove to an area a mile away from her apartment, where a dozen barrels were set up to burn leaves and waste products. She tossed into one of the barrels Lawrence's winter coat and waited until it was consumed. She couldn't take her eyes off the flames. She recalled the bonfire years ago, when her parents thought Will was teasing and touching her inappropriately. But now the fire seemed appropriate for all it represented: passion, destruction, punishment, and purgation—but also, she hoped, rebirth.

She would protect her brother. She knew the killing of Jackson Lawrence wasn't an act of self-defense. Nor did she think her lover had prompted the horrific act. She had no doubt that, in his mind, Will believed he was protecting the person he loved most in his life. Her lover was gone; she knew he was dead before she and Will left the seventh stack level of the Hendley Tower. She wouldn't sacrifice her step-brother, not for the sake of justice, not for any retribution, not for anything. Fortunately, the police failed to ask her the right questions, which would have challenged her decision to hide the truth of what her brother had done. To her, the equation was simple. Jackson Lawrence was gone, and she couldn't afford to lose both these important men in her life.

That afternoon, she asked Will why he had done it.

"I had to. She said the professor had done something horrible to you and was going to hurt you if you told on him."

"She?"

"My girlfriend—the one I've been writing to for over a month now. I told her all about you, and she said she heard that a professor was trying to take you to bed. She told me not to say anything until she found out what was really happening. She said we had to be sure. She said that you'd really be mad at me if I made you think I believed something that wasn't true. But in February when she told me on the phone that it was true and what he did to you, I had to save you. I just had to."

"She told you all this?"

"She did—and she wouldn't lie. She promised me she wasn't lying. She swore she wasn't. Anyway, you'd like her, Sandra. You'd like the way she speaks. She's from England."

• • •

"A brand-new painting?"

"It's the best one I ever did."

"I don't know, Belinda, you've painted some real masterpieces." He felt Elizabeth squeeze his hand.

"Look at it, Daddy." She had painted a bright yellow sun, three birds flying, and two stick figures holding hands." She pointed to the figures. "That's you and Elizabeth, Daddy. Aunt Janis and my cousins are the three birds."

"But where are you, Belinda?"

"Right here."

He had to wipe the moisture from his eyes to see where she pointed. It was at the oval. Her face was inside it.

THE END

NOTE FROM THE AUTHOR

Word-of-mouth is crucial for any author to succeed. If you enjoyed *Secrets of the Chimes,* please leave a review online—anywhere you are able. Even if it's just a sentence or two. It would make all the difference and would be very much appreciated.

Thanks!
John

ABOUT THE AUTHOR

During his career as Professor of English at the University of Georgia, John Vance was the author of six books and numerous articles devoted to literary biography and criticism. He also began indulging his love of theater as actor, director, and playwright, with thirty-five of his plays staged. Now he has turned exclusively to fiction, and is the author of fourteen books, including the historical novel *The King's Favorite,* the humorous memoir *Setting Sail for Golden Harbor*, and the BookBub featured *Death by Mournful Numbers, The Pale Cast of Death, A Bench by Memory Lake,* and *In Mind of the Vampire*. He lives in Athens, Georgia with his wife Susan.

www.ingramcontent.com/pod-product-compliance
Lightning Source LLC
Chambersburg PA
CBHW011132100726
47898CB00009B/2946

* 9 7 8 1 6 8 4 3 3 6 0 2 9 *